Life After Perfect

ALSO BY NANCY NAIGLE

THE ADAMS GROVE SERIES

Sweet Tea and Secrets

Wedding Cake and Big Mistakes

Out of Focus

Pecan Pie and Deadly Lies

Mint Juleps and Justice

Barbecue and Bad News

STANDALONE BOOKS

InkBLOT, cowritten with Phyllis C. Johnson

under the pen name of Johnson Naigle

THE GRANNY SERIES

cowritten with Kelsey Browning

In for a Penny

Fit to Be Tied

Life After Perfect

NANCY NAIGLE

Montlake
Romance

Text copyright © 2015 Nancy Naigle

Published by Montlake Romance, Seattle

www.apub.com

Amazon, the Amazon logo, and Montlake Romance are trademarks of Amazon.com, Inc., or its affiliates.

ISBN-13: 9781477829493
ISBN-10: 1477829490

Front cover design by Anna Curtis

Library of Congress Control Number: 2014958174

Printed in the United States of America

To Pete,

For celebrating the little victories with me along this journey and reminding me to believe in those blue skies ahead.

Thank you, my friend.

You are the real thing.

Chapter One

June days in Georgia were mostly spectacular and sunny, if not a little too darn hot, and on this particular one, the weather wasn't a match for the mood.

Katherine Barclift and her husband, Ron, walked hand in hand up the landscaped path leading to the huge church where the funeral service was being held for their neighbor, Donald O'Connor.

A large crowd had gathered already. As folks filed through the tall arched front doors of the chapel, Katherine spotted Peggy Allen and Shaleigh Wright waiting near the entrance.

She made a beeline for her two friends. "It's so sad," she said as she reached out to hug Peggy. Ron hung back a couple steps.

"Poor Bertie. I can't believe Donald died like that. No warning at all," Peggy said. "I mean, if he were a type A guy I could totally see it happening, but all Donald did was golf and fish. How hard can that be on the heart?"

"I know." Katherine shook her head. "So sad, and he wasn't that old." He was the same age her parents were, and the news of his death had made Katherine worry about them for the first time.

"You've been with Bertie all week, Katherine. She hadn't seen any signs?" Shaleigh asked.

"None." Katherine shrugged. "She said he was perfectly fine. Just didn't wake up."

"He seemed so healthy," Peggy said.

Ron placed his hand on Katherine's arm and said, "I'll go ahead and sign the guest book and get us seats while you talk."

"Sure, honey. Thanks." Katherine watched as her husband walked up the stairs to the chapel. He still had a way of making her swoon. He hadn't had to adjust his wardrobe at all for the funeral today. He sported a nice suit and tie every day of the week. Katherine turned to Shaleigh. "Is it just me or is this the biggest chapel you've ever seen? I always thought chapels were small, with steeples twice as tall as the buildings were wide."

"I think it's just you," Shaleigh said. "Living in that pretend world you like to think is so charming and perfect."

"Perfect is good. Or perfect. Whatever it is, I like my world that way, thank you very much," Katherine teased, but it was only a half-joke. After spending the week with Bertie, helping her figure out her finances and funeral arrangements, Katherine had a long laundry list of things she planned to discuss with her own parents and sister to ensure they were better prepared than poor Bertie had been.

Shaleigh raised a heavily penciled brow. "Well, someone's life ought to be perfect. May as well be you."

No one really knew how old Shaleigh was. Her long dark hair had a youthful sheen and she had only a few tiny wrinkles right around her eyes. But even with those good features, all put together, she was more interesting-looking than attractive. Some would say even harsh-looking. Just as harsh as her reputation.

Rumors in Preakness Heights ran the gamut—from thirty-something to fifty-something. It didn't matter how old she was, though, because the woman was the best divorce lawyer in Atlanta. Local men hated her, because if Shaleigh was representing your former better half, she'd drag your sorry ass through whatever it took to get her client a hefty settlement. Shaleigh seemed to love that she made men cringe, too. Seemed to take a little pride in it, actually—sometimes taking time to point out past prey.

"Can you believe how many people are here?" Peggy, almost six feet tall in her heels, with natural red hair that would send Paul Mitchell into fits of envy, looked around and nodded politely as people passed.

"I know," Katherine said. "No doubt the O'Connors met and mingled with a lot of folks in their lifetime, but we've lived next door to them for five years. If Bertie's seen hide or hair of even a quarter of these people, they must have been sneaking in over the back fence."

Peggy nodded. "Tucker was surprised by how many people were here too. Did Bertie and Donald go to this church?"

"I have no idea. I guess so. Where is Tucker?" Katherine asked.

"Same as yours. Went inside to sit down. I guess he thinks the sooner he's in a pew, the sooner it will be over. You know the world rises and sets on him, right?"

The three women laughed.

"I think everyone from the neighborhood is here. That's nice," Peggy added.

Preakness Heights was filled with busy professional couples, and although Katherine wouldn't call most of them friends, they did look out for one another. Kind of an unspoken law of the neighborhood. Just like Bertie had asked for help from Katherine this week.

"So, what exactly were you doing for Bertie this week?" Shaleigh asked.

"Donald handled all of the finances. She had no idea how much money was in any of the accounts or even how to access them. I went through everything and helped her set up a new budget, locate the insurance papers—the basics."

"She knows you're a project manager, not a banker, doesn't she?"

"Everyone thinks if you work for the bank, you know everything from checking accounts to mortgages and investments. At least this I could handle. Any of us could have," Katherine said.

"True. It was still nice of you. How is she?"

"Sad. Devastated. Lost. But thank goodness she's in financially pretty good shape."

"It's her money, you know," Shaleigh said.

"Bertie's? Really?" Peggy's eyes opened so wide, horizontal wrinkles won against the Botox on her forehead. "I'd just assumed Donald had retired, but now that you mention it, I don't think anyone ever spoke about him having any kind of a career."

"Family money?" Katherine hadn't even considered that, but it made sense now that she knew. "But wouldn't you think Bertie would have been more involved if it was her money?"

"You'd think, but I kind of got the feeling she was a spoiled rich girl when Donald married her. I think his specialty was playing," Shaleigh said. "Not playing like most of the men. Real play. Fishing, golf. I think I remember him saying he collected sports memorabilia. Something like that."

"Well, if he was retired, isn't that what he's supposed to do?" Peggy said.

"Yeah." Shaleigh shrugged. "It just surprises me how many couples still let one person handle all of the finances. It's a big old mess when you're trying to split things up and the two people's interpretation of the financial picture is different. It's just not smart. That's all."

Katherine knew that Shaleigh, with her black-and-white thinking, saw her share of the inner workings of marriages gone bad. She always came down a little on the negative side of it, too.

"I'll be right back," Shaleigh said. "I see someone I need to say hello to."

"I was happy to help Bertie in some little way," Katherine said, then she motioned Peggy closer. "Only I found something that I'd rather not have. I really hate to say anything, but . . ."

"But you're going to. What?" Peggy prodded.

"So . . ." Katherine tucked in closer to Peggy and lowered her voice. "I need your advice."

"What's the matter?" Peggy asked.

"I think Donald had someone on the side."

Disbelief registered on Peggy's face. "Why would you think that?"

"It was the last thing I expected to find going through the checkbooks and working up a budget for Bertie." She glanced around. "But there were monthly checks going to a woman for at least the past two years. Kim Elliona."

"Never heard of her. It was probably a loan or something," Peggy said. "Did you ask Bertie about it?"

"I kind of probed about the amounts, but she didn't seem to know what I was talking about, so I just let it drop." Katherine folded her arms across her chest, hugging herself at the thought. "Why hurt Bertie like that, or embarrass her if she did know? The guy is dead and gone. Water under the bridge. No use stirring up that kind of pain. Hasn't she been through enough?" But, then again, if that woman showed up and befriended Bertie to keep her allowance going, Katherine would be forced to tell her the truth. What a mess.

"Well, for the record," Peggy said looking dead straight at Katherine, "I'd want to know."

Shaleigh came back. "What did I miss?"

Peggy pushed her hair over her shoulder. "I was just saying that if someone knew my husband was cheating, I'd want to know."

Shaleigh cleared her throat and gave Peggy an odd look.

"I would," Peggy said about two octaves too high to be convincing.

Katherine avoided eye contact. This was not a conversation she wanted to have right now, and especially not with Peggy. Tucker Allen was anything but an angel.

Peggy nudged Katherine. "What would you do if you caught Ron cheating, Katherine?"

She sucked in a long breath. "It would be the ultimate betrayal. I'd leave him so fast his head would spin."

"Easy to say," Peggy said. "But you wouldn't want someone to tell you?"

"Oh, I think I'd know." Katherine wished she hadn't let Peggy bait her.

"Y'all don't want to hear statistics on this, and you don't understand until it happens to you. So, come on." Shaleigh took one of each of their hands. "We better get inside."

Katherine thought she might be sick right there, because if Peggy didn't have any idea that Tucker Allen had hit on every woman in the neighborhood and beyond . . . she wasn't about to be the one to tell her. It seemed like most of the women rebuffed his overly flirtatious ways, but the guy had to get lucky once in a while, else he'd certainly have abandoned the tacky actions by now.

Katherine's heart twisted when they walked into the chapel. Bertie looked so tiny in the front pew by herself. No children. No one.

For a fleeting moment she saw herself sitting there. All alone. And boy, did her heart feel heavy, not just for the single loss of a devoted husband, but for the children she'd always wanted . . . thought she'd have by now. She tossed her hair back and swallowed the emotion. She didn't know how Bertie felt about it, but that thought nearly made her crumble to her knees. No, she couldn't give in to that kind of emotion.

Katherine looked toward Shaleigh and Peggy. If they'd felt that powerful punch, there was no sign of it. She forced herself to step forward, leading the others inside. She took the empty spot next to Ron in a pew midway down on the left. He reached out and squeezed Katherine's hand as she sat.

Peggy's comment still nagged at her. Maybe hearing about Donald's infidelity had struck a little too close to home for Peggy. It wasn't like Tucker was discreet. There were rumors. Lots of them, and even if Peggy didn't have any proof, she had to at least suspect something. Didn't she?

Peggy and Shaleigh slid into a pew near the front, next to Tucker. They were nearly the last ones to take their seats.

A short, portly man shaped like a bullet stepped to the front. He didn't wear a church robe, just a dark suit not so unlike every other man in the room. Except for Donald. Although people wouldn't know this unless Bertie told them, since it was a closed casket. She'd dressed him in his hip waders and a fishing hat.

The organist stopped and the preacher's voice boomed across the space with the strength and vibrancy of a man eight feet tall.

His message, and the soothing cadence of the words, despite their volume, sent Katherine's thoughts adrift.

What if it had been Ron rather than Donald who'd had that heart attack? Ron worked so hard. Never slowed down. Long hours. Type A all the way. Bertie had described Donald the same way, but of course that must have been years ago, before they moved to Preakness Heights.

The preacher waved a theatrical arm in the direction of the coffin, and then pulled his fist to his heart. "There's a place inside each of our hearts where love lives on forever . . . always . . . and where nothing beautiful is ever forgotten. Those memories. They will remain with us always."

Always?

Katherine wondered when the last time she and Ron had slowed down long enough to take in the moments that were supposed to become memories. She looked over at her husband. Was he even paying attention, or was he mentally checking off things on a to-do list a mile long? At least he didn't have his phone out.

Katherine choked back a sob, unsure if it was for Bertie or herself. Were most of the people dabbing at tears in this room today missing Donald? Or, like her, was today a reminder of the mortality everyone all must face? The mistakes made. The fear of the unknown.

"As we grieve," the preacher said with such emphasis that Katherine hitched in a quick breath at the power of that word. The finality of it. "Let's share the stories, the hope, the moments that made our smiles touch one another, and be grateful for the lessons that Donald shared with us. Treasure those gifts."

Ron patted her leg. She looked into his face and he gave her that gentle smile that always made her feel better.

"Let us pray." Everyone bowed their heads in a rush of movement like a soft sheet floating in a breeze.

When the amens finally rumbled through the room, the organist played a hymn that Katherine didn't recognize, but it pulled at her core in a way that made it hard to breathe.

The pallbearers came forward to lift the casket and carried it past on the way out of the church.

Donald had been a huge man, but once people die and their bodies are prepared . . . do they all weigh the same?

Could you even google that?

The funeral director, a handsome gray-haired gentleman in a suit only a shade darker than his hair, held out his hand to Bertie.

Katherine stuttered a breath as she watched Bertie place her trembling hand into his. He helped her stand, then walk . . . ever so slowly . . . her lips trembling, her eyes so pink that they looked like they must sting, her hand still clutching one of Donald's handkerchiefs tightly in her fist. So tiny and alone. One woman. No children. All of her family gone.

Katherine looked down at her hands, trying to will away the light-headed feeling she had. If she never had children, she would be alone like this one day. There was no guarantee that your children would take care of you, she knew that, but they'd be there in some form or fashion—even if out of obligation.

She glanced over at Ron. He knew how she longed for a family. Said he did too . . . someday. But for now, her husband was dead set on keeping up with the Joneses . . . no wait . . . make that the Kardashians. Ron was so hell-bent on making as much money as possible that he'd refused to entertain having a child until they were ready. Ready? What the heck did that even mean? She wondered if that's why they'd had fewer moments of intimacy these days. His way of throttling the possibility. Why did he get to decide?

Shaleigh walked by, dry-eyed, leading her row. Tucker followed a tearful Peggy. Her pale complexion was blotched and pink. She'd cried more than her share for someone she wasn't that close to.

Finally their row filed out, and Ron placed his hand on the small of Katherine's back, guiding her to the door. Always making her feel safe. Loved.

"I love you," she said with tears still in her eyes.

He pulled his arm around her and gave her a squeeze.

By the time they got outside, cars were lined up behind the hearse and limo, a processional so long that one car might be at the grave site while the end of the line was still here in the church parking lot.

Would people even realize it was a processional as they drove across town? With daytime running lights, didn't every row of cars kind of look like one? Lately it seemed like things moved so fast that nothing was clear anymore. Like pausing to reflect might somehow take too much time. She glanced at the people shifting with impatience as they waited for the line of cars to begin to move.

Ron held the door as Katherine slipped into the passenger seat. He eased out, nosing his way between two other cars without even a thank-you nod. They weren't any different than the rest of the people rushing through the sad day today. Ron pressed the accelerator and fell in line behind the others as they made their way across town. When they got to the cemetery, cars filled several of the dirt lanes, parking wherever they could.

Ron pulled up as close to the canopy as he could get and then leaned over and laid a kiss on Katherine's neck.

"I'm going to dash," Ron whispered into her hair.

"What?"

"I've got a meeting. I made my appearance. You can catch a ride home with Peggy or Shaleigh, can't you?"

She replayed his words, taking in what he'd just said. Made my appearance. No sorrow. A duty to be here. Why come, then?

"Yeah. I can."

Had things really gotten to this point? That nothing was worthy enough to be more important than his commitment to his job? Somehow that seemed so wrong.

Her eyes burned, but she wasn't going to let him upset her further. Refused to. That service had left her wanting to cling closer to the one she loved, and yet here he was skipping off in a hurry to get to work.

She picked up her purse, got out of the car, and stood there, a little disoriented.

He rolled down the window and stage-whispered, "Love you, babe. I'll see you tonight." Then he pulled off.

She turned around and walked along the dirt lane at Westlawn Gardens Memorial Park, falling in step with the others heading toward the burgundy funeral-home tent.

From where she stood, she couldn't even hear what was being said, and in an eerie way, it seemed overly quiet.

Like even the birds had bowed their heads.

Her chest clenched.

She stepped back, taking in the rows and rows of headstones that surrounded them. Some with flowers, some bare and tired-looking. From here she could see the lovely casket spray she'd ordered for Bertie. Since Donald wasn't a flower guy, Bertie chose to do something more personal. She was very specific, and Katherine had taken a legal pad with all the details, as well as a huge tackle box per Bertie's request, to the florist. Katherine had thought the arrangement might turn out to be hideous, but it was actually quite beautiful, yet masculine, in a whimsical way.

The blanket of white daisies lay atop bright green leaves that peeked out of the edges like the satin border on a blanket. Among the white flowers, hundreds of fluorescent fly-fishing lures sparkled in a rainbow of bright colors, the tiny feathers moving in the breeze and the shiny metal reflecting the light like a thousand tiny brave stars doing a forbidden dance in the daylight: a loving tribute to her outdoorsman husband.

Her mind wandered. She couldn't bear to listen to the preacher, thankful the graveside service was short and people were already starting to peel away.

Conversational chatter filled the air as people hugged and shook hands.

Peggy's red hair stood out across the way. Katherine had always thought her own dark-blonde hair had a reddish hint until she saw a picture of herself next to Peggy. Now that was red hair. Tucker shook hands and patted shoulders, Peggy just moving in his wake.

Katherine picked her way through the crowd toward the beautiful woman. Peggy had model beauty, the kind that made you take a second glance when she walked by. Actually, she didn't walk as much as gently glide—a quality Katherine had often admired about her.

"Lovely, wasn't it?" Katherine said as she stepped next to Peggy.

Peggy nodded, but seemed to be still working through the tears.

"Broke my heart a little, too, and I never really knew Donald well. But Bertie is such a sweetheart," Katherine said. "Can I catch a ride home with y'all?"

"Where's Ron?"

Katherine hated explaining his absence, but she was getting good at it. Everyone knew he was a workaholic, so why people bothered to even ask anymore still puzzled her. "He had a meeting he had to get to."

"Well, at least he didn't turn the funeral into a business opportunity." Peggy pulled her lips into a tight line. "Like some people." She glared at her husband over Katherine's shoulder. "I drove separately. You can ride with me."

"Thanks." Katherine stopped short as someone gave her an overambitious hug from behind. She wriggled from the hold and turned— Tucker Allen was all up in her space.

Katherine caught the read on Peggy's face. Tucker Allen was such a jerk. That stray cat had to be prowling other neighborhoods.

"How've you been, Katherine?" Tucker said, coming alongside her and pulling her close again with an arm sliding too familiarly down her back.

"I'm good, Tucker. Thanks for asking." She took a step, buying herself some distance from him.

He gave Peggy a nod. "I'm going back to the office. I'll see you tonight." He plastered that perfect white smile on his face and seemed to pause so no one would miss it. It was that same creepy grin he used in the commercials for his car dealership. "Ladies." Then he turned and left. Unlike the used car salesman stereotype, though, Tucker Allen was an honest businessman. It was only his personal traits that were questionable.

Katherine and Shaleigh shared a look. It was probably killing Shaleigh not to make a remark, but out of respect to Peggy, they just smiled and said goodbye. The women stood off to the side as the rest of the people made their way back to their cars.

Peggy elbowed Shaleigh. "Katherine saw where Donald was funneling money to someone. Probably a mistress," she said.

Shaleigh rolled her eyes. "What's it matter? If he did, I can guarantee it's over now."

"That's true," Katherine said. "But it surprised me. I mean there were checks every single month. And I'm not talking a couple hundred bucks. They really added up. Whoever that Kim Elliona is, she had a good gig going with Donald." Katherine looked around. "I wonder if she's here."

"She wouldn't show up here," Peggy said. "Wouldn't dare!"

"Things aren't always as they seem," Shaleigh stated matter-of-factly.

"You're just jaded from your job," Peggy said.

"Probably," Shaleigh said. "But you're mistaken this time."

"What do you know?" Katherine asked.

"Well, he's dead and gone, so I'll break the attorney-client privilege. Just between us, though. Donald came to me a while back. Not my area of expertise, but since we're neighbors he was looking for advice about some money he wanted to give to the Chatahoochie Riverkeeper fund. That woman, Kim Elliona, is the chairman of the board of that foundation. She was not sleeping with the guy. I know that for a fact. If Donald was guilty of an affair it was with that river."

"Oh, well, thank goodness," Katherine said, "because I was feeling pretty bad about a forty-one-year marriage that was based on lies. Although there were checks directly to the Chatahoochie Riverkeeper fund too. Those were normal contribution amounts. The amount of money Donald was funneling to that Kim Elliona was a whole lot more than just hobby money. I itemized it all out for Bertie, but I didn't put her on the spot with any questions about it. I just didn't know what to say."

Shaleigh said, "I'm pretty sure Donald was behind that whole thing with them stocking the river. Remember all the local controversy on that. Don't know if you noticed, but he was usually one of the winners grinning with a trophy at those big corporate-sponsored tournaments hosted on the river. He probably knew all the right spots to fish."

"That doesn't sound so awful. At least not compared to what I'd thought was going on," Katherine said.

"Don't give the guy a medal." Shaleigh shook her head. "He was doing it on the sly. You can best believe Bertie will be hot when she finds out that much money was going anywhere other than the foundation her family had set up. She's the last of that family tree, and she takes that pretty seriously. If you ask me, it's not so much different from stealing if you're doing it without someone's consent."

"Well, they were married, so he had a right to spend that money too," Peggy said.

Shaleigh rolled her eyes and then settled her gaze on Katherine. "If you ask Bertie about continuing those payments, I bet you'll see a side of Bertie O'Connor you've never seen before."

Katherine's stomach turned. If someone would keep something that minor a secret, what other secrets would he carry? "I don't know, Peggy.

We're talking some significant money. Money that Bertie could use. She's okay, but the money he siphoned off to feed his ego over fishing could have made her life a lot more comfortable long-term."

Why did death always seem to prickle her moral compass? Make her want everything in a tidy line like pretty little maids in a row. But she knew most people didn't have the kind of life she did. Call it luck, hard work, or clean living, whatever it was, she was thankful for it.

"What a day," Peggy said. "Death is exhausting."

"Probably not for Donald," Shaleigh said.

"Shaleigh! You did not just say that." But Katherine couldn't hold back the laugh.

Shaleigh crossed one black platform heel across her other and folded her arms across her blazer. "Hey, he didn't have to even pick out an outfit, and someone else made sure he was here on time. Plus, whatever he'd been doing, he's gotten away with it now."

Katherine had to admit, Shaleigh had a good point.

Chapter Two

The scent of antiseptic and adhesive hit Derek Hansen as he walked through the back door of the medical center. You'd think a doctor would get used to it, maybe not even notice the smell after a while. He wore boots, and his footsteps echoed through the empty space, like he were a cowboy walking off paces in a duel.

The nurses back at Duke University Hospital used to tease him that they didn't have to look up to know when he was coming down the hall. Even when he had the paper booties over them, his boots had a distinct sound.

He missed the old gang, but his passion for his career at Duke changed when Laney got sick. So here he was, back in his hometown of Boot Creek, North Carolina, doing general practice. It was a far cry from the work he did at the cancer institute, but after losing Laney to the very disease he specialized in fighting, what good was it to treat a disease that fought you back on a personal level? It was like cancer had decided to even the score.

The change of location and focus hadn't dulled the loss of Laney though. He missed her. Every single day. Still, after nearly two years, he'd sometimes wake up and turn to her side of the bed, thinking she might be there, her hair sprawled across the pillow. And every time, that reminder dug into him—the wound just as raw and pink as the day he laid her to rest.

Derek stopped in his office and snagged his white coat from the hook, pulling it on over his shirt and tie as he walked down the hall. In the small practice, the nurse, Wendy, ended up also playing reception-ist most days.

"Good morning, Wendy. How was your evening?"

"Great. I went over to the annual open house night at Criss Cross Farm last night. I can't believe how much they've done over there since last year. After bottle-feeding the calves, I might never eat a burger again."

"Somehow I doubt that," he said with a wink. She ate burgers nearly every single day of the week. Extra pickles. Not that she'd ever told him, but he could smell them when she ate at her desk.

"You're right, but those big brown-eyed babies were so sweet." Her mouth twisted up a little. "Although it *was* kind of like giving a bottle to a grizzly bear. Nothing gentle about it. They are really strong at just a few days old."

The image of Wendy, barely five feet tall, wrangling a calf into sub-mission with one of those giant bottles tickled him. "Glad you had a good time. I haven't been over to the beefalo ranch since I've been back." He tugged his ink pen out of the pocket out of habit. The same Mont-blanc that his dad had given him the day he graduated from medical school. "So what's our morning look like?"

"Not too busy if we don't get many emergencies. A couple rechecks, labs, oh, and Jeb Crossley put his back out again. I told him to come in whenever he could make it." She lifted a stack of charts and handed them to him.

"Of course he did." Derek shook his head. Jeb Crossley had been the wrestling coach back when Derek was on the team in junior high and that man refused to give in to the aging process. "What's that? The third time this month?"

"Fourth. He came in and saw your dad last week."

Jeb should ask for a frequent visitor discount. Derek would almost be obliged to consider it.

Derek flipped through the first two charts. Routine stuff. Then he glanced at the next file. His gut twisted. "I'm going to look these over. Let me know when the first appointment arrives."

"Yes, sir."

Back in his office he looked closer at the file on Kelly Jo Keefer. She was one of his dad's patients. Cancer. Stage four. Derek's teeth clenched. When cancer took Laney from him, he'd made the decision to transition back to a general practitioner.

Researchers had made a lot of progress since he started in the field, but for all the new discoveries that would someday save lots of lives, the truth was the disease was relentless. For those needing a cure right now . . . it was hard to deliver the news that there still were not a lot of answers.

Now his days were filled with vaccines, scrapes, and the occasional stitch or two. Things that would put a bother in your day, but for the most part weren't life-threatening. And that was a much better place to be in his life right now.

He sat back in his chair and read Kelly Jo's chart until Wendy knocked on the door to let him know his first patient was ready.

Just reviewing Kelly Jo's chart, so like Laney's, was already chafing those still unhealed two-year-old wounds.

He saw the first four patients. A cold. A case of jock itch. Chiggers, and one sprained ankle.

Then he tried to calm down his next patient's mother, who was clearly more upset than her son was about his predicament.

"I bet he can *bear-ly* breathe with this gummy bear up his nose," Derek said, trying to put a light spin on the situation to calm down Ryan's mom while he dug out the culprit. Finally, he got a grip on the squishy piece of candy and tugged it from the boy's nostril. "A green one at that."

"Ryan? Why in the world do you keep doing this?" She gave an exhausted sigh. "Why couldn't I have had girls?"

Derek smiled at the irritated mother. "I think there's a misconception that boys do this more than girls, but that's not the case," he said. "It's common in kids under six. For items found in the ears, girls equal boys, but for the nose, it's a two-to-one ratio in favor of girls." He laughed. "It could've been worse."

Derek gave the five-year-old the speech about sticking foreign objects up his nose and then sent them on their way. Before seeing his next patient, Derek headed straight to his office, pulled open the left desk drawer, and chucked the bag of gummy bears stashed there right into the trash. "Won't be eating any of those again for a while."

The nurse knocked on his office door. "Mrs. Keefer is here. Room seven."

"Thanks, Wendy. I'll be right there." Derek took in a deep breath and counted to five.

With the chart tucked under his arm, he walked down the hall and gave the door to Room 7 a quick double-knock. "Good morning, Mrs. Keefer."

"Hi." The dark, bruised-looking rings under Mrs. Keefer's translucent skin made her look fifteen years older than her thirty-one years.

"Dr. Hansen is off today so I'll be seeing you. I'm his son, Dr. Derek Hansen." Derek's being back allowed his mother to spirit his father away from the clinic on any number of couples' trips.

"Nice to meet you." Even her smile took an effort.

"You're new in town?" he asked.

"Staying with my Great-Aunt Naomi. She lives down at the creek."

"Mrs. Laumann is your aunt? I'm surprised you and I never met. I grew up around here. All of us used to hang out at the falls down near her place. Good lady."

"She is," Kelly Jo said. "I only spent a couple of summers here. She speaks quite fondly of you, and your dad, of course. He's been great." She fidgeted, seeming to be as uncomfortable as he was.

"Thank you. I think he's pretty amazing. Now let's take a listen to that heart." He placed the ear tips of his stethoscope in his ears and pressed the diaphragm to her chest. "Good. Now a deep breath in." He moved his stethoscope and closed his eyes, listening. "Another."

"Lie back for me," he said.

He pressed his hands along her abdomen. "Any pain or discomfort?" She shook her head. "Just the normal stuff."

"The new medication helping with the nausea?" he asked, seeing his dad had switched medications for her after her previous visit.

"Yes. Pretty much." She showed hardly any emotion as he went through the examination and asked a few more questions.

"Good." He stepped back, and then sat down in the rolling chair; for a split second he felt like he was back in Raleigh with Laney at the point of no return. No more hope. Just waiting. That feeling, fear wrapped up in helplessness, surged like electricity through him. Making him want to run for safer ground. He took a moment to pull himself together as he checked off the updates on the report. "You can sit on up." He forced what he hoped was at least half of a smile, and scanned the list to be sure he covered all that was expected in today's visit. "Okay, I'm going to write your refills for you, and we'll get those labs done today."

"Thank you."

"Any other complaints today?"

She sucked in a long breath. "Wouldn't do to complain." She laughed, but it lacked joy. He recognized the look of exhaustion. "I know your wife had cancer."

He tried to recover from the stab those words had delivered.

"I'm sorry for your loss," she added.

"Thank you." He didn't even recognize his own voice when he uttered the words.

"I'm done with the treatments. I'm just coasting. It's not better, but it's not worse, and for a while . . . every day was worse than the last."

"I understand." He already knew the details from the chart. And he did understand, more than she could ever imagine, but damn if that didn't make it only harder to talk about. "Only you can make the right decisions for yourself," he said, as if that might somehow comfort her. "We have a lot of new things we can prescribe to help make you more comfortable. If something's not working, we can try something new. I see you've refused hospice help so far—if you want to talk about that . . . let me know."

"I'm not ready for people hovering. I just want to be alone." She laced her fingers. "Quite honestly, I keep praying I won't wake up."

He'd heard Laney say the same thing. Seen the look of disappointment in her face when she opened her eyes and saw him looking at her. Sometimes the most helpful thing to say was nothing.

She swallowed, and then said, "Thank you for not pushing. I was worried when I realized Dr. Hansen, your dad, wasn't in today." She paused, catching her breath. "He's been so understanding."

"No problem. You change your mind anytime about anything, you know how to get us." Derek wrote out her prescriptions and handed them to her. "Here you go."

"Thank you so much."

She looked relieved that he hadn't pressed her for more details. "You take care," he said, and left the room, taking her chart and the prescriptions to Wendy at the front desk, and then retreating to his office.

Behind that closed door, he pulled off his jacket and loosened his tie.

His skin prickled as if he was under a Jamaican sun, but he knew the air was working. Sweeping a hand across his sweaty brow, he picked up the picture of Laney from his credenza, one from before she got sick, before treatments. He wanted so badly to remember her like this. Beautiful. Healthy. Instead all he remembered were her last days, when she looked not so unlike Kelly Jo just now.

No color. No energy. Not much life left in the container God had lent her. The one that cancer had sucked the beauty from so heartlessly.

It took him a few minutes to pull himself together; then he went back out and continued from room to room, handling the patients until there weren't any left to be seen.

"That's it?" he asked as he approached the front desk.

"Yes. Nothing else on the books." Wendy smiled. "Our lucky day."

"I'm going to run over to the diner and grab something to eat. Text me if you need me." He patted his hand on the counter and headed down the long corridor.

Derek made one last stop in his office to hang his white coat back on the rack.

He glanced at his degrees on the wall. He was going through the motions, keeping his medical license intact. For now. Until he figured out what the rest of his life would be. There'd been lots of days since Laney had died that he'd considered chucking it all. He'd spent the six months after her death hopping from conference to conference and class to class, trying to stay as busy as he possibly could getting his general practitioner CMEs up to date.

His future had once been all laid out. Not so anymore. Not since the day Laney died. He was only certain of one thing: he couldn't work in oncology.

Balancing the wins and losses had become impossible, and the losses were sucking him under like quicksand. He knew that it was the time to switch gears, and leave that area of medicine to others.

There was a time when he'd have pushed his opinion on Kelly Jo. Touted the help she'd receive at highly acclaimed facilities like his. And for a moment those thoughts flew through his mind, but they didn't emerge from his lips. He didn't have it in his heart anymore. There were a few drugs they could use to slow things down a little, but from the look of Kelly Jo's last scans, there wasn't much hope for any relief that would improve her quality of life in those additional days.

"Are you clear on all of your options?" he'd asked.

She'd held up a hand. "Completely. Please don't—"

"That's fine. I understand."

She'd breathed a noticeable sigh of relief. She was so tired. It was as if Laney were sitting in front of him. The life no longer danced in her eyes. The rounded slope of her shoulders evidence it was too much to hold a straight line anymore.

No. Cancer wasn't for sissies. This gal was no sissy. She'd fought her battle, and she'd chosen what she was willing to give. It was okay. It wasn't easy. Not for the patients. Not for their families and the physicians and nurses who kept an eye on "quality of life" even when the end was near.

When Laney got worse, he'd shifted most of his patients to the care of one of his partners, keeping only a handful who were so far along in their treatments that it seemed unfair to ask them to trust someone new.

By the time Laney died, all of his other patients had too, and so had a big part of him.

———

Mentally exhausted, he walked over to the Blue Skies Cafe. It was a straight shot, back door to back door, between the medical center and the diner. He'd walked it so many times that he knew where all the potholes and divots were in the gravel parking lot.

The oppressive heat made his shirt stick to his body, though it wasn't even a fifty-yard walk.

In the diner, the sizzle on the flattop grill softened the conversations between the people already starting to fill the booths for supper. Ol' Man Johnson gave Derek a wave and a nod.

"I'll get my own drink," Derek said grabbing a glass at the beverage station.

"Doggone right you will." The hefty man toddled off toward the grill, his laugh like the howl of a beagle on the scent of a white tail. Nearly as wide as he was tall, he blocked almost the entire view of the long cooktop, though the smell of herbs and onions wafted up around him.

Without one complaint from the cafe's owner, Derek could tell the poor guy's gout was flaring up again. "If you'd stay away from that shellfish like I told you, you wouldn't be hobbling around like you are."

"Shrimp scampi. Worth every bite. It's the special. There's more. Want some?"

"Sounds perfect. Got any of those cheese grits?"

"You know it."

And that was just about how ordering at the Blue Skies Cafe went for Derek every time. He rarely had to choose his order, just let Ol' Man Johnson tell him what was cooking, or let Angie decide. His best friend from high school knew his likes and dislikes as well as he did.

Still, those shrimp and grits were hard to pass up. Derek figured Johnson had probably had a double helping to cause that gout flare-up, but Derek had to admit the guy was in good shape for someone easily ninety pounds overweight. Even his cholesterol was better than most of his patients who were on a prescription for it. Just goes to show you that you can't always tell what's going on internally from the outside of a person.

This diner was no different. From the tired turn-of-the-century storefront, you might expect a typical greasy spoon.

Not the case.

Ol' Man Johnson's daughter had gone to some fancy interior design school up in New York City, and he'd let her practice on his restaurant to help build her portfolio.

Over one summer, the Blue Skies Cafe had gone from leave-no-impression to y'all-come-on-back-now-and-set-a-spell. It proved that a little thing like ambiance could change the clientele. The light that streamed in the windows used to about blind the customers. His daughter solved that by contracting an artist out near Blowing Rock to do stained glass panels. As dividers between the booths, the panels diffused the rays through the colorful glass images like a church on Sunday. Almost heavenly, and that was exactly what a Food Network star had said about the food when he came in and sampled the Blue Skies Cafe's signature dish—Carolina Beefalo and Browns.

No dish screamed Southern more than Ol' Man Johnson's CB&B. It included a small medallion of fresh beefalo cooked just to your liking. Yes, beefalo—a cross between a domestic cow and an American bison—grown right up the road on Criss Cross Farm, served with hand-sliced fingerling hash browns, and then married up with whatever fresh local vegetables were available that week. A picture next to the register flaunted the cafe's Food Network episode and bragging rights.

Derek watched Angie serve supper like she had a hive of bees behind her. Her dark hair shone, and he knew she was flustered when she shoved it behind her ear. A tell. They'd been friends so long sometimes he thought he knew her better than he knew himself.

She whisked down the aisle toward the drink station, her expression transforming, her real smile appearing, as soon as she saw him.

"Good day?" he asked.

"Busy." She set a water pitcher down on his table just long enough to push her dark hair back over her ear again, and nodded toward a booth at the front. "Cranky travelers." She rubbed the back of her hand across her forehead. "On top of everything, I had to walk to work this morning. My car took its last breath last night. I swear I can't catch a break."

"Why didn't you call? I'd have given you a lift."

"The walk was fine. That wasn't the point. I'm just tired of everything always being a struggle."

"What's wrong with your car this time?"

She seemed to deflate before his eyes. "Who knows? I only just had the oil changed and the engine all checked out." She let out a groan.

"Let me get this lady's Arnold Palmer before she has a fit. Seriously. If you can drink an Arnold Palmer, you can drink sweet tea. What is it with people?"

She rushed off, and it was only a couple minutes later when Angie slid Derek's dinner in front of him. "Heard you saw Kelly Jo Keefer today."

"I did. How'd you know?"

"I was over at Naomi's this morning," Angie said. "Kelly Jo is married to Todd Keefer."

"Todd? I hadn't made the connection." The distance Derek had been trying to force between him and her case suddenly got harder. "Man, I haven't seen Todd since we watched him play ball in the minors. It's been a while. So they're back in town?"

"He's not. They were living in Tennessee when Kelly Jo got the news that her cancer had metastasized to the liver. She came to live with Naomi so Todd wouldn't watch her die. She thinks she's doing him some kind of favor." Angie folded her arms. "I'm not sure if that's the craziest or the most unselfish thing I've ever heard somebody do."

Derek remembered the day that Laney took his hand. Her words had barely been more than a whisper when she'd said, "Seeing the anguish in your eyes every time you look at me is worse than the pain of dying." That had just about killed him. Even the memory weighed heavy on his chest.

Kelly Jo hadn't been looking for any miracles or promises of hope today. She'd accepted what was in her future, but still, hours after she'd left, he couldn't forget her. He knew from experience what was ahead of her. It wasn't going to be pretty.

"She might be doing Todd a favor." He suddenly wasn't very hungry. "Watching Laney's decline was the worst part of all. It gives you such a helpless feeling."

She sat down and reached across the table and took his hand. "I know you still miss her."

"Every day." He held her gaze. She'd been a great friend through Laney's illness. "There's nothing Todd can do to change it. If it's what Kelly Jo wants, who are we to say it's not the right thing."

"It just seems so unfair."

"Cancer doesn't fight fair, Angie. You know, when Laney turned that last corner, there was nothing else that could be done. I knew it. She did too. It was a damned death sentence, yet even with the combined experience of all of my colleagues, we had no way of knowing just how long she'd have. There's nothing you can do but wait, and sadly no way to make the days good enough to matter."

"Can't you help Kelly Jo?" Emotion and hope hung on her expression. "Somehow?"

He cast his glance toward the front door. "Kelly Jo is in that stage now, Angie. She's dying, and there's nothing anyone can do to stop it. All we can do is buy her calendar time, not quality time. She's already figured that out for herself."

"But what about Todd? It's unfair that she's shut him out of her life. I told her that just because she left, it doesn't mean a switch turned off for him. He's still suffering. Missing her."

"Oh, I'm sure he's in a living hell right now." But Derek knew Todd would be in a living hell either way. There were lots of days that Derek wished he had the memories of the Laney who was all beauty and confidence. Instead, the images of her dying right before his eyes remained at the fore . . . blocking the beautiful memories. You just can't erase those. But then he couldn't have left her side. Didn't until her last breath. Wouldn't have for all the money in the world.

"She doesn't let anyone come visit her." She grabbed his hand and held it. "Maybe you can share something with her that will make her realize it's okay for Todd to be a part of it. Or something. I don't know. I just want something good for her. And him. I want him to be okay."

"Your heart knows no boundaries. I love that about you." But he knew there was no making things okay for Kelly Jo or for Todd. He knew exactly what Todd was feeling.

"But . . ."

"But this is a personal decision for them. What we think is right may not be right for them. We have to respect that."

"I hate it when you're practical." She looked out the window. "I just feel so helpless." She turned and looked at him. "And Derek, I feel helpless for you, too. I hate seeing you so sad. Your life didn't end."

"I know." He cleared his throat. "I'm okay, Angie."

"Okay is just okay, and that's not good. I just want to help," she said. "You and Kelly Jo. It shouldn't be so hard to help people you care for. Kelly Jo used to love my chicken salad, but she couldn't even eat it last time."

He leaned forward. "Taste buds change," he said.

She turned and looked at him. "Is that code for something?"

"No. You said you wanted to help Kelly Jo. When the cancer is that far along, with all the treatments she's been through, her taste buds have changed. Things she never much liked might suddenly taste good. A lot of my patients say things like tomato soup and sauces are very palatable. You might try something like that. Couldn't hurt."

"I would have thought that tomato soup would be way too harsh on her stomach." She smiled. "Tomato soup. I'll try it. Thank you."

"It's not going to change the end game, Angie." He tilted his head to the left and then to the right. Every muscle in his neck crimped and pulled. "She's dying." It sounded crass. He knew it, but it needed to be said.

Angie threw a towel over her shoulder. Her eyes glassy, she touched her nose with her other hand, like that would somehow stop the tears. "That's what she said to me, too."

"Say it," he said.

"She's dying." Tears spilled down her cheeks, and she choked against them.

"It's okay. Tears are okay, Angie. It's sad as hell."

She tore the ticket off of her pad and slid it under his plate, then got up to go back to work. "I hate it when you're right."

Derek pushed the shrimp around his plate. They were good, but the last one he'd eaten seemed to be still sitting in the middle of his chest. He tossed his payment and tip on the table and walked out.

What were the odds that two guys who played high school ball together in the same small town would lose the loves of their lives to the same cancer? It wasn't geographical. Neither Laney nor Kelly Jo was from Boot Creek, but it had happened and there wasn't a thing he could do to change the outcome.

Chapter Three

When Katherine opened her front door, the last person she expected to see in the middle of a Thursday afternoon was Peggy Allen. Unlike the others in the neighborhood, Peggy was a housewife, but between her volunteer work, time at the club, and social calendar, she worked harder at not working than any of them. Too bad it didn't pay a salary.

"Hey, Peggy." Katherine stepped back from the door, but Peggy's normal beauty queen smile was missing. "Everything okay?"

"Not by a long shot."

"Come in." Katherine motioned Peggy inside. "Coffee?"

"If you have some already made, and it isn't any trouble."

"I'm working from home today," Katherine said. "Just made another fresh pot." She motioned Peggy inside, but the woman who was usually as effervescent as the fizziest champagne wasn't sparkling and that made Katherine nervous. After spending the week with Bertie, the last thing she wanted to hear was more bad news.

The two of them walked back to the kitchen. Katherine grabbed the coffeepot, glancing out the window at the behemoth brick house next door. The grandest in the neighborhood, Peggy and Tucker Allen's house was just as flashy and loud as he was.

"Something's wrong," Katherine said. "I can see it all over your face."

Peggy hiked herself up onto one of the counter-height barstools at the granite island. "Before you say anything, I want you to hear me out. All the way out."

"Okay." Katherine poured the coffee into two tall blue and white mugs. "You're scaring me."

Peggy took a sip of coffee and then sucked in a deep breath and closed her eyes. "I know Tucker is cheating on me," she blurted out, then opened her eyes and looked at Katherine.

Katherine knew she should look surprised. But she wasn't. "I—"

"Let me finish." Peggy held her hand up like a traffic cop. She looked like she'd practiced this speech in the mirror and committed it to memory, and any interruption might mess her up. "I didn't mean to put you in a weird position yesterday at the funeral. You know, when I said I'd want to know if Tucker had been unfaithful."

Katherine took a sip of coffee, hoping the hot liquid would soothe the burning that had just started in her gut. Guilt. Remorse. Whatever it was, it left a bad taste in her mouth.

"I've known for a while. I mean he was always a flirt, and that was embarrassing at times, but it's how he won my heart initially. And when we're alone, he acted like the sun rose and set on me. He still does, only now I know it's all just a big game to him."

Defeat hung over her friend like a dark cloud. Unlike Peggy and Tucker, Katherine and Ron had met and fallen in love as teenagers. They'd grown up together. They'd never flirted with other people. But then Tucker and Ron were different as night and day.

"I thought I was special."

"Oh, Peggy. You are special. Don't let him ruin your self-esteem."

Peggy's chin trembled. "I believed he loved me. I believed . . . with all of my heart . . . that he'd never cheat on me. Maybe I just needed to believe that. I don't know. Maybe he gave me all he was capable of giving. I'd convinced myself that the flirting was innocent and those little extra ego strokes were kind of the fuel that kept Tucker going."

Oh, he was getting stroked. Katherine held her tongue, but a million thoughts were flying through her mind. How does a woman *not* know when the person who is sharing your home, your life, your bed . . . is carrying on with someone else?

Flirting was one thing, but that guy never turned it off. And it wasn't cute. He got right into your personal space.

Maybe it was a blessing Peggy asked her to just listen because the thoughts running through her mind right now were probably not as supportive as the ones Peggy needed to hear. None of those "look at the bright side" comments like *at least now you know* seemed appropriate or helpful.

Katherine walked over and grabbed a box of tissues from the small table in the hall and put them between them on the island.

Peggy plucked one from the box and like a switch had been triggered, a single tear spilled down her cheek. "Shaleigh has been helping me for weeks. We're getting all of our ducks in a row. I'm filing for divorce."

"I'm so sorry, Peggy."

She shrugged. "I'm not so much hurt as I'm just downright pissed off. I'll start over, and I'll do it with half his stuff. That'll be the least he can do for me after making me a fool in front of everyone."

"You're no one's fool."

Peggy rolled her eyes with a reassuring grin. "It's an expression, Katherine." She snickered, but the pain in her eyes wasn't a joke. "I'm fine. If you want to worry about someone—worry about Tucker. He's going to pay for this the rest of his life. I'm going to make damn sure of that."

"Well, Shaleigh is the best." Even if Katherine thought she could have talked Peggy out of it, there was no reason to. In good conscience she couldn't say anything nice to soothe the situation about Tucker, because she just wasn't that good of a liar.

Peggy would be better off without him, and not one person in Preakness Heights would feel sorry for Tucker when they heard. She was older than Katherine by at least ten years, but she wouldn't have any problem finding someone else. That is, if she even wanted to. How does someone get over that kind of betrayal?

Peggy leaned her face into her hands.

"It's okay," Katherine said, scooting around to her friend's side. But it wasn't okay. It was wrong in so many ways, and although it wasn't a surprise, the truth of it felt heavy on her heart. Her own tears fell, and her voice shook. "Peggy, you don't have to put on a strong face here." She was so lucky to not be walking in Peggy's shoes. Or Bertie's for that matter. Even if Donald hadn't been cheating on Bertie with another woman, he was taking her money and keeping secrets. What was the world coming to when the person you committed your whole life to wasn't even faithful with that precious gift?

The two of them hugged and Peggy's hot tears reminded Katherine that even those that seemed to be the strongest around you needed someone on their side. Bertie. Peggy. Even her sister had been feeling dejected after her recent breakup. After her divorce she'd dated a few guys, but having a toddler made it hard, and more often than not those dates didn't result in much more than a second and final one.

"Aren't we a pair," Peggy said, looking in their reflection of the glass front cabinet and running her fingers under her eyes to whisk away the mascara now streaking her porcelain skin.

Katherine plucked some tissues from the box and handed half of them to her friend. Both dabbed at the tears, and then Katherine stepped over to the cabinet and took down a bottle of Baileys. She didn't bother to ask, just tilted a splash into each of their mugs. "Shaleigh is the best divorce lawyer in the city. You're in good hands," Katherine said. "I'm so proud of you, Peggy. You seem to be handling this with such grace."

"Thanks. I don't feel very graceful," Peggy's voice squeaked at the end like she was losing air.

"Oh, honey." Katherine pushed the concoction in front of her. "Drink up."

"Leave the bottle out."

"You got it." Katherine sat back down. "But I have to ask, did you really not suspect a thing?"

"Not a thing." Peggy took a slow, deliberate breath. "Until I got the email asking us to rate our visit to the Opryland Hotel in Nashville."

"I love that place," Katherine said. Good memories. She and Ron had been several times.

"I've never been there," Peggy said.

"Oh."

Peggy's wedding rings sparkled, but they spun on her finger. Now that Katherine looked closer, Peggy had lost some weight. Probably the stress of it all. "I called the hotel and got them to send me over the registration. It was Tucker's signature, all right, and his dealer tag on the valet records."

"Ouch."

"That was just the beginning. The deeper I dug, the more there was. It's just so humiliating."

Katherine shook her head. What do you say to comfort someone? It was awkward in so many ways and mostly because what she really wanted to say was good freakin' riddance to that jerk for hurting her friend. But being a good friend, she wanted to try to at least be supportive either way. "What did he say?"

"Tucker? I haven't even talked to him about it."

"What if it's a mistake?"

Peggy lowered her chin and shot her a look. "Seriously?"

Katherine wished she had something nice to say, something that might help diffuse things for her friend.

"It's no mistake," Peggy said. "Trust me. I've dotted i's and crossed t's on this. Shaleigh's tracked down more on him since that first little dribble of information. She has a team of investigators she can pick from. She just picks up the phone, and days later you have more details than you ever wanted to know. Besides, does any man ever come clean when you ask him about something like this?"

"I guess not."

"Right. Men deny it or beg for forgiveness. I don't want either, frankly. Shaleigh said there's no sense in letting him know we're on to him until we have everything squared away. Then he won't have time to hide assets or screw me over in any other financial way."

"I guess there's something to be said for that." Katherine pushed her coffee aside. "I'm sorry this is happening to you."

"Me, too."

"Were you happy? I mean before you found all this out?"

Peggy wrinkled her nose. "I was happy enough."

What did that even mean? But then maybe all people settled a little when things got comfortable. "Maybe now you'll find real joy."

She rolled her eyes. "I don't know if I even have the energy for all of that."

"You're too young to just throw in the towel. I know it's hard to even fathom now, but maybe things will be better. New doors and all of that."

"Yeah. All of that. It seems like a lot of work to start over," she said. "Tucker isn't perfect, but we've been together so long that it was easy. Comfortable. Maybe that was part of the problem. I'm thinking alimony for a good long time will make me feel better. Then we'll see how things go."

Guilt weighed on Katherine's heart for suspecting and not saying anything to her friend, but she'd always thought Peggy must not have wanted to see the truth. It seemed so easy to see from the outside. "It's not you who's broken, Peggy. It's him. You know that. Right?"

"Absolutely, and this could be so much easier if I moved out, but I can't. I haven't worked a real job since college. Besides, I worked with the architect on that house," she said pointing toward their home just across the lawn. "I handpicked every color, every tile—every decision that went into this house was mine." Peggy gazed out the window. "That is my house. He needs to be the one to leave."

The front door slammed, and the jingle of Ron's keys hitting the hall table stopped Katherine and Peggy's conversation.

"I better go," Peggy said, opening up the balled-up tissue to dab at her eyes again.

Ron walked in and stopped, raising an eyebrow in surprise. "Well, to what do I owe this pleasure? Two lovely ladies in my kitchen at the end of a hard day." He smiled and kissed Katherine on the cheek as he walked by to get a cold bottle of Coke out of the refrigerator. "Drink anyone?"

"No, I'm just leaving." Peggy forced a perfect smile.

"Don't leave on my account," Ron said.

But Peggy was already hightailing it to the door. Katherine followed her. "Please let me know what I can do," she whispered. "Anything."

Peggy reached out for Katherine's arm and leaned in. "Tucker will get the papers at work tomorrow morning. Watch for any fireworks over at my place tomorrow night. He's not supposed to come back to the house, but I'm a little worried about his reaction. Shaleigh arranged for someone to come pack up all of his things during the day. I have no idea where they'll take them. His office, maybe." Her words held a tension Katherine had never heard before.

"I will keep an eye out. You don't think he'll do anything crazy, do you?"

"Probably not. Everything else will settle in good time. Thanks for letting me bend your ear, and Katherine . . . I understand your not telling me."

Only Peggy saying it was okay made Katherine feel that much worse.

She walked inside and closed the door. Leaning against it, she wished she'd been a better friend.

She stepped into the downstairs bathroom and used a cool wash-cloth to repair her makeup damage from the tears she and Peggy had shared. She picked up the new lip color she'd just purchased and swept it onto her lips.

When she walked back into the kitchen, Ron was nursing his drink.

"You worked from home today?"

"Yeah. Figured it'd be easier if Bertie needed anything."

"You look pretty. New lipstick?"

"Uh-huh."

"I like the color." He leaned closer and kissed her.

His kisses still sent shivers of desire through her.

He pulled back and smiled. "That color makes your mouth look sexy."

It was probably the tears that made her mouth look sexy. Her lips always swelled when she cried, but she took the compliment anyway.

"What's up with Peggy? She looked upset." He lifted his drink to take a sip.

Katherine leaned her arms across the island. "She is. Tucker's cheating."

He paused, and then took a big swig. "Well, I'm sure it doesn't mean anything. You know how he is."

"Yeah. I know how he is, and I've never said anything to Peggy."

"What was there to say? Your husband feels up all the women in town? It doesn't mean anything. He's just overcompensating by being overly friendly."

"There's more to it. Don't you think that's obvious? I mean even a blind squirrel finds a nut now and then," Katherine said. "Maybe if any of us had half the guts to tell him to keep his hands off, he'd have quit acting like a jerk before anything happened."

"Or not. It's just who he is. Peggy had to have known that when they got married. They've been married forever. All I'm saying is there could be more to it."

She regretted mentioning it to him now. What was it? A guy code. She wasn't about to get into it with Ron tonight. Sometimes it was like no matter what she said, or what side she took, he was going to argue with her. Usually it was when he was tired. Tonight, it seemed he was in one of those moods.

In two days she'd learned two neighbors had deceitful husbands. She really didn't have the energy to entertain that topic any longer. "You're right. How was your day?"

"Hectic as hell."

"Why don't you take off early tomorrow? Maybe we could steal away for the weekend. I want to go down to Hilton Head and just putz around. Chill out a little. I could use the break after this week." She walked over and stepped between his legs, nuzzling close to him. "We could make a romantic weekend of it."

"Can't. Have meetings tomorrow."

"We could leave after work."

He handed her the glass and tugged his tie loose. "We'll see. Let's talk about it tomorrow night."

She stood there holding his glass as he turned and left the room to go upstairs. She could hear him taking the stairs two at a time, like a kid; sometimes he was still so seventeen. The water in the shower came next.

She put his glass in the dishwasher and then ordered a pizza. Medium sausage and hot peppers. The way Ron liked it.

With her laptop in front of her, she responded to the last few emails that had come in while she was with Peggy. Then, she boiled water on the stovetop to make a pitcher of sweet tea to drop off over at Bertie's tomorrow.

She picked out a bottle from the wine cooler—one from when she and Ron had met up in Napa while they both were traveling for business on the West Coast. She poured a glass and took it out on the screened porch off of the kitchen while Ron showered.

The sun dipped behind the tall oaks that bordered their yard—how long the days were this time of year. She wondered what the night before your marriage ended must feel like, especially when one person has no idea it's coming.

She sipped the wine, and as the sky grew darker, she could see shadows move behind the curtains of the Allen house. Tucker and Peggy going through their regular routines. One last time.

The pizza arrived and Ron called out to her.

"Going to watch the game with me?"

She carried the wine back inside and snuggled on the couch next to him. For now, anyway. As soon as his baseball team did something stupid, he'd be jumping up.

He got so wound up during those games. Didn't matter if it was from his armchair. He was just as animated at home as he had been in college. Watching him was usually more fun for her than watching the game.

She loved this side of him. Going to sporting events together had always been so much fun, especially on the nights their team won. You'd think he was getting a bonus check for every run or score. Too bad it had been so long since they'd been able to work a game into their schedules.

Katherine got up and walked back into the kitchen to pour another glass of wine. "Want anything while I'm up?"

"Just you back here by my side."

She lifted the glass in the air in the kitchen, with a smile playing on her lips at Ron's words. Looking across the lawn toward the Allen house, she said, "To your future, Peggy. May you find joy. Here's to Tucker paying through the nose for cheating on you, and getting what he deserves."

Usually Katherine worked from home on Fridays, but this morning she had to go into the office for a couple quick meetings. Most people were of the TGIF variety, but fighting summer traffic on Friday afternoons wasn't anything to celebrate. She'd take Thursday traffic over Friday traffic anytime, which was why she was thankful she had the flexibility to work from home most Fridays. That flexibility was the least the bank could do given how much she traveled these days. It was beginning to get a bit comical because when she was traveling, Ron was home and vice versa.

Hopefully she'd get in and out of the city before everyone else and miss the crazy turtle crawl out of town.

She was ready to cut her schedule back a bit. Ready to start that family she and Ron had always talked about; but they were living up to their income, which was only going to make it harder to cut back and slow down for a family.

How long were they going to keep going through the minutiae of tasks, and work, and 24/7 stress? To hell with the Joneses. Her fancy red Mercedes was just one more reminder of Ron's obsession with flaunting their success.

Katherine had been perfectly happy with her Ford. But when bonus time came around at the bank, Ron had practically insisted she treat herself to the expensive ride. So she had.

When she was in college, her visions of joy had been simple, and not nearly this much work. Sandy beaches, sunshine, pretty drinks with umbrellas, tender hugs, and sharing beautiful moments.

But then if anything was going to change, she'd have to make an effort to make a change too.

She got through her meetings and was out of the office by eleven.

Still feeling hopeful that she could somehow wrangle a romantic weekend for the two of them, she headed for Ron's office. Nothing like a surprise on a Friday to put a smile in someone's day. A quick lunch at their favorite little restaurant, and then they could plan the weekend.

If not a trip to Hilton Head, maybe at least a little day trip to do something together.

Her mood buoyed. Even the crazy afternoon traffic wouldn't bother her today. She took the exit for Ron's office. In this section of Atlanta, the tall buildings shaded the road from the hot summer sun, but the air still undulated above the hot pavement.

She sat at a stoplight just a few blocks from Ron's building with her blinker on. The guy in the car next to her smiled and waved. He must have been wondering why she was sitting in traffic with a big goofy grin on her face.

The streets crawled with businesspeople in a hurry to squeeze in a quick break, or a working lunch. She was thankful the LOT FULL sign wasn't up at the parking garage. Sometimes it was nearly impossible to get a spot in this part of town on a Friday. She got lucky and found one on the second level of the parking garage. As she took the stairs, rather than the elevator, she smiled at a woman who was also walking up. These days, with all of the hours you spent behind a desk, you had to work in a little exercise any way you could.

Katherine headed up the block toward Ron's building. Unlike in the bank, anyone could go up and down the elevators. She dialed his cell but there wasn't an answer. She called his office line and his secretary answered.

"Hi. It's Katherine Barclift," she said as she wove through the maze of elevator banks to the one for floors 11–26, and pressed the button. "Can I chat with Ron?"

"I'm sorry. He's in a meeting."

"Oh. That's okay. I've got some time. I'm here in the city. Maybe I'll just come up and wait."

"You know, it's one of those all-day things. I don't know when he'll be available."

This was exactly why she didn't usually do spontaneous. It rarely worked out for her. Nope, she should have made a plan. "Okay, will they be breaking for lunch?"

"They'll have to eat, I suppose. Maybe at the top of the hour?"

Clueless didn't begin to explain this girl's reaction. Katherine hated it when people seemed to be winging it. "Just let him know I called, then."

"I'll tell him."

Katherine had her doubts she'd even deliver the message. She'd just call him herself in about thirty minutes. Where to wait, though?

The arrow lit, and the elevator door opened. She nodded to a couple of Ron's exiting coworkers she didn't know by name, but recognized from the Christmas party last year.

She decided to head on down to her and Ron's favorite little bistro and order a salad or appetizer while she waited. If she called at the top of the hour, maybe she'd catch him and they could meet for a short lunch.

People were coming in and out of the building so fast that the revolving door looked like it would never stop spinning.

She timed her entrance into the swift moving contraption and it catapulted her back out onto the street. Heading east a couple blocks, she spotted the familiar bright red awning of the Carpe Diem Bistro.

A young man in black pants, a white shirt, and a red bow tie greeted her immediately. "Just one?"

"I'm meeting someone," she said, and then quickly added, "He's running late."

"No worries. I can seat you now."

"Can I get a booth? With a little privacy."

He gave her a wink. "I have just the one. Follow me."

Feeling a little more confident that she might be able to salvage the not-so-impromptu lunch date now, she relaxed a little and followed him to the corner booth.

"Can I get you something to drink while you wait?"

"A glass of chardonnay would be great."

"On its way."

She settled in and checked her phone for an update from Peggy. She hoped things were going okay. Knowing that your husband is unfaithful had to be the worst feeling. But there weren't any messages or emails from her.

A different waiter brought her a glass of wine. "I'll be back in just a bit for your order."

She sipped her wine until it was just a few minutes until the top of the hour. She'd try calling Ron then. Hopefully he'd pick up his personal cell phone, or she could at least leave him a well-timed voice mail.

At exactly one o'clock she dialed Ron's phone. He finally picked up on the fourth ring.

Her mood lifted. "Hi. How busy are you?"

"Hey, Katherine. Everything okay?"

The meeting must still be going on. He sounded hushed and in a hurry.

"I'm fine. Finer than fine." She lifted her shoulders and let them drop. "Fantastic. I thought we could get together for a quick lunch."

"Oh, hon. It's not a good time. You should've called."

"I left you a message. I guess you didn't get it." She shifted gears. "When will you be done? I can wait."

"No. I'm in an all-day meeting. I just stepped out here in the hall to take your call, in case it was important."

"There's kind of an echo," she said, pulling the phone from her ear.

"Must be the hall."

Only it wasn't. Because it wasn't echo so much as stereo. She edged forward and looked across the way to the booths over and behind her.

The waiter approached her with a "you ready" look.

She held up a finger and he disappeared.

The man in the blue button-down shirt with the sleeves turned up just-so who sat across the way . . . he didn't need to turn around for her to know who he was.

The way his hair waved in that one spot, and the way his watchband hung like it was a little too loose on his left arm, which always drove her a little crazy, was all it took.

She pulled back into her seat, clutching the phone close to her ear, trying not to completely lose it right then and there.

Chapter Four

Katherine slid further toward the wall in her booth. Not just to hide, but to catch her breath. The smells of the food in the bistro made her stomach roll like oil in a fryer.

Breathing, that thing your body knows how to do without thought. Her body had suddenly forgotten how.

She sucked in a deep breath and risked leaning out to look again. Katherine watched her husband hold his shiny red iPhone case to his ear. He reached his hand across the table to hold someone else's, and his cheeks tugged in a smile.

"An all-day meeting?" she repeated, watching intently to gauge his response. "They won't even let you out for like a fifteen-minute lunch break? I don't mind waiting. I could meet you somewhere. Just a quick bite in your office, even."

She watched the line of his jaw as he spoke. Though she couldn't see him face on from her angle, the words coming across the phone line synchronized with his every movement.

She lifted a finger to the corner of one eye, and swept at the tears that were making her vision blurry.

So this is what it looks like to have no idea at all.

Thoughts of Peggy flooded her mind, and that place in her gut that was so hungry just a few minutes ago tightened into a coil. The blood pulsing through her veins was so loud she'd missed half of what he'd just said.

"And I'll probably be late tonight. You know how these things are, babe."

Babe? "Of course. Yeah. Sure."

She watched him shove the phone in his pocket and slide his arms across the table toward that woman. There was no explaining it away.

Late? How many times had he been late recently?

She sat there staring.

At him. Her husband.

At that woman. Younger than she was. The woman had short, wispy dark hair. Her total opposite. Ron about came unglued every time Katherine had a hair appointment. He liked her hair long and simple. He loved blondes. That woman was not his type.

At least that's what she'd thought.

But Ron's attention was so focused on the woman that he didn't seem to notice a thing around him, including her.

Her body refused to budge to get out of his view. All it would take would be one glance across the aisle and he'd be looking right at her, slack-jawed and all. She gasped, sucking air, but seemingly unable to get her lungs to take it in. They . . . her husband and some other woman . . . sat there with nearly empty plates in front of them. The image of them bounced around in her head, burning into her brain. An image that didn't belong.

With her back to them in the booth, she lifted her phone above her head and snapped a picture. It made that loud, old-timey camera sound.

She practically folded in on herself as she yanked it from the air. So much for being sneaky.

She hit every button she knew of on her doggone iPhone to quiet it. Then she held the phone again like she was going to take a selfie . . .

only the camera was reversed, facing across the way . . . toward Ron's table. Silently, she captured the image.

A moment later they slid out of the booth.

She snapped another as they headed for the front door, as she pretended to make her way to the ladies' room.

He held the door for her, that woman. His smile, the one that normally charmed her socks off, made her teeth grind. The woman ducked under his arm like she was doing a well-executed cross-body lead in a sexy mambo. When was the last time he'd held the door for her?

Katherine tilted her head down, pretending to focus on her phone, all the while snapping a loop of pictures of them as they crossed the street. Holding hands.

And then as if there were any inkling of hope in her heart . . . she watched them as they stood at the crosswalk. Ron lifted his hands and placed them on the sides of the woman's face. And then he kissed her.

Katherine's mouth dropped open.

She knew that move. She could almost feel the heat of his hands against her cool cheeks. His warm mouth. It melted her heart the first time he'd ever done that to her. It had melted her heart this morning . . . again . . . for the last time.

Click.

She stood there, frozen to the spot. A tear of frustration traced her cheek to the corner of her mouth. She swept it away and ducked inside the bathroom. The pounding in her head blurred her vision with each beat in a dizzying effect. Her heart felt like it would explode out of her chest.

Her watch read 1:09 p.m. A quick glance at her most recently dialed numbers showed she'd called him at 1:01 p.m.

Those eight minutes felt like eight hours of adrenaline-forged hiking.

She stepped out onto the street to find them, but however long she'd been in the bathroom pulling herself together had been long enough for them to get a pretty good head start.

Standing there with no idea what to do next was like being stripped naked on Main Street.

Katherine walked up to the next block, but still didn't see them. Her mouth was so dry she could barely swallow. She stepped inside the Starbucks and paid for a bottle of water and a biscotti.

On the street she scanned the people again. No sign of them.

She unscrewed the cap off the water bottle, and of course the flimsy plastic collapsed, spurting water across the front of her shirt. She took another sip and then shoved the bottle in her purse.

Slowly moving up the block, she manipulated the biscotti in her hand, the crinkle of its cellophane wrapper bringing her some kind of weird peace as she tried to figure out what her next step was.

She'd prayed for a change. Practically danced across the parking garage at the thought of it. Now this? Had God answered the wrong prayer? Maybe she hadn't been specific enough. And damn if those words that she'd thought about Peggy weren't raging in her head, slashing at her with a big fat don't-judge reminder from her mom. How could she not know?

That last conversation with Peggy and her own unspoken judgment felt like payback. Maybe everyone else knew about Ron and what he was doing too. Maybe it wasn't even the first time. Would that make it worse? One time was enough damage, wasn't it?

The tsunami of thoughts flooded her brain.

He couldn't or wouldn't give her even fifteen minutes, but he sure did give Miss Thing his undivided attention. Seriously? He could have squeezed her in, kept his secret, and still played playboy for a long lunch . . . if he'd wanted to. If she'd been important enough.

No one was that busy. It was just a matter of where you were in his priorities. It was that simple. He hadn't been willing to give her an inch.

The biscotti crumbled inside the plastic wrap. She hadn't had any intention of eating it anyway, but she'd about tortured the innocent almond pastry into a limp heap.

She debated confronting Ron.

What purpose would that serve? Maybe she should have done that in the restaurant. Stepped pretty as you please right up to his table, and then said, "Hello, dear." Laid a big wet kiss on his mouth and told little Miss No Good, "I've got this." Shooshed that pixie-haired woman off with a flip of her hand like she was nothing.

What did she expect to get out of that, though? An apology? She'd more likely get an excuse. Was that what she wanted? And even if she got the apology or the excuse, was it enough?

She pressed the button on her phone and pulled up the pictures she'd taken. She tapped the screen and spread her fingers to enlarge the image.

He looked perfectly happy. Not even guilty. You'd think he'd have had the decency to at least find a new restaurant, not recycle her favorite lunch spot with that woman. Was nothing sacred?

She was pretty. Katherine wanted to think she was ugly. Pretty is as pretty does, Mom had always said. Did she know he was married? Did she even care? Must be nice to have such long manicured nails. She glanced at her own nails. Void of polish. It was too hard to keep them looking nice with all the typing she did.

Maybe that woman didn't even work. Maybe she had all day, any day, to spend with Ron. How do you compete with that?

Katherine brought up Shaleigh's number on her phone. She'd know what to do, but Peggy had said they'd been gathering things for weeks to get ready for her separation from Tucker.

There was no way Katherine was going to keep her cool that long. Peggy probably deserved an Oscar. Besides, why suffer through even one weekend of silence when she could face Ron head-on and be done with it.

She tossed the crumbling package of biscotti into the trashcan. He didn't need to bother coming home tonight. Late or otherwise.

Katherine made her way back to Ron's office on heavy legs. She paused to lean against the hard concrete of the black-glassed building she'd always called Darth Vader. Weighing her options, her mood was as ominous as the dark building.

She stood there in Vader's shadow. *May the force be with you.* The words echoed in her head as she pushed herself onward.

She pushed through the spinning doors and right into the same elevator to Ron's floor that she'd almost gotten on earlier.

Two o'clock. Too much to take in.

The receptionist smiled politely when Katherine walked in, but Katherine didn't bother to stop to chitchat or ask her to announce her arrival. She whisked right by her instead.

Katherine knew the way to Ron's office. She'd helped him hang the pictures she'd picked out for it when he got his last promotion.

"Mrs. Barclift," the receptionist called as she closed in on her from behind, her high heels making little scuffing noises in the plush carpet as she ran down the hall. "I'm sorry. I can't let you just come back here."

Katherine put her hand on the knob of Ron's office door, and threw it open without so much as a glance back at the girl.

The office was dark. Not a paper or laptop on the desk. Not a darn paper clip out of place.

She turned and stared at the receptionist, tilting her head as if the thoughts in her head would just somehow inform the girl what she was thinking.

With a quick intake of breath, like someone getting ready to dive into icy waters, the girl said, "He's been gone most of the day."

"The meeting?" Katherine choked out.

She shook her head. The lie creeping in in the form of a red rash up her neck. "I'm sorry. I don't know. He said he wouldn't be back in today." The girl looked afraid. Probably afraid for her job. Maybe afraid of what Katherine was going to do. It was probably wise, because Katherine wasn't quite sure what she was going to do either.

"Can I have one minute?" Katherine tried to sound calm.

"Of course," the girl said with a look of panic. "Just don't break anything. Please?"

Katherine stepped into the office and closed the door behind her.

The smell of Irish Spring soap and Ron's aftershave intermingled in the air. She walked over to his desk.

The picture of the two of them on their honeymoon wasn't on his desk anymore. Neither was the one where they'd been in the Caribbean celebrating Christmas island-style.

Slowly looking around the room, there wasn't one picture of her. It was like she'd never existed. The thought made her throat ache with regret. No evidence of their life together. Except there, on the bookshelf, was a picture of her new car. Thanks, man.

She picked up a piece of paper and an ink pen. *What do I even say?*

She sat in his chair, and spun toward the large windows that overlooked the city. She couldn't even cry.

She turned back around and leaned forward. Her fingers stroked the fine leather of the desk pad she'd bought him on his birthday last month. The bomber-jacket leather was so soft. It had been a fun splurge. He was hard to buy for because they really bought whatever they wanted when they wanted it, but when she found this . . . she knew it would be perfect.

He'd barely been able to keep his hands off the fine soft leather when she'd given it to him. Not unlike the way he seemed to be with that woman today.

She reached into her purse and pulled out her new lipstick. Bright magenta with just a hint of sparkle to it. He'd said it made her mouth look sexy.

She twisted the lip color up and scrawled L i A R in big letters across the entire thirty-six inches of the desk pad.

The letters looked fluorescent against the dark leather. The letter *i* had come out a little short.

She stared at it. That little *i* taunted her. *No surprise, because I am feeling right small today.* Rather than extend the *I* to the height of the rest of the letters, she lifted the lipstick to her mouth and ran it across her lips in a thick layer, then leaned forward and dotted that lowercase *i* with her lips. "You don't deserve me. Kiss that."

She hoped the hot pink never came out of the leather.

"Bye, love," she said as she headed for the door.

Standing at the door, she took one last glance back. There was something calming about what she'd just done. She straightened herself and pasted a perfect smile on her face.

The receptionist, on the other hand, looked so pale Katherine wondered if she might get the poor girl some water.

"I'm sorry," the girl mouthed.

"No. He is." Katherine strode out of the building, not bothering to look back.

When she got to the parking garage, she stepped out of her heels and ran the stairs. It was a relief to burn some of the adrenaline that was making her body ache, the exercise releasing some of the anxiousness in her gut.

She stood next to her car wondering if Ron's receptionist was hard at work trying to remove her message. She had a feeling the girl may have just gone home sick right then and there, and the way she looked, no one would have questioned her sincerity.

Katherine started the car, and silenced the radio, needing to steer clear of the happy music that she'd been dancing her way through the morning to. She didn't feel happy, didn't want to feel happy, and didn't know if she'd ever smile a real smile again.

Now what? Change the locks on the house? *Can I even legally do that?*

Would she even need to? Clearly his preferences lay elsewhere. Once he knew that she knew, he might not even show his face.

He could have his little mistress. More power to him. She probably didn't even have a job. Little Twinkie. No. Ho Ho. Yeah, that was more like it. She hoped the girl drained him for every penny he'd ever saved. It would serve him right. What kind of woman slept with another woman's husband?

The lowest of low.

Katherine didn't know her next step, but did know that she needed time. Time to figure it all out. This was the kind of problem that required a plan.

Without a second thought, she dialed her boss.

"Didn't you just leave out of here?" Dave Harris asked.

"Not too long ago. I had something come up. A family emergency."

"Everything okay?"

"Not really. I'm on the road, heading out of town. I need to take a leave of absence. I'm sorry it's such short notice. I need at least a month. I can explain later if you need—"

"No explanations necessary, unless you just need the ear."

"No. I can't talk about it yet."

"Katherine, you take care of your family. That's the most important thing. We'll cover things here."

"I might need the whole ninety days." It was one of the benefits, although it was rare anyone ever took advantage of it, especially since it was without pay.

"We can cross that bridge when we get to it. Do what you need to do. Touch base with me later."

"My laptop is locked in my desk if you need to secure it."

"Good, that will save you the trouble of mailing it in while you're on leave."

"Thank you so much, Dave." Katherine knew she was lucky to work for him. Some people wouldn't have a benefit like this so easily initiated, even if most companies dangled it as one.

"Is there anything I can do?"

He was always so supportive. Not just a coworker, but right up there on the friend list. He'd be shocked when he found out. Or maybe he wouldn't. Maybe it was a man's code or something. "No. Nothing anyone can do. Time's what I need right now." That wasn't entirely untrue.

"Make it be on your side then, gal."

"Thanks." She hung up the phone and closed her eyes. One five-minute phone call and she had a leave of absence. *That was almost too easy.*

She put her car in drive and navigated the tight curves toward the garage exit. At the crossarm, she took her credit card from her wallet. Just as she was ready to swipe the card in the machine, she hesitated, and then switched it out for Ron's. She never used his credit card. They had each other's cards, just in case, but they'd just always settled their own spending. Not today. No sir.

If Ron had any doubts that it had been she who left that four-letter message on his desk, in case multiple women were competing for his affection (the thought!), the twelve-dollar parking fee on his credit card would solve that little puzzle for him pretty quick.

"Thank you very much," she sneered.

Cars packed her in on all sides, but at least traffic was moving. She drove in silence. Twice she picked up her phone to call Shaleigh, but then decided she just wasn't up to discussing things with anyone, not even her lawyer, yet.

When she pulled into her driveway, she didn't bother putting her car in the garage. Partly because it always drove Ron crazy when she didn't, and partly because she wasn't sure she planned to stay. She stared at the house. It wasn't a home anymore. He'd just ruined that.

She switched off the ignition and sat there.

Just this morning she'd wanted nothing more than to spend more time with her husband and strengthen their bond. Maybe start that family.

If anyone had asked her this morning, she'd have sworn on her life that she'd have a forty-plus-year marriage like Bertie and Donald's. They'd always seemed so happy, but then even they had secrets.

And now . . . it was making her physically ill to even think about seeing her husband's face one more time. She'd always sworn she wouldn't have a marriage like her own mom and dad. They never talked about anything. Nope, they just complained about each other to everyone. She'd always thought if there was any kind of problem, she and Ron would be able to talk about it, and solve it. But then she hadn't even realized there was a problem, had she? Had she been too busy to even notice?

Katherine sat in the driveway for so long she began to sweat. On a hotter day, she could have suffocated in the car. Wouldn't that have been a surprise for Ron when he got home? No, she wasn't the type to go wallowing in self-pity. Lock *his* ass in the car to suffocate? Maybe.

She pulled herself together and got out. As she walked up the sidewalk, she heard Peggy calling her name as she made her way across the yard.

"I was beginning to think you'd passed out in your car," she said.

Peggy must have seen her drive up. She looked better than she had yesterday afternoon. Today she wore a crisp white blouse and lots of silver jewelry. "How are you doing?"

"Good. Tucker got his papers this morning." Her wrists jingled from the row of bracelets. "Lord, he hit the roof. Movers left like twenty minutes ago with all of his stuff. That was a weird feeling. To watch someone pack up your husband's stuff. I mean it's not like he's dead. Or maybe he should be. I mean not dead-dead. Dead to me. Wait . . ." She reached for Katherine's hand. "Are you okay?"

A choked cry escaped from her. And that was it. She hadn't cried when she caught Ron. Hadn't cried when she scribbled the message on his desk. Hadn't broken down all the way home, but one look into Peggy's eyes and she'd lost all of her restraint, and she couldn't even catch her breath to explain.

"Oh, my goodness. Katherine? I'm so sorry. I was just rambling. All about me. I didn't even notice. What is going on?"

Katherine folded to a heap on the front porch.

"Did something happen to Ron? Oh, God. He's not dead, is he? You know how I'm always saying things like that. Has something happened to him?"

Katherine let out a halfhearted laugh through her tears. Oh, something had happened to Ron all right, was happening pretty frequently to him, too. But not like Peggy was thinking.

"Let's get you inside," Peggy said.

"I can't." Katherine shook her head and clenched her keys tighter in her hand. She couldn't go inside. There was nothing in there she needed. Nothing but more lies. She leaned forward on her knees and cried.

Peggy sat down next to her and rubbed a hand along her back. "Honey. What's wrong?"

"I'm so sorry. You're going through all of this stuff, too. It's not fair. I'm so sorry about Tucker."

"Oh, Katherine, you're more upset than I am. Honey, don't do this to yourself. I'm going to be fine. Yes, he's going to be a big fat pain in the ass about it. Already conjured up a lawyer to do battle with me, but I'm not the least bit worried. And no matter what he does or how long he drags it out, it's going to be on his dime." She grabbed Katherine's hand. "It's okay, honey."

"No. It's not." Katherine ran a hand across her face.

"Let me at least go in and get you some tissues."

Katherine handed over the keys and Peggy went inside.

By the time Peggy came out with a glass of water and a box of tissues, Katherine had pulled herself somewhat together. "I'm sorry, Peggy."

"Don't be. We're friends. Now what in the heck has you so upset?"

Katherine tugged two tissues from the box, and then squeezed them into her hand. "Peggy, I saw Ron with another woman today."

Peggy's lips pulled into a tight line. She shook her head, then tilted it slightly as her eyes softened in response.

Katherine hated to ask, but she had to. "Did you know?"

Peggy lowered her chin. "No, honey. I didn't know. Ron isn't Tucker. I'm sure Ron was very discreet. Are you sure what you saw was . . . you know."

She nodded. "No question about it." She pulled her phone out and scrolled to the picture of Ron kissing the woman. "Right in the street." She shoved the phone into Peggy's hands.

Her friend took a long look at the picture, even zoomed in, and then dropped her hands to her lap. "No way to really wiggle out of that one." The redhead tilted the phone to the left. "You don't even do CPR in that position."

Katherine took the phone back. She took one more look at the picture, resulting in a groan, and then pressed the power button. Even the red slide to power off prompt annoyed her right now.

"Maybe you can work things out. Couples do it all the time. You know middle-age craziness and all that."

She flashed Peggy a look. "Seriously? I could never forgive this."

"Me either. I just wanted you to consider it." Peggy wiggled her toes, the nails bright orange, in her sandals. "What are you going to do?"

"I'd like to run away."

"Then do it." Peggy leaned her head on Katherine's shoulder. "You have a career and you can take care of yourself. Trust me: I'll be in an ugly, nasty fight with Tucker for months, maybe years, over all of this. He's going to nickel-and-dime me to death. You don't have to go through it. If I were in your shoes, my ass would be in that cute little sports car and I'd be halfway to somewhere else by now." She wiggled her toes again. "Well, right after I got a nice new pedi to match the car. I wouldn't want to clash." She laughed and nudged Katherine. "Come on, honey. Giggle a little. We have to stay positive. Somehow."

"Really? You'd up and run away?"

"Yeah. Really. I mean, call Shaleigh and let her do all the legal stuff, but you don't need to put yourself through all of this. Can't you work from anywhere? With all the travel you do for work, I'd suspect so."

"I can, but I actually called my boss right after everything went down and asked for a leave of absence."

"Oh, girl. You are crazy if you don't get out of here right now. What's stopping you?"

"I don't know."

Peggy stood up. "Come on. If you're one-hundred-percent sure you don't want to consider forgiving him . . . then leave."

Could she really do that? Did she want him to come home and grovel and swear his allegiance on their relationship? Well, yeah. But would she ever believe him again? No. "I'm leaving."

"Good. Let's go pack your stuff. You can be out of here, and licking your wounds in a super-nice suite with room service, before Ron ever gets home tonight."

Katherine sniffed back the tears, and stood . . . ready to forge ahead. "You're right. I don't want an apology. I don't want to hear an excuse, or have him turn this around to be my fault. What's done is done."

Chapter Five

"Come on." Peggy hopped up and opened the front door.

Katherine paused in the foyer. Like she was a visitor in her own house. She turned to her friend. "Peggy? I'm so sorry I never told you about Tucker crossing lines with women. I mean I never knew he actually did anything, but all the wives complained about the way he was overly friendly, and not one of us did anything to stop him. I'm so sorry. Will you ever forgive me?"

"I know," she said quietly. "It's funny how crisp and clear hindsight became once I knew the truth. I wouldn't wish it on my best friend. I'm sorry you were put in that position with Tucker. I'm sorry you're going through this too. I wouldn't wish this kind of betrayal on anyone."

But Katherine had to wonder if it was some kind of karma retaliation. If she'd been a better friend. If she'd kneed that son of a gun Tucker Allen right in the family jewels and told Peggy, maybe her own situation would be different. Something she'd never know now.

Katherine looked around her home in a new light. It was funny how one teensy thing could change everything. Well, it wasn't really all that little. When it came to lies, this wasn't an itty-bitty one.

The pictures of their happy moments sat on the mantel and tables, and now they looked like the ones that came in the frames when you buy them. Like a good-looking couple you don't know who needs to be replaced with real people.

"You and I don't deserve this," Katherine said.

"You're right." Peggy took both of Katherine's hands in her own. "Don't forget that. We deserve better. Trust me, there will be days when you'll find yourself searching for what you did wrong. This is their problem. Their shortcoming. Not ours."

"Easy to say." Katherine sucked in a deep breath. After all, if she'd been enough, been perfect, would he have ever needed to stray? She could have stroked his ego more. It was probably hard on a he-man's ego to have his wife make more money. Not that they ever talked about it. "You're right. It's going to be hard to not blame myself."

"But don't. Promise me," Peggy said.

Katherine wasn't about to make that promise. She'd just be a liar if she did.

She scanned the room. How do you pack just a few things? Memories, treasures, pieces of her whole life were in this house. "How do I even figure out what I need?" She walked past so many things that held importance it was hard not to want to scoop up every little memory and take it with her. But then she'd need a moving van, maybe two, and there'd be time to come back for that stuff. Right now, she just needed space. "I guess this is like 'what do you grab in a fire drill?' Only the critical stuff."

Katherine stood at the base of the stairs and clutched the handrail. Had he ever had that woman here, in their bed? While she was traveling? Opportunity. She'd certainly given him plenty of that, if not reason. She lifted a heavy leg to the first step on the stairway and then trudged upstairs.

Peggy followed and helped Katherine fill her wheeled travel bag with casual wear and underclothes; then she took to the bathroom and grabbed the makeup and personal items Katherine might need.

"Just a minute," Katherine said as she eased past Peggy into the bathroom. She looked around: her favorite perfumes and the embroidered hand towel her grandmother had made for her as a wedding gift were on the counter. She touched the worn fabric. It was hard to leave anything behind. Her attention settled on Ron's toothbrush.

Peggy stepped behind her.

"He has the best smile," Katherine said, tears welling at the conflicting emotions coursing through her. "Damn him."

Peggy snatched the toothbrush from the holder. "Do you have any white vinegar?"

"Yeah. In the kitchen. Why?"

"Come on." Peggy raced down the stairs and Katherine followed her. "Get me that white vinegar." Peggy grabbed a coffee cup from the sink drainer and stood at the ready. Toothbrush in one hand, coffee mug in the other.

Katherine slammed through two cabinets and then walked over to Peggy with the vinegar. "What are we doing?"

Peggy tossed the toothbrush tip down into the mug and then glugged out enough vinegar to cover the whole head of the toothbrush. As she swished the tight blue and white bristles through the vinegar, the smell wafted in the air. "It's harmless. I promise, but toothpaste reacts to this vinegar and it will put a taste in his mouth that he is not going to forget for a long haul."

Katherine smiled. "Really?"

"Oh, honey. The worst. We used to do this all the time at summer camp. It's a little evil but so worth the price of a cheap bottle of vinegar."

"And a perfect comeuppance for that tooth-obsessed husband of mine. Did I tell you that the woman had teeth so white it looked like they were painted?"

"Don't think about her." Peggy swished the toothbrush again. "Too bad we don't have her toothbrush!" She lifted the toothbrush out and carried it like the Olympic torch up the stairs with Katherine at her heels. She set it back in the holder and they both stepped back with a satisfied grin.

"Sometimes you just have to have a little win," Peggy said.

Katherine reached under the counter and took his teeth whitening kit. "May as well make that two." She shoved the whitening kit into her bag. "I can't do this. Whatever I've got, I've got. I'll be back," Katherine said, because if she didn't leave now, she'd never be able to.

"No. Not by a long shot. You need to grab all of your personal documents. The last bank statements, titles, all the important papers. Better to have them with you than to trust he'll produce them."

"We have them in a safe downstairs."

"Leave the safe. Take the papers. He probably won't even realize they're gone for a while and that will play in your favor."

"How do you know all of this stuff?"

"Shaleigh has been taking me through these paces for weeks. I paid for this advice. I'm giving it to you for free."

They took the suitcase downstairs and Katherine grabbed another tote bag from the hall closet and went into the office and filled it with the papers.

"I'd move half the money today, and anything you don't have, just buy. On his credit card. Not yours," Peggy said.

"Not sure I would really do that." Although she had put her parking on his card, but that was twelve bucks . . . and a statement.

"Do it. Trust me, if he turns into a jerk you'll be happy, and if not you can always pay the bill."

"Good point." She pulled the zipper closed on her bag. "Thanks for everything. I'll call and check on you. You'll call me if you need to talk."

"I will. We're both going to be okay."

Katherine gave the place a look around.

"It's just stuff," Peggy said. "I wish I'd been able to do what you're doing. I'm so envious of you right this minute. No arguing. No bickering or name-calling." Peggy hugged Katherine. "Call me. Anytime. Day or night. And if you need to come back, you can stay with me. Although I guess it could be a little awkward being right next door." Peggy took the tote bag and slung it over her shoulder.

"True. Thank you so much for being here today." She grabbed her laptop bag, balanced it on top of the wheeled bag, and headed to the car with Peggy at her side. She put her suitcase and laptop bag in the trunk. Peggy tucked the tote next to Katherine's suitcase, and slammed the trunk closed.

Peggy dipped her hand into the back pocket of her capri jeans, and pulled out a tiny bow made from a thin, soft yellow ribbon. She handed it to Katherine.

"What's this?"

"For good luck," Peggy explained. "When I first found out about Tucker, I went to an infidelity support group."

"There's a support group for that?"

"Yeah. I didn't stick it out, but one lady, the one who gave me that ribbon . . . she had some good advice."

"I can't take it then," Katherine said handing it back.

"You sure can." She pushed Katherine's hand back. "I heard the message firsthand. I want to share it with you. You tuck that in your pocket, just like she told me to."

"Okay. I like the yellow," she said giving it one last glance before putting it in her pocket.

"The woman said yellow is the color of hope and optimism."

"And caution," Katherine said, immediately regretting the snark in her voice.

"Can't argue that, but you're going to struggle with what's happened. There'll be good days and bad days. You're going to want to know why it happened, and you'll probably blame yourself. Don't. Trust me, I'm just ahead of you on this path. It's hard. It strips you of your confidence some days, and makes you as angry as a hornet on others. Neither is good. Cheaters cheat. They are broken. You are not."

"Thanks, Peggy."

"You go out and find the life you were meant to have. And anytime you doubt that you can keep moving forward, you pull out this ribbon as a reminder that there's hope for something better."

"Thank you, Peggy. I'll keep that in mind." Katherine took the ribbon back out of her pocket. "That's a lot of responsibility for one little piece of ribbon." She always joked when she was upset. It was an awful coping mechanism, but Peggy meant well, and she didn't have any better plans, so she held the ribbon in her fist and clutched it to her heart for a long moment.

"Seriously. I don't ever want to feel this way again. Thank you for sharing this with me." At that she tucked that ribbon into her front pocket and got into her car.

She waved to Peggy, and then headed down the street, not allowing herself to glance back even once. There would be no looking back from now on.

A few miles up the road, Katherine pulled into the parking lot of the bank branch nearest to her house with only a few minutes to spare before closing time. At least it wasn't the bank she worked for. She worked at the corporate office of one of the biggest banks in the nation. No, Ron had been adamant about keeping their funds in this small local bank because he had hopes of being on the board of it one day. That and he sure liked being the big fish in the little pond. His dad had been on the board of their hometown bank and he'd do anything to match or better his dad.

She glanced at her watch. The tellers were going to want to kill her for showing up at the last minute on a Friday night, but it was better to get this transaction done while she had the gumption to do so.

She clutched the scrap of paper with the magic number on it, praying they hadn't already locked the doors.

"How are you today, Mrs. Barclift?" the branch manager said, recognizing her as soon as she walked in. If the late entrance frustrated him, he didn't show it.

He didn't seem to notice her strained smile either. "Great. Things are great. I need to make a withdrawal from our savings today. Something special is going on." She let out what she hoped sounded like a playful titter of excitement.

"Come with me. I can help you with that."

Katherine had probably contributed sixty-five percent of the balance in their savings account, but Ron had paid for the vacations, so it would even out. Probably more in his favor, but she didn't want one penny of his. She didn't even want to breathe the same air that he did.

She followed the branch manager into his office. The desk was piled with stacks of papers. A bookcase in the corner couldn't have had more than a dozen books, but it was filled with family pictures. There was one of him with his wife. Him with his kids. The whole family. Him with the dog. Him with his boat. Every single picture included him. The whole world must seem to revolve around him.

She'd been in the very chair she was sitting in dozens of times. Why hadn't she noticed this about the photos before? All she'd ever noticed was that he seemed to have a really happy and busy family.

At least this guy had pictures of his wife in his office. She'd disappeared from Ron's. How long ago had he done that? She couldn't quite remember the last time she was actually there.

She tugged the corners of her mouth into another smile. Not fair to judge everyone based on the behavior of a few.

"I need this amount." She pushed the paper across the desk.

"Cashier's check okay?"

"Just fine."

"Who should we make it out to?"

"To me." He looked curious, but she wasn't about to start offering up a story. He'd know she was lying anyway. "Easiest that way."

He plucked away on his keyboard, and then got up from his desk and went to the cashier's window. A few minutes later he came back with the check in his hand.

With the cashier's check in an envelope, Katherine got back in her car. She tucked the envelope into the owner's manual in her glove compartment and locked it.

While she'd been waiting for the branch manager to get her check, Katherine had decided she'd head north. Might as well. It was June and the south was only going to get hotter by the minute. She'd head up toward Charlotte. She knew that route like the back of her hand from going there for work so often and trips to see her parents. It would be an easy drive and she knew she could grab a room and make the rest of her plan from there.

For now, all she had to do was drive.

She wondered how long it would take Ron to notice she was gone. Did he even know that she knew? If he'd been to the office, he might not come home at all.

"I'll probably be late tonight," he'd said.

Then, "You know how these things are, babe."

No. She didn't know what it was like to go out of your way to cheat on and betray someone. And she never wanted to.

She headed north, making good time compared to the heavier traffic in the opposite direction. She rolled down her window and let the wind blow through the car; it was warm, but less confining.

An hour in, she took an exit to grab a Diet Coke from a drive-thru. After she placed her order, she thumbed through the old emails on her phone until she found the one she needed.

She pushed speed dial to call the cell phone of the only person who needed to know what was going on. Shaleigh.

The phone rang, but it went directly to voice mail.

"Hey, gal. It's me. I guess there's something in the water around here. I need your professional services. I want the fastest divorce you can serve up. I don't want the house. I don't want half of his anything, just what's got my name on it. I just withdrew half of all of our savings. God, this sucks. Call me and let me know what you'll need from me. I'll be on the road. Use my cell."

She pressed END, and expended a long exhale like she'd been sucker punched. At least she hadn't broken down and cried.

A sucker punch would be easier to explain to people. What would she say to her mother, her friends? How do you tell people that your husband is a liar? And why hadn't he just left, rather than lie? She'd like to think that if he was unhappy, they'd have amicably divided and gone their ways.

There was no going back.

Forgiveness? Second chances? Those were for people who made mistakes, not for those who had done what Ron had just done.

It was probably for the best that he hadn't made her the priority when she'd called. If he had given her that fifteen minutes she had begged for while he sat just across the way, even after seeing him with someone else, she might have reasoned with herself that *she* was most important. That it hadn't meant anything. There was no question about where things stood. His actions had made that abundantly clear.

She clung to her phone like it was an IV pumping fluids that would keep her alive. Forcing herself to put the phone down, she clung to the steering wheel instead. While sweat, or maybe it was tears, wet her face, her mood ebbed and flowed as she passed each exit . . . further from what used to be home.

By the time she hit Charlotte, the emotion of the day was starting to catch up with her, but she still felt strongly about what she was doing.

She took the next exit and pulled into a gas station. After filling her gas tank, she got back into the car and called her mom.

"Hey, Katherine, sweetheart, how're you doing? I was just sitting here talking to your little sister, and Chloe's been singing to us."

Great. Here it comes.

"When are you and Ron going to give me some more grandchildren?"

Right on cue. Katherine never could live up to her sister. Jacqueline farted rainbows in Mom's eyes. Always had. Giving their parents their first grandchild four years ago was like getting extra points for fertility; and even when Jacqueline had divorced that husband of hers, everyone was so quick to blame him. Never her. At least Katherine wasn't the first to get a divorce. That had to count for something.

From the looks of things now, Katherine would never have a family. By the time she found someone new and started over, her eggs would be scrambled or hard-boiled. It was really going to suck to admit Ron cheated in front of Jacqueline.

"I'm in the area. I know it's late, but I thought I'd stop by. Can I bring some chicken or pick up a pizza?"

"You're here? In Charlotte?" The phone went muffled, but Katherine could still hear her mom telling her sister that she was in town, as if Jacqueline couldn't have already figured this out by listening to the other end of the conversation.

Her mom got back on the line.

"Yeah. So you'll be up for a while?" Katherine asked.

"Yes! We're delighted. Oh, but your sister says she doesn't want pizza or fried chicken. Can you pick up something healthy to snack on?"

She'd kind of hoped her sister was on her way out, and wouldn't be there when she got there. She should have known. Her luck wasn't good right now. She should have just made idle chitchat first before saying she was in town. There'd be no wiggling out of a visit now. "Sure. I'll see y'all in a little while."

Katherine stopped and picked up some food and then drove across town to her parents' house. It wasn't the house she and Jacqueline had grown up in. Mom and Dad had only moved there a few years ago to be closer to Jacqueline after her divorce and help out with Chloe.

Her insides swirled. Why had she even mentioned food? It wasn't like she'd be able to keep anything down. But then if she hadn't, Mom would have spent the whole visit prepping something and that really would have just been too much. It would be so much easier if she didn't have to tell them, but she knew she had to. They'd know soon enough that something was going on when they called the house, or worse, called her at work to find out that she'd taken leave. No, she didn't have a choice. She had to tell them now.

Katherine walked up the long sidewalk to the front porch. She could hear her mom and Jacqueline playing with Chloe just on the other side of the door. At least Jacqueline had gotten Chloe out of her failed marriage. That little girl was the most special gift, even if she was the spitting image of her sister.

At least Jacqueline should be sympathetic. Her husband hadn't been a cheat, but he'd squandered away all of their money and left them in one heckuva financial bind. They'd almost lost their house at one point.

When Jacqueline finally decided to leave, she'd been so depressed that she and baby Chloe had moved in with her and Ron. Through Jacqueline's months of depression and anger, Katherine had never judged one decision she had made; Katherine just helped her move forward. Ron had even come up to Charlotte every other weekend to do the honey-dos and get her house ready to sell. It would be good to have Jacqueline be there for her now.

She lifted her hand and knocked on the door.

Her mother threw the door open with Chloe at her side. "You're here. Honey. Let me look at you." Mom's face dropped as she gave her the once-over. "You look beat."

"I am. Kind of." Katherine pushed past Mom, handing her the bag, then stooped and pulled little Chloe into her arms.

"How is my sweet angel girl?"

"That's me," Chloe said. She wrinkled her nose and put her arms around Katherine's neck. "I love you, Aunt KK."

"I love you more," Katherine said.

Jacqueline walked over and waited for her turn for the obligatory hugs. "Hey, sis," Jacqueline said, then scooted Chloe off to wash her hands. "Mom's right. You do look worn out. You're working too hard again."

Katherine dropped her purse on the hall table, and then plopped down on the couch in the living room. "Probably, but it's what I do. Right?"

"Yeah. You always have, but look what you have to show for it. That car is to die for."

"No it's not. Trust me. It gets me to and from work just like the Ford did."

"Well, I'd die for it."

Dramatic. Jacqueline had always had a flair for it.

"Come on, girls. I've got everything laid out."

They gathered around the kitchen table and Chloe said grace.

"Where's Dad?" Katherine asked.

"He should be back soon. He's over at Jacqueline's mowing the lawn and doing a few things."

Of course he was. It seemed like he was always doing something for Jacqueline. She couldn't remember the last time Mom and Dad had even made the trip down to Atlanta. "When will he be back?"

Jacqueline said, "He met with the roofer to get an estimate on a new roof for my place. You know Daddy. He's probably talking a mile a minute to that poor guy."

Of course he was. *Probably going to pay for it too.*

"Ron and I are getting a divorce," Katherine blurted out.

"What?" Her mother glanced at Jacqueline, then Jacqueline picked up where Mom had left off.

"He's leaving you?"

"No," Katherine said emphatically. "I'm leaving him."

Jacqueline stabbed at a hunk of lettuce. "Now that's just the most stupid thing I've ever heard you say. Why in the world would you leave Ron? He's perfect."

"He's far from perfect, Jac."

"Well, honey, you do live a rather wonderful life. What has you up in arms? Is it that time of the month? Or wait, are you pregnant? Are your hormones all haywire?"

Mom looked so hopeful that for a moment, with the nausea swirling in her gut, Katherine wished she actually was. At least then she'd have something good to focus on.

"He's cheating on me, Mom."

"No. There's some mistake." Her mother shook her head, dismissing the idea completely. "I'm sure there's an explanation."

"There is. It's simple. He betrayed me. He's a liar." The letters she'd scrawled across his desk danced in her mind.

"I'm sure it didn't mean anything. He loves you."

"No. I'm pretty sure that is not the case. And how much can your husband really love you if he can be with someone else? I don't know about you, but I draw the line there. I'm leaving him and I'm filing for divorce."

Mom put down her fork. "Well, where will you live? Who will get the house?"

"And the car," Jacqueline said.

"Seriously? You two cannot be serious right now. Those are things. I don't care about the things."

"Things make life nice. You only say they aren't important because you've always had them," her sister said.

"And I worked my ass off for them. All I wanted was a husband who loved me, and a family. He made me wait for the family, and now I've wasted all this time just to find he doesn't love me the way he should."

"Is this about not getting pregnant yet?"

Jacqueline got up from the table. "Wait a second. I have what you need." She went into the kitchen and came back with a small turquoise cosmetic bag. "Here. These will calm you down. You can go back and smooth things out. I swear. After I had Chloe, my emotions were so whacked out. It was either antidepressants or these things. They're all natural. You'll be fine in a few days." Jacqueline smiled and acted like she'd just solved the whole thing with a row of homeopathic pills. "You can have the case and all."

Katherine unzipped the bag and dumped the assortment of bottles on the table. She sat there staring at the generic bottles of St. John's wort, soy, and nerve tonic. Nerve tonic? It was like something out of *Doc Scott's Last Real Old Time Medicine Show.*

"Here." She shoved the pills back toward her sister. "You keep these. There is nothing wrong with me. It's Ron who's screwed up. Maybe you can hook him up."

"Quit being so selfish, Katherine." She swept the little bag back in front of her and meticulously placed the contents back inside before zipping it up. "It'll sort itself out."

"Selfish?"

"Yes. You live in that gorgeous house without a worry in the world. You have no right to be unhappy."

"And what. You do? Let me tell you that when Ron is traveling, I go out and mow the damn yard of my gorgeous house myself. I don't ask my father to go sweat it out in ninety-degree heat. He's got a heart condition, Jac. What the hell are you thinking? You want to talk about selfish and ungrateful. Do not even get me started." She rested her hand on her hip, thinking it was a good thing that yellow ribbon wasn't bigger or she just might strangle her sister with it.

"Girls. Stop it." Katherine's mom reached over and held Chloe's hand. "I will not have you fighting like this in front of Chloe. Now, Jacqueline, your sister is going through a tough time. She does not need you judging her."

Katherine sucked in a satisfied breath.

"And you, Katherine, need to pull up your big girl panties, get in your car, and get your butt back home in bed with your husband. He is probably stressed out and you being on the road all the time doesn't help. You are the wife. It is your job to make that home work."

Him stressed at his job? Her job was equally demanding. Maybe more so. And she wasn't off gallivanting like a groupie after a rock band; she was traveling for work!

Chloe looked confused. "May I be excused?"

"Yes, honey. You go play with your dolls in the living room." The little girl leapt from her chair and ran away like there were snapping turtles at her heels.

"You two scared her to death. You should be ashamed of yourselves."

"Did you not hear the part where I said he was cheating on me?" Katherine wasn't even sure if she'd spoken the words at an audible level. "Fidelity. Isn't that just the minimum price of entry to a marriage?" Katherine pushed away from the table, but her mother and sister continued to eat as if she hadn't spoken. She walked into the living room feeling completely let down. The verbal beating was almost worse than finding out Ron was a liar.

She sat down on the carpet next to Chloe. "I'm sorry we yelled."

Chloe lifted her sparkling blue eyes from her Barbie dolls to meet hers. "Are you running away from home, Aunt Katherine?"

Squeezing her tight, Katherine inhaled the sweet innocence of her. Whoever thinks children aren't wise to what's going on are just not paying attention. She *was* running away. Running away from everything—Ron, work, her sister and mom, too. Everything that was making her perfect little world feel pretty darn rotten right now.

She only hoped this time it wouldn't be like when she was eight and ran away to the curb, only to regret it come dinnertime and have to drag her suitcase back to the porch and ask to be let back in. Her mom and dad had stood there looking at her like they were trying to decide. It had been the most frightening thing to think they might say no. Which, of course, would never have happened, but it was one heck of a head game.

"I love you, little angel," Katherine said as she picked up her purse. "I'm going to be missing you."

"I'm already missing you." The little princess put her hand to her mouth and blew a loud kiss, followed by an excessive amount of giggles.

That joyous sound even temporarily lightened her broken heart. Katherine didn't bother to say her goodbyes, just picked up her purse and left.

She had Chloe to thank for her heading further north up I-85 tonight.

Chapter Six

Tonight's meeting at the Boot Creek Volunteer Fire Department had been deemed mandatory for all members on the final preparations roster for the Blackberry Festival fundraiser. Over forty men and women mingled, most hovering in front of the industrial fans near the tall garage door of the station to catch some relief from the summer heat.

Derek had shed his tie in his truck, and turned back the sleeves on his white dress shirt as he walked up to gather with the others.

"Anyone heard from Justin on his honeymoon?" one of the guys was asking as Derek approached. Derek had joined the fire department at Justin's urging; Justin had been a volunteer since back when Derek had first gone off to college.

"Not me," Derek said. "I bet she hid his cell phone, because I didn't even get a text from him when the Nats beat the Braves, and you know how he loves to rub that in."

Someone made a whip sound, and most of the guys laughed.

Sandy was one of three women who had joined the department over the past two years. As she walked by Derek, she said, "Mighty pretty girl Justin had you lined up with at the wedding there, Derek. Y'all made a nice-looking couple."

He'd already heard the same comment from his mother, and Angie, earlier in the week about the cousin of the bride. A California girl, and she looked the part. Not his type, a little too on the high-maintenance side, but she'd flown across the country alone and it'd been nice to have her company at the reception. "She's married."

"Too bad," she said.

He could see her wheels turning. Why was it all the women he knew were worried to death about him being alone? Did he look so desperate that he needed a hookup? He'd been charming once. Laney used to say he was. If and when he was ever ready to let someone back into his life, he could do it.

But there it was again. That swell in his heart, his soul, whenever love went through his mind—Laney was the only one he could picture. Probably always would be, and he was okay with that.

A couple more people straggled in, including Derek's dad, who only showed up at the minimum number of calls a year. But that was one thing about the volunteer fire department: Most people were willing to at least do a small part, and that's what made it work.

"Did I hear Sandy trying to set you up on a date?" Roger Hansen asked his son.

"No. Still talking about the girl from Justin's wedding. Old news." But Derek knew his dad would run right back and tell his mom and get her hopes up. If he'd been widowed at the age of sixty, no one would think a thing of him spending the rest of his life alone; but because he was still in his thirties, people acted like he needed to be with someone to be happy. Just because he and Laney hadn't been together for decades didn't make their love or the loss any less.

"Let's call this meeting to order," the captain said.

The group quieted down, and each of the officers gave their reports and the committees gave updates on their progress with the various efforts the volunteers had taken on in the community.

The captain moved to the front of the group. After thanking everyone for their reports, he said, "Okay, now that all of that is done, let's handle the final details for the Blackberry Festival tomorrow."

Everyone applauded. "This is so much better than the boot drive," someone yelled out.

"True," the captain said. "More work, but more return on the investment too. I appreciate you all coming together to make this so successful."

"We're ready!"

The captain said, "If we do as well as we did last year with this fundraiser, we'll exceed our needs for this year and even be able to do a little something extra. Maybe add a couple families to the Christmas fund or do something extra at blanket drive time."

"We got this," Patrick hollered like a JV cheerleader.

Derek laughed at the new recruit's enthusiasm.

"All right. I've got everyone's assignments for tomorrow, and a few of you had also agreed to do some things tonight. Let me know if there are any discrepancies with time or task." The captain began calling out names, and one by one the volunteers picked up their assigned duties.

"Game on, Hansen," Patrick yelled from across the bay. "Who got the Turn-out Gear Challenge? That's right. Me! You're not hanging on to that title again, Derek! It's mine this year."

Derek knew he'd be competing, since he did hold the best record in the entire company, but until now he didn't know who he'd be facing. Clearly, if enthusiasm meant anything, he'd just met his match.

Once everyone had a chance to review their assignments and swap or rectify any mistakes, the whole group gathered around long tables under the trees out behind the fire station for a chicken barbecue.

After dinner, Derek headed straight over to the festival grounds. Since he had no one waiting at home for him on a Friday night, he'd offered to take on a few of the tasks so the others could spend time with their families.

Derek parked at Justin's place. Justin lived right on Main Street in the middle of the festival path, so it was easy for Derek to walk from there to the gazebo in the middle of town square. Tomorrow it would be the information booth. The festival had gotten that big over the last few years.

But tonight, people picked up their assignments at the gazebo, and checked back when they'd completed them to ensure everything was done and ready to roll in the morning.

He exchanged hellos with a couple of people he'd gone to school with, and then nodded to Ryan's mom, who was putting bottled water in a cooler for the folks helping set things up. She looked a lot more relaxed than she had in his office.

A nagging loneliness caught him off guard.

The guys down at the firehouse were always trying to fix him up on dates. That was nothing new, but he hadn't had the appetite for that kind of thing yet. Although ever since Justin's wedding last weekend, he yearned for a little company. And although appointments like the gummy bear incident with little Ryan yesterday made him sometimes second-guess his desire, he did long to have a couple kids someday.

Boot Creek's Annual Blackberry Festival was held the second Saturday in June every year—rain or shine. This year was supposed to be the biggest year yet. They'd even outsold all the previous years' ticket sales just in online preorders—and online sales was something they'd only started doing the previous year.

Word of mouth made the festival bigger every year, but the article in *Our State* magazine hadn't hurt, and when the Food Network had popped in on the Blue Skies Cafe, Ol' Man Johnson had worked in a little plug too. That's when the town really saw a jump.

Derek wove between groups of people, the members alternately working and lollygagging. The streets were alive with activity. Men worked at securing tent poles, and women set up tables for their wares. Tomorrow everything from bird feeders and jewelry to pottery and quilts would fill the streets. And food incorporating blackberries any way you could dream of, and a few ways that even the best imagination wouldn't have pictured, would be the biggest draw.

He stood in line, waiting for his turn at the information booth. The girl in the booth had a system, and she was checking in people ahead of him and sending them on their way in a jiffy.

"Derek Hansen checking in," he said.

"Hey, Derek. How have you been?"

"Good." He recognized her voice, but he'd be darned if he could place her face. This was when nametags would be nice.

She scanned a long list of tasks on her clipboard. Then she pulled an index card from a box and handed him an XL t-shirt with the festival logo on it along with the card with his assignment. "Check back in with me when you're done, please."

"Yes, ma'am." Her serious tone tempted him to give her a salute, but then with more than one hundred and twenty-five vendors to set up tonight, he probably shouldn't razz her for being a little frazzled.

And it wasn't just locals either. This festival had become so popular across the state that vendors planned a year in advance to be among those selected to participate. That added complexity to the situation.

Derek's task card said that he was to set up the tables in the fire department tent area and assemble the t-shirt grids. No problem. He got right to work and it really didn't take too long to get it set up.

When he moved the last piece of grid wall into place, a bright-green tree frog leapt from the white plastic covering to the top of his boot, and then to the still hot cement pad.

"You could probably use some water on this hot night, couldn't you?" Derek poured a little from his bottle next to the frog, and darned if that little guy didn't jump right into the middle of the puddle like a kid on a rainy day. "There you go, buddy."

The tiny frog's mouth seemed to open and close like he was giving Derek a thank-you nod for the cool down.

"Later, dude," he said to the frog, then walked back along the festival route. He dropped off his completed task card at the booth and offered to take another.

Someone needed help with hanging tent sides. He could handle that. It was clear at the other end of the spread, so he took his time checking out what was in place so far.

Even in the crowds of people getting ready for the festival, in dozens of hellos from old friends and acquaintances, loneliness taunted him.

———

Saturday morning, Derek drove back down to Justin's and parked in the lot out back. He tucked his keys into his front pocket, then took the cones out of Justin's storage building and, like Justin had asked, marked off the lot so only the residents could gain access during the festival. In just a few hours it would be in full swing and continue well into the evening.

A giant flag with a big purple question mark now flew high above the gazebo in town square, signaling it was the place to go for answers to questions, share information, and reunite with lost children, keeping things running smoothly from start to finish.

The place had transformed overnight. The streets were no longer filled with boxes of inventory or half-put-together stands. Even the lights that would brighten the night had been strung across the streets by the guys from the electric co-op. Why it took a week to put up the holiday lights, and only a few hours for this, he couldn't explain, and no one else would even notice them until tonight. They had always been one of Laney's favorite parts. The purplish lights at night. He shoved his hands in his pockets and walked on. Being here alone felt like being shortchanged.

Today, every booth was tidy and ready for the crowd. Signs boasted bragging rights and balloons bounced in the breeze. The rainbow of colors assaulted him, with the smells not far behind—ranging from salty to sugary sweet—enough to make your mouth water and you dig into your pocket.

Derek walked over and picked up one of the colorful, slick tri-fold brochures from the information booth. Just yesterday afternoon Boot Creek was only a small town with a few cars parked along the curbs. Today, it buzzed with nearly as much excitement as the State Fair.

He walked up the couple of blocks to the fire department booth. All of the tables and grid displays he'd set up last night had been transformed into a nice little store selling fire-department-themed items, including wooden sculptures that the guys had been making with chain saws for the last couple of months.

"How's it going?" Derek asked the girls still straightening out the shirts.

"Great."

"It looks good."

Patrick looked up from the chain saw he was working on. "Hey, Derek. Good to see you, man. Figures Justin would plan his honeymoon right through our busiest fundraising weekend. You ready for me to take your title?"

Derek gave the rookie a nod. "Let's wait and see how it all shakes out."

Two other firefighters joined the conversation. One of them elbowed Patrick and said, "Justin's going to be having way more fun than us today. If you know what I mean."

Derek knew exactly what they meant, but somehow he had a feeling that Justin was probably wishing he was back in Boot Creek, even if only for a few hours, to hang out with the guys after nearly a week of lovey-dovey honeymooning.

Patrick cursed as he worked a wrench on the chain of his chain saw.

"What's the matter, man?" Derek walked over and watched for a moment. He remembered what it was like to be the new guy in the department. "You need a new chain."

"I know. I should have brought one with me. I don't know why I didn't think about it. I've got two in my locker at the station. Just forgot to put them in my bag. I don't have time to get them. I have to do the announcements for the next hour."

"I'll drive over and get them for you," Derek offered. "My round isn't until one o'clock. I've got plenty of time. Hang tight."

Derek walked back up the street, stopping at one of the stands to get a blackberry limeade along the way. The flavor was so fresh that it reminded him of the days he and the guys would walk out behind the fence at school and pick thumb-sized ones right off the wild bushes at lunchtime.

Those were good times, well, not the picking part. Blackberry picking was kind of like going for the prettiest girl. Between the stickers and the chiggers you were likely to get hurt or not be able to ignore the itch, but you wanted to get to the prize. And it was worth the aggravation.

He made the drive across town to the firehouse, then stopped for gas on the way back.

Derek pulled his white King Ranch pickup to the pump. As he started fueling up, a sporty red Mercedes pulled up.

He half-expected a sparkly, jewelry-dripping doctor's wife to step out of it. Several of his doctor friends' wives in Durham drove these cute little rides, and they'd all been that type. But to his surprise, the woman that stepped out was more like the girl next door. She pushed her sunglasses on top of her head as she walked around her car to the gas tank. She barely wore any makeup and even though she was wearing a skirt, it wasn't a tight sexy number. It was long and looked so light that even the slight breeze this morning moved it as she walked.

She clicked the lock button on her key fob and put her credit card in the pump.

City girl, he thought. No one around here would lock her car just to pump gas. "Nice morning," he said casually.

"Hi. Yeah. Not bad for June." She pivoted her back to him. "At least there's a little breeze."

"You in town for the Blackberry Festival?" And where the heck had that come from? He wasn't one to just strike up conversations with strangers, but then something about being at the festival this morning had him yearning for some interaction.

"Just passing through," she said with a shake of her head.

Her voice had a nice southern drawl. He cleared his throat. "We have the biggest Blackberry Festival in the state. People come from all around for it." Okay, that was just lame.

She smiled, but didn't encourage any further conversation. Maybe he wasn't as charming as he used to be.

"Free blackberry cobbler while it lasts . . . and it usually lasts." He nodded toward the traffic. "We could probably rack up one of those Guinness World Records for the amount of cobbler they prepare. All-day party and then dancing in the streets under the moonlight."

"Dancing in the streets?"

"Yeah." He didn't need help with a hookup, but then why did he suddenly feel his palms sweating a little? He'd started the conversation. "And blackberry wine. You should check it out."

"Maybe I will." She ran a hand through her hair, and adjusted her sunglasses.

He pushed his sunglasses to the top of his head, mirroring her. "You won't."

She swiveled her head around, and this time her eyes locked with his. Pretty brown eyes. "And what makes you so sure?"

"I can read people."

"You a psychic or something?"

Oh, great. Swing and a miss. Now he was coming off as the creepy guy. "Nothing like that. I just have a knack for knowing when people are giving lip service." It was an occupational hazard. He couldn't help it. He shrugged in an effort to look more casual. "Being polite."

Her tank was already full, his probably not even halfway, but he had her attention. He could tell by the way her arm flexed in that sleeveless white blouse when he'd said she was just being polite. He'd struck a nerve.

"Nothing wrong with a little politeness." Her stare held his gaze for a moment too long.

"Right. Yeah. No. Polite is good." And what the heck was he doing? Just mumbling random words.

She put the nozzle back on the pump, and rubbed her hands together. "Where is this amazing street festival that no one should miss out on?"

"Up this road just over a mile. And it stretches further than that. Just head out of the lot that way." He propped his leather cowboy boot up on the yellow painted curb. "There are signs everywhere. You can't miss it."

She nodded. "Good."

He held her gaze a moment longer than he intended, but then she smiled. And that was reward enough for the awkward moment. "Good. Maybe I'll see you there." He didn't bother filling the whole tank. That took way too long. He stopped pumping his gas and tore the receipt from the pump.

"Maybe you will."

He hopped into his truck and pulled around in front of her car; she was just starting to get in. "Oh, and some local advice. Don't pay more than three dollars to park. Trick is if you go all the way into town, through all of the festival stuff, you can park in the market or church parking lots for just three bucks. Everyone always thinks that it will be more expensive closer to the action and they get sucked into the private five-dollar parking. The three-dollar parking is closer to the action."

Now what? All that for . . . what the hell was all that? Practice?

Chapter Seven

Katherine was so hungry that she'd have eaten that crunched-up biscotti from yesterday at this point. She'd been just a moment away from running inside to grab a candy bar or chips when the guy in the truck decided to give her the chamber of commerce spiel. Of course, if he was any indication of the bell curve on good-looking men in this town, the town of Boot Creek probably had a pretty catchy slogan. Berry good-looking men came to mind, and that made her laugh. And a laugh felt pretty darn good right now.

"Lighten up," she said out loud. This situation wasn't going to get any easier if she allowed herself to get caught up in the drama of it all. Let Mom and Jacqueline fear the worst. Heck, they did it way better than she did anyhow. Today she needed a well-deserved break, and Peggy's words reminded her of that.

What better place for something different than a festival? After all she'd been through, she deserved a little fun.

Besides, why should she miss out on a giant cobbler? Wasn't that her right as an American? It wasn't like she had anywhere to be.

Katherine took the stranger's advice and turned left out of the parking lot. She cruised right past the action to the very end of the festival route. A huge Baptist church up on the rise had a big yellow sign that read PARKING $3.

"Just like he said." She pulled into the lot and paid a white-haired man three dollars to park. He handed her a brochure and waved her up toward the front of the parking lot.

The slick pamphlet listed the events, times, and locations of all the activities. There were a lot of them, too. On the back, a hand-drawn map of Boot Creek and the festival layout appeared across all six panels.

She spun it around, trying to get her bearings. The church parking lot she was standing in was well marked. Grabbing a pen from her purse, she starred the location where she was parked so she'd be sure to find her car later, then took some cash from her purse and tucked it into her front pocket. Her hand grazed that little yellow ribbon.

She wondered how Peggy's day was going. She hoped it was better than her evening with Mom and Jacqueline. She took her phone out of her purse, and then put her purse in the trunk.

Music and the sweet smell of sugary treats filled the air.

She let the crowd just move her along, then stopped to watch a group of kids lined up at long tables, hands tied behind their backs, at the ready for a blackberry-eating contest.

At the blow of a coach's whistle that reminded her of her days watching Ron on the college swim team, all heads went down. Only instead of hearing a splash, there were loud, wet slurping sounds and there wasn't a face to be seen across the table. Just the bobbing of heads and the sound of parents laughing as they cheered the contestants on.

Katherine placed her fingers between her teeth and let out a whistle. She was rooting for the little towhead boy, third from the left. His hair was so white that she wondered if the blackberries might stain it for good. Though he was little, he'd looked determined.

She'd been a blondie like that as a child, and short. He was the spitting image of the little boy in her fantasies of being a mom.

At last, an air horn blew and the contestants raised their messy faces.

The whole crowd cheered, but the little blondie she'd been rooting for had been defeated. His face was purple and most of his hair was too, but he was grinning like he'd won the whole thing anyway.

A girl in a giant blackberry costume hobbled toward the winner and lifted the kid's arm with a victorious *whoot-whoot*.

Katherine moved on. There didn't seem to be much rhyme or reason to how the booths were set up. Food was next to art, which was next to candles, which was next to a yoga demonstration. This setup might be to the vendors' benefit, since people would hate to skip even one for fear of missing out on something superspecial.

Ahead she saw a banner that read LARGEST PATCHWORK BLACKBERRY COBBLER IN THE WORLD.

As she got closer, it was clear what all the fuss was about.

The guy at the gas station was right.

This had to be some kind of record. According to the banner floating above the flatbed trailer, there were two hundred and twenty individual casserole pans of homemade blackberry cobbler nestled into this one giant blanket of yumminess.

The creation covered a whole flatbed trailer that couldn't be less than twenty-six feet long from the looks of it.

"Is this really the biggest one in the world?" she asked a man in line.

The man looked at her like she'd just called his dog ugly. "It is until someone steps up and says it ain't. It's over 26,000 square inches of cobbler. Just sayin'."

Clearly, this guy had done the math beforehand.

Her mouth watered at the sight of the perfectly browned crusts, and the variety in the pans was what made the plethora of goodness look so pretty. Some cobblers had crumbles on top, some looked more like pies, and some had crisscrosses of pastry that had black gooey syrup baked right into it. She stepped up to the counter.

"Ice cream or whipped cream?"

"The works," Katherine said.

The girl dished the cobbler into the bowl, dropped a scoop of ice cream on top, and then squirted four little flowers of whipped topping around it. "Enjoy!" she said as she tucked in a wooden spoon.

Katherine smushed the ice cream down into the cobbler and took a bite. The warm crust and tartness of the berries against the cold ice cream flooded her mouth.

She tugged her phone out of her pocket and took a picture, then texted it to Peggy.

KATHERINE: Hope things are going okay. Wish you were here to have some of this cobbler. It's as amazing as it looks.

PEGGY: Where the heck are you?

KATHERINE: North Carolina.

PEGGY: Your mom's?

KATHERINE: No. That was a disaster. Headed north.

PEGGY: Hugs. Kind of a disaster here too. Will catch you up soon.

The old saying that misery loves company had always sounded so mean, like you wanted other people to be miserable, but the truth was, it was somehow calming to know someone else was going through similar things. An understanding ear. A shoulder to lean on.

Katherine strolled down the street enjoying the diversity of the vendors. Someone was even grilling blackberry-basted chicken, but she'd already filled up on cobbler. There were lots of crafts and even a fortune-teller. She felt bad for making that snarky remark about being a psychic to the guy at the gas station. He'd just been trying to be nice. She didn't have any right to take out Ron's bad behavior on every man she bumped into. Even if it did make her feel just a little bit better.

Suddenly the low-pitched vroom and buzz of a motor came from the end of the street.

She opened the festival brochure and scanned it for the details of what was going on. She looked at her watch: she was shocked that she'd already spent more than two hours here, but she didn't feel ready to leave.

SPACE 64—CHAIN SAW CARVING DEMONSTRATION—BOOT CREEK VOLUNTEER FIRE DEPARTMENT

Could be interesting. She'd seen an ice-carving competition once at the Hilton in Atlanta during some endless work conference or other.

She followed the sound to two men with chain saws fired up, hacking at stumps of wood. She wasn't quite sure what it was they were going to end up with, because at the moment it just looked like they were making big wood stumps littler.

A large digital timer ticked away off to the side. Both guys were in great shape, but then weren't firefighters always in good shape? Wasn't like you could rush into burning buildings with a beer gut.

The men's chain saws roared, sending splinters of wood flying from the lifeless stumps, until right before her eyes two bear cubs were facing her. In less than five minutes that wood was art.

All the proceeds from the sales of the cute critters would go to the local volunteer Boot Creek Volunteer Fire Department, so she figured she'd buy a miniature one as a souvenir. People hung around the tent watching the artists add expressions and even personalize a few carvings that were ordered onsite.

Katherine paid for hers, and then stepped back, right into someone. She spun around. "I'm so sorry."

"I'm glad you took my advice."

It was the guy from the gas station. His eyes were even bluer than she remembered up close. North Carolina Tar Heels blue. "You made it sound so good. How could I not?"

"Did I lie?"

That word shook her. Lie? "No." She swallowed back the sick feeling the word conjured up. "No," she tried to lighten her tone. "It's pretty amazing."

"I'm Derek." He stuck a hand out.

"Hi." His smile was gentle. Perfect teeth and white, but not that trendy bleached-out white like Ron's. Better looking than Ron too. And that was saying something. Ron was good-looking in a preppy way. Derek had rugged movie-star qualities that had her imagining him sweeping her into his arms in one of those over-the-threshold moves.

Her eyes met his and for a moment she felt trapped. Like she'd been caught, like he somehow knew what was on her mind. The urge to bolt surged, but that was just silly. She tried to look at ease, but who didn't hear their parents' chorus of don't-talk-to-strangers even as adults?

She took his hand. She'd always liked a man with a firm and confident handshake. Like Ron's, only Derek was naturally rugged. Ron had taken to that scruffy look recently. Maybe it was his attempt at looking rugged, but she'd never liked it on him. Maybe he'd grown it for that other woman. Was that how it was going to be now? Was every little thing Ron had done recently going to just make her have more questions?

"This is where you tell me your name," he said. Not even a hint of a whisker.

"Oh, yeah." What did it matter? She'd never see him again. She was passing through and he knew it. "Katy." But the truth was she hadn't been Katy since college. Not since Ron had made such a big deal about how she'd never be taken seriously as a successful woman in the business world with a name like Katy. "My friends call me Katy."

"Nice to meet you, Katy." He smiled, and what she wouldn't give to reach out and just touch his smooth cheek.

Katy. Derek repeated her name to himself to commit it to memory. When he had seen her standing in his booth, he'd had a rush of adrenaline that could only compare to the first sixty seconds gearing up for a multiple-alarm fire, and that had been unexpected.

She looked like a Katy. Fresh, vibrant, but there was caution in her eyes.

"Having fun?" he asked.

"Yes. And you're right. That cobbler was a must-see."

"I told you. Did you get some?"

"Best I've ever had. Didn't look like they'd run out anytime soon either."

"Well, what's a blackberry festival if you can't guarantee everyone some cobbler?"

"Good point."

"Glad it was worth the ride into town."

"Definitely. Thanks for telling me about it." She glanced across the crowds of people. "So you live here?" she asked.

But before he could answer, Patrick called his name over the microphone. "I see Derek Hansen over there hanging in the wings. Wave to the crowd, Derek."

Derek waved his arm in the air toward Patrick, then glanced over at Katy sheepishly. Why did he feel like he'd just been caught flirting with another woman?

Patrick's voice bounced across the street, and the crowd started pulling in toward the fire department's tent. Maybe Patrick had been a carnival barker in a past life. "I know y'all aren't going to want to miss the Turnout Gear Challenge. Derek Hansen of our own Boot Creek Volunteer Fire Department is the reigning champion of the Turnout Gear Challenge."

A wide grin spread across Katy's face. She looked him right in the eye. "That's you? How fun." She clapped along with the crowd, then asked, "What's turnout gear?"

Patrick shouted, "Y'all cheer Derek on. Let's get him to come up here for a minute. Y'all need to meet this guy while he's still champion. Because that title just might be going to someone new here shortly." Patrick encouraged the crowd to cheer, and they did. "Get over here, Hansen."

Derek felt a blush rush his cheeks.

Katy's smile made him grin. How could he say no to that? "Will you wait here?"

"Sure."

Her energy pushed him. "I'll be right back." He rushed off, then took one quick look back, praying she'd still be standing there. She was, and for a moment he didn't feel like the lonely guy that started out here this morning. He could get used to that.

Katy watched Derek make his way to the roped-off area in front of the tent. She worked her way closer, watching as Derek carried over a bundle of equipment. One of two that had been prepared especially for the Turnout Gear Challenge.

His muscles flexed as he reached the guy with the microphone and placed the equipment down. That conjured up a few wolf whistles from the ladies in the crowd.

Even Katy was a little tempted to whistle.

"Yeah, so this huge bundle is what each of us has either at the station or in our personal vehicles, or both, so we are prepared to gear up and go to your rescue." Patrick winked at a young blonde in the front row and took her hand. "Come see how heavy it is."

He played to the crowd, and did his share of flirting with the girl, who could barely lift the heavy bundle.

"You're going to have to be able to lift that if you want to be a fire-fighter, girl," Derek said, leaning into Patrick's mic. "You can do it. We have a couple of great gals on the roster."

"Tell them about what we have here," Patrick said, handing off the microphone to Derek and abandoning him as he walked the girl back to where he'd found her.

Katy wondered if Derek would flounder at the impromptu handoff, but he didn't. He was a great speaker. "The fiberglass helmet, Nomex hood, bunker coat and pants, gloves, spanner belt, ax and boots . . . the whole getup. Every piece of this equipment serves a role in protecting the firefighter. It's fun here today, but every second we can save in preparing to take action could be the difference between life and death."

Patrick jogged back over and grabbed the microphone from Derek. "How much do y'all think this gear weighs?" Patrick walked through the crowd, sticking the microphone in front of people's faces for guesses. They ranged from as low as three pounds to three hundred pounds.

"Derek here is the reigning champion. No one can get in or out of gear as fast as this fireman."

The girls screamed their approval, one shouting her undying affection for him. Derek blushed at the attention.

Patrick waved his hand in the air to get them to quiet down for a minute. "Derek, tell them how much this stuff weighs."

"This gear weighs over twenty-five pounds, but we didn't mention one of the most critical items. The SCBA. That's our self-contained breathing apparatus, and it adds about another twenty pounds and gives us over thirty minutes of breathing time. So, altogether we're talking fifty-ish pounds."

Someone from the crowd yelled, "We love you, Derek."

"Is your mom out there?" Patrick teased.

"Apparently," Derek said. He glanced her way and smiled.

She waved to him; it seemed like all those squealing women were now looking her way with a little jealousy. The smile on her face wasn't hiding how that made her feel, and when she tried to stifle it, she felt the dimple in her left cheek give her away.

Patrick played up to the crowd. "Who will be back for the Turnout Gear Challenge?"

The crowd cheered.

"Good. Derek will try to protect his title, and he's going to need some help, because did I mention who his competition is?" He looked at Derek.

"No, don't think you did, except for the million times you've bragged about it to me already," Derek said.

"That's right, it's me!"

Katy laughed at how obviously uncomfortable Derek was with the antics of the other guy. If that guy jumped in the air for one of those belly-bumps, Katy knew she'd probably fall out from laughter. But she wouldn't be surprised. Poor Derek.

Patrick waved an arm in the air and shouted, "See y'all right here at one o'clock sharp!"

Derek walked back over to Katy, his face still a little red, which she found cute.

"A turnout gear race? So, basically you can get undressed and dressed faster than anyone else?"

"Impressed?"

"I'm not sure," she said, and was he flirting with her?

"It's fun here, but it really is a critical skill."

"So, you're a fireman."

He nodded.

"Now I'm impressed."

"Don't be. I can't carve a bear with a chain saw."

"Have you ever tried?"

"Yeah. It wasn't pretty. Came out looking like a termite-ridden beehive."

"I've always been real fond of bees." Okay, that just sounded stupid, but he was smiling. It was probably about time to move on.

"Will you stick around?"

"I don't know. I—" I what? I'm married. My husband just cheated on me and I just need some attention to remind me that I've still got it? I'm flirting with you and you're really hot, but this is not going to happen?

"I've got to get over there and get ready. It won't take long." The guys yelled over for him, and he looked like he didn't want to leave. "Don't go anywhere, okay?" He flashed her a smile, as he started backing up. "I'll show you how we dance in the streets around here later. It'll be fun."

She smiled his way, but as soon as that little contest was over, she'd get lost in the crowd and disappear. It was the right thing to do.

Maneuvering through the crowd, she jockeyed for a spot with a decent view of the competition.

Derek was on the left and the other guy on the right, both at the ready, dressed in their everyday clothes. Only Derek was wearing cowboy boots, which had to be a disadvantage.

At the siren, the Turnout Gear Challenge began and it happened so fast that it had barely been worth the time she'd spent to get to the front of the roped-off area.

Derek was the clear winner, by a long shot, at an amazing thirty-six seconds. Both guys went from everyday clothes to ready-to-go firefighter, including the SCBA tank, in less than a minute.

A different siren blared, and red emergency lights bounced from all corners across the crowd, while the song "Fire" by the Ohio Players came through speakers so loudly it probably filled the air for three city blocks.

Derek pumped his fists in the air.

Fifty-plus pounds of gear? It was a wonder anyone ever got rescued!

While Derek changed out of his gear, the loser, Patrick, played up to the crowd like a stripper, carrying a boot to collect money for their fundraiser.

Katy's phone vibrated in her pocket. She slipped back in the crowd and jogged over to the side, hoping it was Shaleigh calling her, but when she looked at the screen, Ron's face stared back at her.

All the happiness and fun she was just having slammed to a stop in her throat, making it hard to swallow or breathe. That lighthearted feeling of being Katy, rather than Katherine, flagged.

She silenced the ringer and made her way through the crowd over to the curb so she could sit down before her legs gave out on her. At least if she hyperventilated right there, across from the fire department display, there'd be someone to rescue her.

Her phone made a *buh-doop*. He'd left a voice mail.

Katherine covered the phone with both hands, hating that churning feeling in her gut. She stared at her hands, unsure she even wanted to hear what he had to say, but then it couldn't be any worse than the go-round at her mom's last night.

She wanted to hate him for what he'd done. Wanted to so badly.

Then a text came across.

RON: You went without me? Sorry I was so late last night.
Hope you're having fun in HH. I'm stealing an afternoon to
golf with Bart. <3 TTYL.

He didn't even know that she knew. Son of a gun.

Her teeth clenched. Really? Here she was dealing with all of this emotion and he was still just gallivanting about?

Golf? Was everything he ever said a lie? Hadn't he already stolen an afternoon just yesterday? How many holes would he play today? Probably the same one as yesterday.

She dropped her head back, staring at the beautiful blue sky, but feeling like a heavy gray cloud was about ready to rain on her like no tomorrow.

She pushed herself up from the curb and headed for her car. If she had her bearings right, it should just be a block over.

The crowd was thinning at the firemen's tent so she slipped behind a huge big rig serving ribs and race-walked, distancing herself from the crowd.

By the time she reached her car, her hand was so sweaty that her phone was slipping in her hand. Her heart raced, but probably not from the walk. She was in good shape. No, it was the adrenaline, fight or flight, and doggone if she wouldn't like to fight him in a battle to the death right about now. Her throat was so dry that she couldn't even swallow.

She revved the engine on her car and headed back in the direction she'd come from. There was a McDonald's on the first corner. She needed something to drink.

Snagging a parking space in front, she went inside and headed straight to the ladies' room. She pulled a handful of paper towels from the dispenser and cooled them under the water. She held them to her face, praying her heart would slow down.

She needed to lie down.

Her phone rang. She fished the phone out of her purse to see who was calling.

"Shaleigh? Thank you for getting back to me." Katherine stepped out of the ladies' room and sat at a back table.

"What is going on?"

Katherine ran her fingers under her eyes, then spilled every last detail to Shaleigh. And when she finally took a breath, Shaleigh said, "Oh. My. God. I'm just not even believing this. Of all the married couples I know, I just always thought yours would be one that would last."

"Believe it. I have the pictures to prove it."

A decisive harrumph came from across the line, then Shaleigh said, "Good. Send me those right now before you say another word. I'll wait."

"Hang on." Katherine pushed the button for the camera roll on her iPhone and selected the pictures. "Okay, I just set it up to send as soon as we hang up." Katherine hated to ask. Wasn't even sure she really wanted to know the answer, but she had to. "Did you know?"

"What do you mean?" Shaleigh's voice held a distant hesitation.

Would she even admit it? "I mean like Tucker. Everyone knew about Tucker except for Peggy. Did you know about Ron?"

"Oh, Katherine. No, I wouldn't have kept a secret like that from you. Tucker's behavior was so blatant that it was clear Peggy didn't want to know, regardless of what she's saying now. But if I'd suspected Ron was up to no good, I promise I would have told you. We've always been upfront with each other. You know that. Now, are you sure you've thought this through?"

"I'm positive."

"What did he say about it?"

"I didn't bother to ask. He's just going to make an excuse, right?"

"True. Most of them do, or come clean because they want to leave. So you just left, without a word?"

"Well, no. I left a word. On his desk blotter. The word *LIAR* about two feet tall in lipstick."

Shaleigh laughed out loud. "You did not."

"I did. In 'Through the Grapevine' magenta. Tell me that wasn't meant to be."

"Poetic."

"Yeah. Big ol' kiss over top of the *i* . . . as in kiss my—"

"I gotcha. You're mad."

"Yeah, but here's the kicker: I just got a text from him. He hasn't even seen the message. Not only did he duck out with another woman, but he never even went back to the office. He thinks I just went to Hilton Head on my own since he and I didn't nail down the trip together. He's clueless that I left."

"Good. He's playing wild and loose. Better for you. He'll make mistakes."

"Mistakes? Yeah. He's already made a few doozies, if that's what you want to call them."

"Where are you, Katherine?"

"A small town in North Carolina. Boot Creek. It's off I-85. Somewhere." She tried to place where on the big map she was. "North of Charlotte. Not even sure where I'm headed."

"You sound exhausted, honey."

"I am."

"I don't guess you'd want to go back home and face him."

"No way. I'd like to just crawl into a cave somewhere and hibernate."

"So do it. Go get yourself a little room in one of those cute small-town inns and just sleep. Lick your wounds. Console yourself. Honey, you deserve it. You don't have to put on a brave face. He's the one that did you wrong."

Brave wasn't how she felt. Mostly she felt like she was swinging from huddled mess to dangerously pissed off. Neither of which were particularly appealing.

"It's still hard for me to believe he would do this. We had plans. Big plans. I mean he had stuff planned out down to the month for things we'd buy, places we'd go, things we'd do."

"These things rarely make sense. I've got your back. He'll be pleading for mercy before this is all over."

"Thanks, Shaleigh."

"I'm serious. Go get a room. Call me when you get checked in. You shouldn't be driving around. I'll handle everything from here, and I'll let you know when we're ready for some signatures."

"I don't want to get into anything ugly with him. I just want out."

"That's fine, but let's not go giving everything away until you'd have had some time to think things through and we hear what he has to say. You're hurt right now. There isn't any hurry."

"That's why I called you. I trust you." Shaleigh was going to handle things, and that was a comfort.

As soon as she hung up, the phone reminded her that those awful photos were on their way.

She walked up to the counter and ordered a medium drink. After handing the gray-haired woman at the counter her money, she asked, "Are there any nice places to stay around here?"

The woman's eyes glistened in bright excitement. "Yes, there are. My sister owns a wonderful inn not all that far from here." The woman leaned forward. "She'll fix you the best country breakfast every morning. Part of the deal. You may not ever want to leave."

"That sounds perfect. Can you give me directions?"

"I sure can. Heck, I'll do you one better than that." The woman pulled out a paper sack and drew a map on it. "Straight back out down this road. Then take these turns and you're there. Her place is right on the creek. Lovely. And if you get lost," she said as she scribbled a phone number below the drawing, "here's my number. Tell her Nell sent you. Her name is Naomi. We're identical twins." The woman laughed and Katherine could picture that spry woman having a hundred memories of using her and her sister's identical looks to trick people. She had that mischievous look.

"Thank you so much." Katy turned to leave, knowing this was just the first step in leaving Katherine behind.

Chapter Eight

Just past the festival, the streets became nearly ghostly quiet.

A gas station that looked like it had probably been there a hundred years or better hailed the cheapest prices off the interstate, and a large redbrick warehouse filled the whole next block. A roundabout with a huge statue in the middle seemed to only slow things down. Apparently, Boot Creek was home of the Grand Ole Opry Hall of Famer Dillon Laumann. A bronze statue of him in his younger days, complete with a fringed western getup, rose from a fountain with a small walkway around it. Katy circled the roundabout, then exited and went straight for the next three blocks, just like the woman had drawn on her map. Tiny stores nestled right next to each other with matching signs gave the street a movie set vibe.

Each building was painted one of three colors, and every building had the same black chalkboard-looking sign above its door. Vivid colors popped, like in those drawings you did as a kid where you used every crayon in the box to fill up a piece of paper, creating a psychedelic place mat, then carefully covered it in black paint. Once it dried, you created a picture by scraping off lines in the paint, exposing a surprising rainbow of colors. Even a stick figure looked cute in that medium, and it was no different for the signs here. Cute, playful, and crisply uniform.

The route on the little map on the hamburger bag sure didn't appear as long as the drive was. Katy was beginning to think it might be easier to turn around, get back on the interstate, and drive to the next big town to find a Marriott. She had enough reward points to probably stay a month for free.

Finally she crossed the bridge Nell had drawn on her map.

Lush greenery hung over the side of the bridge from below.

She slowed for the turn. The trees bent over Blackwater Draw Road like a tunnel. The digital display for the outside temperature dropped three, four, five degrees in just a matter of seconds as she made her way toward the shaded hillside.

A small sign about the size of a pizza box, painted bright blue, simply read FALLS followed by an arrow. She wondered if that was a lane to the house of someone by that name, or if perhaps there was a waterfall down the path.

Katy slowed as the road elbowed, just like the crude drawing had said it would.

Another snaking turn caught her a little off guard, and then trees seemed to stand back from the road, letting a glorious stream of sunlight flood over it.

A yellow road sign indicated a drive to the right ahead.

It was marked with a city sign, but in fact was dirt and gravel. PINEY CREEK LANE. A small sign under the street marker read, NO OUTLET.

As she took the turn, her tires crunching against the rough terrain, she wondered just how long this road with no outlet was.

The creek came into view. She'd always thought of a creek as a small trickle of water, but this one spanned a good distance to the other side. Although it was so rocky, it was doubtful you could do anything but walk or fish in it.

The inn sat off to the right-hand side.

LONESOME PINES.

The sign was just like the ones in town, only instead of a rainbow of bright colors, it had hues of greens, deep reds, and golds against the black.

For some reason, when the old woman at McDonald's had spoken of the inn, Katy had pictured a historic home with a room or two for rent. Lonesome Pines Inn had two full stories and dormers at the third level with such intricately carved trim that they looked like big Yosemite Sam mustaches.

Two long wings extended from each end of the main house for as far as the foliage would let her see.

Katy drove down to the water, and got out and walked to the edge, near a small dock that had seen better days. Large boulders peeked above the water line as the current rippled and splashed against them in a hurry to follow the flow . . . to somewhere. She knew the feeling. It's exactly what had led her here in the first place.

Chirps, beeps, buzzes, and pops filled the humid air with a cheerful hum. A splash across the way caused her to spin, only to find that whatever it was had already disappeared. For such a serene landscape, it sure was filled with busy sounds.

But maybe those sounds of nature would quiet the noise in her head. More important, she had no one to judge her. No one to answer to. And that made it the perfect place to hunker down for a few days.

She lifted her phone and snapped a picture of the creek. Maybe she could figure out what a future without Ron in it even looked like. It wasn't something she'd ever even casually entertained. She turned and took a selfie with the water behind her.

Her smile looked forced.

She walked back to her car. Before getting back in, she took a picture of the inn, then pulled into the driveway.

A woman stood at the door.

"Hi," Katy said as she climbed out of the car. "I just met your sister over at the McDonald's up the road. She told me you had a vacancy."

The woman stepped onto the porch. "I do. That Nell could keep my house fuller than a Holiday Inn if I let her. She doesn't even work there. Her husband owns the place. She helps out when she gets bored. *She* calls it help. *They* probably call her a nuisance. Come on in." She motioned her inside. "Welcome!"

"You really are the spitting image of her."

"Thank you, dear. I happen to think my sister is quite lovely, so I'll take that as a compliment. I'm Naomi."

"It was meant to be one." Katy followed the woman inside. "So nice to meet you." The house was very clean and inviting. Ron absolutely refused to pick up after himself, so she'd given up on trying to keep her house clean, and finally gave in to the maid that Ron had wanted her to hire anyway. It still baffled her a little that a house with just two people in it, who travel half the time, could be that much work.

"Traveling alone?"

Katy nodded. "Yes, ma'am."

"I have a beautiful room down here on the first level. It'll give you plenty of privacy and it even has a reading nook. Or I have one up on the top floor. It's a little smaller, but it has a great view of the water. Would you like to see it?"

"I'll take the room with the reading nook. That sounds very nice." Suddenly, all she wanted was to go to sleep. "I've been driving for hours. You'll probably barely see me the next few days."

"You've come to the right place. I'll be quiet as a mouse." She waved a bony finger in the air. "Oh, but shall I wake you for breakfast in the morning?"

"Yes, that would be lovely. Thank you."

"Excellent." Naomi opened a leather-bound journal. "What's your name, dear?"

"Katy."

"With a K?"

"Yes, ma'am. K-a-t-y."

Naomi wrote meticulously slowly. So slowly that it took everything Katy had not to snatch the pen from Naomi's frail, wrinkled hands and finish for her.

"Last name?"

Lord have mercy. It would take a year. "Bar." Good enough.

"Two r's?"

"Just one." Katy gave her a little wink, encouraging her to get a move on with her entry. If she'd let Naomi spell out the whole name, Barclift, she'd fall asleep right here at the counter. She probably should have just used her maiden name after seeing how slow she wrote *Katy*.

She hadn't even thought about a divorce meaning a name change. They didn't have kids, so no reason to keep his, even though when she'd married Ron, she'd been so glad to be rid of her maiden name. Wild. That last name came with plenty of jokes through the school years, but now it seemed to have more appeal. Short, easy to spell, and it was hers. Not Ron's.

She could leave all the monogrammed stuff behind. Well, except for the little hand towel in the bathroom that Grandma had embroidered. That was special.

Katy glanced down. The woman was still carefully scrawling letters. Could she be any slower?

Naomi's lips recited each letter as she wrote it. "How long will you be staying?"

"Let's start with three nights. Then I'll let you know, if that's okay."

"It'll be fifty dollars a night, but if you decide to stay a week, I'll give you the discount on the other nights."

"That's fine." Katy paid Naomi in cash, and then went back to her car and brought in her things.

"The room is ready." Naomi turned and headed down a hallway to the left. "Follow me."

At the end of a long corridor decorated in a bold jewel-tone blue, Naomi took both hands and swung open a set of French doors.

Naomi looked around like a proud mother. "This is my favorite guest room. There's a nice little patio through those doors too if the weather cooperates. You can only see a little glimpse of the water, but the sounds are so relaxing. You don't even have to really see the water to enjoy it."

"Thank you. This will be perfect."

"You can bring your things in and get settled in." Naomi waddled back out to the foyer. "Would you like a quick tour of the rest of the place?"

Katy didn't have enough polite energy left in her to go through that. "Can we do it another time?"

"Of course." Naomi walked over to her and said, "We're huggers. Hope you don't mind, but you sure seem like you could use one." She held out her thin arms and Katy walked right into them.

The older woman was right. She did need that hug. "Thank you. Thank you so much."

"Make yourself at home, dear. I keep the small refrigerator in the library right off this hall filled with water and sodas. There are always snacks under glass on the sideboard there too. I bake something fresh about every day. Gives me something fun to do."

"That sounds wonderful."

"If you're up to it later, the Blackberry Festival is the entire weekend. It's really quite a celebration in the evenings. You might consider going down there."

"I'm just going to head on down to my room. Thank you for everything." Katy walked back to the bedroom and shut the French doors behind her. It wasn't just a bedroom; more like a suite, and that reading nook had a window seat nestled in the center of the wall of books. Hardbacks, paperbacks, and floor to ceiling.

She walked back to the door that led outside and unlatched the deadbolt. Her skin became instantly damp in the humid air, but the foliage was in full bloom and she couldn't resist stepping outside for just a minute or two.

Her mind immediately went to what it would be like to have been here with Ron. She forced that image from her mind. *Why'd you have to go and ruin everything, Ron?*

She sat on the edge of the bed. Had there been times when she'd felt things weren't quite right? If she hadn't seen him sitting there with that woman yesterday, would that phone call have made her wonder if something was wrong?

Her fingers traced the hand-stitched quilting. The fabric was in good shape, but silky soft against her fingers from years of washing. Good quilts lasted forever. She used to think good relationships were like that. She was beginning to wonder if there was even such a thing.

There was a soft tap at the door.

"Yes?" Katy said.

Naomi eased the door open and slipped inside the room carrying a delicate teacup. White polka dots danced on a blue background and flowers ran around the edge. "I brought you a cup of tea to help you relax. A decaf called Midsummer's Peach. One of my favorites."

"That was so thoughtful." She reached for the cup and saucer, and inhaled the warm aroma. "Wow, that really does smell like fresh peaches, too."

"That teacup always lifts me up when I'm feeling a little blue." Naomi's eyes reflected kindness.

"Is it that obvious?"

"You look troubled." Naomi began to leave, but paused in the doorway. "Sometimes getting away will bring a better perspective. This is a good place for that. It's quiet."

The tea shook in Katy's hand. "I hope you're right."

"Take your time, dear. And if money is a problem, we will work something out."

"Oh, no. That won't be a problem. But thank you."

Naomi patted the edge of the door and gave her a little wink. "I'll leave you be, but if you wake up hungry later, come on out and join us. I don't usually serve supper, but I have some regular guests passing through tonight. They won't make it for breakfast, so I'm doing a little breakfast-for-dinner kind of thing special for them. You're more than welcome to join us."

"Thank you. I'll keep that in mind." Only, Derek's face popped into her mind as she said it. She wondered if Naomi could also tell she was just being polite.

So where exactly was the line between lying and polite?

"Get some rest," Naomi said.

What a lucky day to land in a spot like this for just fifty dollars a night. Comfort equal to the Ritz-Carlton, and a therapist/grandma here to comfort her. It was like a recovery clinic for the rich and famous.

She sipped the tea, closing her eyes and wishing for emptiness.

But that wasn't meant to be.

Her mind was still filled with the image of Ron and that woman, and the voices of her mother and sister. And a dozen questions that she'd probably never get the answers to.

She climbed out of bed to unpack. She put her laptop on the dresser, and then took her toiletries out and set them on the counter in the adjoining bathroom.

The old claw-foot tub was so deep she might need a life preserver. With a twist of the old white porcelain knobs the water rushed into the tub. She splashed her hand under the stream to check the temperature, then pushed the plug into the drain. A hot bath would relax her. She took advantage of the wooden scoop that hung from a huge old jar next to the tub, and tossed a scoopful of rose petals into the steaming water.

Katy got undressed and then stepped into the cast iron tub, letting the flowery water wash over her like a warm embrace.

When was the last time she'd slowed down like this? Probably not since college. Not since she'd been Katy, not Katherine, and her life had been a lot simpler.

She unwrapped a small disc of soap from a tray of them next to the tub. The wrapper, a simple square of fabric, had been held together by a round sticker that boasted a local farm, Just Kidding Goat's Milk Baa-aath Bar.

She held the soap to her nose—like honeysuckle on a warm summer night. She swished the soap in the water, then slipped it into the washcloth and gave it a twist; tiny bubbles oozed into a rich creamy lather. It felt smooth on her skin.

She lay there until the water went cool. A renewed spirit trying to rise from the broken mess.

Time. Time is what she needed.

She stepped out of the bath feeling relaxed. She toweled off, catching a glimpse of herself. A beautiful old mirror stood strong and tall, like a lover, in the corner of the bathroom. Watching her.

Katy lowered her eyes, and then looked up again. The ornate wooden frame, mahogany maybe, held twisting vines captive in its delicate carvings. The glass was wavy, but even so her body seemed unfamiliar. Her tummy was still flat, but gone were the days when at this time of year, she'd have been tan, with lines where her bathing suit would have been. No, now her skin was one continuous canvas of ivory that hadn't been kissed by the sun in at least two years.

She hugged the towel close to her body. Naomi sure didn't scrimp on linens. Everything about this place was very high end. The towel was not only soft, and thick, but it was big enough to dry two people at once. She grabbed two ends and tied a quick knot, then twisted it and looped it over her head like a sarong as she walked back into the bedroom.

She pulled on a pair of light blue panties, then dropped the towel to pull her nightgown over her head. It fell over her rosewater-soft skin in a gentle swoosh.

Katy hung her towel over the bar in the bathroom, turned out the lights, and slipped between the covers.

She whispered a prayer into the darkness, "Oh, Heavenly Father, please give me the strength to fill my thoughts with the right things. I'm sorry for judging others. I'm trying so hard not to solely focus on the wrongdoings. I know exactly how Peggy felt now, but also know that being in a relationship with someone who is not committed to me is not how you meant marriage to be. Please help me find the right answers."

With tears on her pillow, she closed her eyes and was asleep before the water made its final gurgle down the drain.

Chapter Nine

Katy sat up and hung her legs over the side of the bed. From the edge of the bed she could see her reflection in the mirror. She swept a hand through her hair. It had curled from the dampness of the bath. She sat up, thinking she should've blown it straight before she'd slept because there'd be no taming it now.

Ron had always preferred her hair sleek and straight. All the more reason to let it go. She fluffed her fingers through her hair. "Good enough."

She grabbed for her phone and checked the time. To her surprise she'd only slept a couple of hours, but boy, had she slept hard.

After applying a little bit of makeup to cover up the sleep lines on her face, she dressed in capri pants and a flowered, short-sleeved white blouse. She cinched her belt, and ran her hands down the front of the pants to smooth the fold lines.

The door to her room creaked when she opened it. She hadn't taken Naomi up on the offer for a tour, so she just quietly wandered out to the main part of the house.

Other than the guests Naomi had mentioned, she had no idea how many others were staying at the inn, although there had been a couple cars parked out front.

She backtracked to the entrance and then walked through the house toward the soft sound of music. Country music.

The dining room was empty, but the table was set. The long table would have been overwhelming in a normal-sized dining room, but the room was more like a ballroom. As it was, the table felt like the one in the Last Supper. You could probably seat as many as sixteen or more quite comfortably, but this evening there were only five place settings around one end of the table. One at the head and two on each side.

As she stood there, a couple and their daughter walked into the dining room.

"Good evening," she said as the family joined her at the table. "I'm Katy. It's my first time here."

The woman, who looked to be in her mid-fifties, said, "Hi there. I'm Anne. Naomi was telling us she had another guest. If it's your first time, it won't be your last. Right, Sam?"

Her husband nodded.

"First time in this area, in fact." Katy settled into one of the chairs with an empty place setting. "I'm traveling alone. Will Naomi join us?"

"No. Don't think I've ever seen her eat. She'll come visit with us, though." The woman pulled her lips into a thin line, and glanced toward the kitchen door, lowering her voice. "That seat would be for Naomi's grandniece, Kelly Jo. She probably won't make it for any meals." The woman leaned forward and whispered, "She has cancer. Very fragile."

Katy's heart clutched. "I'm so sorry to hear. I didn't know."

"Poor thing was here the last time we came through. How long ago was that, Sam?" The woman looked to her husband, who was a bit older and had a distinguished speckle of salt in his peppered hair, for concurrence.

"Just back in May."

"Yeah, Naomi says she's really taken a turn for the worse."

"It's an awful disease."

Anne nodded. "So now you know. We stop here every year on our way up to see my parents. More often if we get the chance. Where are my manners? This is my husband, Sam, and our daughter, Rachel."

The daughter rolled her eyes at her mom's chatting. Clearly visiting her grandparents wasn't at the top of her list for summer vacations.

Katy extended her hand across the table to Sam. "Katherine. Katy. Everyone calls me Katy."

The girl plopped an elbow on the table, and then pulled it down when she caught the side glance from her father as he shook Katy's hand.

Anne looked like she'd had that attitude from her daughter about one too many times already, but even as aggravating as it must have been, Katy was envious of the family.

Anne tore her stare from her daughter. "So what brings you to town, Katy?"

"Just passing through. I'm on an extended vacation."

Anne seemed to be waiting for more, but Katy wasn't about to start spilling her guts to complete strangers, so she just let the silence hang.

"When did you get in?" Sam asked.

"Earlier today."

Rachel got up and started roaming around the room.

Naomi whisked into the room with a tea service. "Tea, my dears?"

She filled the cups without a dribble or a splash, then moved a lovely ruby-red Depression glass tray from the sideboard to the table. "Fresh cream, local honey, and sugar and a pretty rainbow of all the fake kinds of sweet stuff the business types love to use." She gave them a big wink. "Me. I'm just a good old-fashioned sugar girl."

"You are after my heart, aren't you, Naomi," Sam said.

"I know you like the blue packets, Sam." She gave his back a little rub and squeezed his shoulder. "I'm so glad you were able to make me part of your travels again. It's so good to see y'all. Rachel, you are more beautiful every time I lay eyes on you."

Anne gave her daughter a glare from across the table.

"Thank you," Rachel said with only a halfhearted smile and plopped back down in her chair.

Naomi winked at the parents. "I'm not serving juice tonight, because I made a wonderful berry French toast dish. Juice would just make you pucker. So what's your pleasure? You sticking with tea or is anyone up for milk? I've got white or chocolate."

Sam and Anne both said, "Tea."

"Milk for me," Katy said. "Chocolate."

Rachel looked at her with some surprise. "Chocolate moo juice for me, too."

"Great." Naomi extended two fingers on each hand as if to help her remember their preferences by the time she got back to the kitchen. "Give me just a minute and I'll get you all served up."

Sam took a sip of his tea. "If you're going to be here for any time at all, you have to go on the watershed project hike along the creek. It's a good workout, and the scenery is peaceful."

Anne's face lit up. "Yes. It's amazing. We even saw an eagle when we went last time. Didn't we, Sam?"

"We did, and if you're looking for some good southern cooking for dinner one night, go to the Blue Skies Cafe."

Rachel nodded. "Oh, yeah. That place is off the hook. Best fried chicken in the world. But be prepared to wait for it. It takes them like a half hour to cook it."

"Worth it," Sam said.

Katy just nodded and listened, committing the suggestions to memory. An all-American family. She'd never get Ron to stay at a B&B. He was too impatient to conform to the schedule, and way too much in a hurry to just meet and mingle with new folks.

Naomi came back in, a sweet scent following along. She slid the strawberry French toast casserole into the center of the table. She then left and came back out and put a warm carafe of maple syrup in front of Rachel.

"Can you serve, Katy?" Naomi asked as she disappeared once again into the kitchen.

Katy took the silver serving spatula and carved a slice, then reached for Sam's plate. Once everyone had a nice portion, Katy took a small serving for herself.

Naomi pushed backward through the kitchen door, carrying the two chocolate milks. "Anything else I can get you kids?"

"Not a thing." Katy put a forkful of the strawberry French toast into her mouth. "Oh, Naomi! Nell was right. You do make an amazing breakfast. Even if it is dinnertime. Thank you for this. I was really hungry."

"That's what brings pleasure to my heart, young lady."

They all dug in and Katy was thankful the idle chitchat slowed to a halt.

As soon as she was done, she excused herself under the guise of needing to make a few phone calls and took a cup of tea out to the porch off of her room.

Out of habit she'd tucked her phone into her pocket. She sat down in a blue rocker next to a pot of bright-red geraniums, placing her teacup on the small nail keg that served as a side table, and began to look through her messages. Shaleigh had called. She listened to her voice mail, which told Katy to check her email for some details.

Katy flipped through the email messages to find the one Shaleigh referred to.

There were a few papers to sign, and then Shaleigh went on to advise her that she should call and let Ron know why she'd left and what her intentions were.

Katy slouched in her seat. The last thing she wanted to do was talk to him about this, but the reason she'd called Shaleigh was because she was the best doggone divorce lawyer around. It wouldn't do her any good not to follow her advice.

She plucked a geranium bloom from the pot and twisted it between her fingers.

She responded to Shaleigh's email.

Shaleigh,

Sorry I missed your call. I'll get these papers filled out and back to you tonight. Meanwhile, I'm staying at the Lonesome Pines Inn in Boot Creek, North Carolina. Have not told anyone else where I am, but if you can't get me on my phone . . . call here.

I'll make sure Ron knows what I know before he hits his desk Monday morning. Should get interesting.

Katherine

She put her phone facedown in her lap, then pushed off the porch floor with her foot and let the rocker do its thing, move at the speed it wanted to. It was soothing. Her phone vibrated and she flipped it over to look at the text message. Short and sweet. From Shaleigh.

Take care, sweetie.

Katy's skin grew clammy. Probably more a symptom of the situation than the warm weather, but she went back inside to try to cool off.

She took the little cross-stitched DO NOT DISTURB sign from the back of the door. Katy admired the handiwork, and thought about hanging it out on the crystal doorknob, but the truth was, that email from Shaleigh had amped her up.

It wouldn't take long to fill out the papers. She had most of the information in the stuff that Peggy had told her to grab. She grabbed her laptop and sat cross-legged on the bed. As her fingernails clicked against the keyboard, she had a little satisfaction in knowing she was taking a solid step toward some kind of end to this matter.

By the time she'd completed the forms, the sun was setting, and although that French toast had been delicious, she felt snacky. No surprise;

stress usually did that to her, only she didn't have a stash of comfort food with her.

There had been plenty of comfort food at that blackberry festival. Part of her wanted to stay in bed until everything was behind her, but she knew that wasn't about to happen. Surely, gorging herself on comfort food wasn't going to be a long-term solution. Even a festival full of it might not be enough to conquer the emotional beating she'd taken, but it was better than wallowing in self-pity. "Think long, think wrong." Daddy had always said that about things. Of course, it may have been his way of surviving in a house with three women all those years.

It was a weird feeling to be able to just get up and go out without having anyone to answer to. Maybe there would be some plusses to her new situation. She grabbed her keys and headed out. She had a good sense of direction, and essentially it was only two turns back to where the festival was.

The roads had turned dark. No streetlights in this little town. It made her appreciate the nicely finished roads and lights of her neighborhood back home.

There were a lot of decisions to make—where she would live, what kind of place it would be. She loved having a house and a yard, but they required a lot of upkeep. Was she really ready to handle that all on her own? On one income, even if it was a good one, was it smart to spend money on a landscaper when she should be tucking it away for retirement?

Thinking of her dad cutting Jacqueline's yard made her cringe. She'd never ask that of him, no matter what.

She drove to the same church where she'd parked that morning and pulled up to the parking attendant.

He pointed to her parking pass from before, and waved her through.

"A deal." She didn't get as good a spot this time, though.

She texted Peggy.

KATHERINE: Just checking in on you.

PEGGY: Awww. Thanks. I'm okay. It's crazy here. No one's talking to me. Silent treatment is deafening.

KATHERINE: Shaleigh got things started on my end. I'm at a blackberry festival. Go figure.

PEGGY: First day of the rest of your life, girl. I'm living vicariously through you. Have a ball!

KATHERINE: Hugs.

The first day of the rest of my life.

What did that even mean? It sounded a bit overwhelming, but she took multimillion-dollar projects from totally offtrack back to success. How was this so different? If she could just take the emotion out of it and break everything down into tasks, she should be just fine. Just one more project, albeit a personal one.

"I'm young. Smart. Successful. I will be fine." And with that she got out of the car and headed to the festival again.

Earlier there'd been a mishmash wave of weird-wonderful music—rock, country, bluegrass, and some new age stuff all mingled together, alternately taking over the lead as she'd moved by the row of multicolored tents and displays.

Tonight, a single flow of music rolled in like a tide the closer she got to the action.

She hadn't noticed the strands of lights overhead as she'd walked down the streets this afternoon, but now the strings of blackberry-blue colored lights strung across the road between the merchants like tightropes were aglow like psychedelic stars.

The song "Hot Hot Hot" by Buster Poindexter suddenly filled the air and Katy clapped as a conga line started forming right in front of her. She laughed and continued to clap, singing along. She made her way to a tent and bought a glass of blackberry wine.

"Four dollars," the bartender said.

She handed him a five and took a sip. "That's great!" She danced her way back to watch the fun in the streets with her glass. Way better than being huddled up in the fetal position.

The black-light effect of those blackberry lights made her white blouse glow. There was something about black lights and wine that could buoy your mood on any day. Maybe she should buy a case of those purple bulbs.

Someone grabbed her arm and she spun around.

Derek grinned, his cheeks still smooth, not even a hint of a five o'clock or seven o'clock shadow. "Come on. Thought you'd left!"

What were the odds he'd have still been there, or even spotted her in a crowd this big. "I'm back." She wasn't sure if it was the blackberry wine, or the light, but the way his mouth moved when he talked made her want him to just keep on talking. "Hi." The tingle that tickled her nerves made her laugh from the nervous excitement.

He pulled her into the middle of a giant twisting conga line that seemed to weave in and out of the entire block. "It's fun. See!"

She could barely hear him above the hooting, hollering, and loud music, and the sound of her own laughter. That blackberry wine definitely had a little something to do with it too.

Above, the soft breeze blew the strung lights like psychedelic fireflies over their heads as they congaed through the streets.

She set her plastic wine glass down on a nearby table, then looped her fingers through his belt to not lose her grasp. They skipped and kicked and by the time the music shifted, they'd made it darn near to the other end of the block, and she was out of breath from laughing so hard.

That DJ must have played that song back-to-back three times.

The tempo dropped from the fast, almost-Caribbean sound to Jimmy Buffett's "Margaritaville."

People started peeling away and she let go of Derek's waist. "That was fun." She stepped back and started to walk toward the curb.

"Uh-uh. Get back here." He tugged her hand and gently pulled her into his arms and swayed to the beat of the music.

Nose to nose, she recovered from the quick surprise of his unexpected move. "You can dance."

"I'm not sure I'm good at it, but I think it's fun." When the song stopped, he placed his hands on her shoulders and spun her away around, facing away from him, then leaned into her neck and said, "Come on. I want to show you something."

She let him guide her forward until they made their way out to the edge of the crowd of enthusiastic festivalgoers.

"Are you hungry?" he asked, stepping around her to take the lead moving through the crowd before she could even answer.

Eat? That was like a date. She was married. Kind of. What the hell was she doing? "For a snack, maybe. What do you have in mind?"

He was moving faster than her feet would go, making her do triple steps to keep up, like he was sensing her trepidation.

He laughed as if sincerely amused. "You always answer a question with a question?"

She squeezed his hand. "Why do you ask?"

"Good one." He glanced down at her and snickered as he pulled her hand tighter into his own. "What, are you a lawyer or something?"

Game on. She was determined to come up with another question to his question if it killed her. "Do I look like a lawyer to you?"

"You're killing me," he said, but with an easy smile that melted her defenses.

She took satisfaction in the little victory.

"Come on," he said with a gentle squeeze to her hand. "Don't want to lose you in the crowd."

He tugged her toward a small building with a brick front and pushed the door open. "It's a lot quieter in here."

She pointed over her shoulder. "But all the action is out there. I thought we were going to get some festival food." She didn't even know this guy. What was she doing?

She withdrew her hand and turned back toward the crowd.

"I'm sorry. Did I scare you?" He paused and stepped back, giving her room to breathe.

"Well . . ."

"Sorry. I didn't mean to frighten you. This is a restaurant—Bella's." He pushed the second door open and there were several tables with some people seated at them, but not many. "See?"

She let out a sigh of relief, and let her arm, which had tensed at his last tug, relax.

"Same dishes right here, and a few even better ones," he said, leading her to a table in the middle and pulling out a chair. "And you don't have to balance a paper plate and eat with a plastic fork."

"Oh. Okay. Yeah, count me in, then." Seemed innocent enough, and she'd never been a real fan of plasticware.

He led her to a table and pulled out a chair for her.

She sat and placed a cloth napkin in her lap. "Come here often?" she teased, trying to make up for acting like he was an ax murderer.

"Some. Can I order for us?"

"By all means. Have at it." It was nice to just let go of the wheel. Katherine might have thought she needed to control the situation, but Katy was enjoying it immensely.

A waiter stepped to the table with two martini-type glasses of a frosty purple concoction. "Complimentary."

"Thank you," Katy said and took a sip. "Fabulous."

The waiter nodded, looking pleased that she liked it. "Enjoying the festival?"

"Very much," she said.

Derek didn't bother with the menu. "We'll have the blackberry spinach salad, pork chops with blackberry port sauce, and sweet potato–quinoa cakes."

"Sounds delicious," Katy said. "But it also sounds like a ton of food."

He folded his hands in front of him on the table. "Not that much. You're in for a treat."

"Thanks."

"So you are just passing through?" He placed his napkin in his lap and pushed the candle between them off to the side. "I'm glad I bumped into you."

"Me too." She sipped from the frosted glass. "I really needed this."

"Where you headed?"

"Just taking some time off," she said, choosing her words carefully. He seemed to be waiting for more, but what more could she say? If she said she had no idea where she was going, she'd sound like a fruit loop. Even just thinking it in her own head sounded a little ridiculous.

"What do you do?"

"Nothing for the next few weeks if I stick to the plan," she said. "I'm on a little hiatus."

He lifted his glass to hers. "To vacations. And fun. And new friends."

She took in a deep breath. "To new friends."

The waiter came back to the table. "You liked the drink?"

"I did," she said.

"Would you like another, perhaps with a little shot of something fun? Or we have blackberry wine as well."

"Oh, blackberry wine sounds great." She looked to Derek. "I just had my first taste ever out there. It was amazing."

Derek looked at the waiter and held up two fingers. He was off without a word and back before they had even picked up a new thread of conversation.

Right behind that the food arrived.

Katy leaned over the plate. "Who knew you could make so many things with blackberries in them? I mean, desserts, yes, but main courses . . . vegetables . . . who knew?"

"That's why it's worthy of a festival. And the chef here, Roarke, he's one of the best chefs in the region. He worked at the Biltmore for years before retiring here."

"The Biltmore? Impressive. What brought him to Boot Creek?"

"His daughter moved here. He wanted to be near her and his grandchildren after his wife passed away. He named the restaurant after her. That's why it's called Bella's."

The romantic notion made the cold edge of her own heart soften a little.

He leaned toward her. "Where are you from?"

She knew he meant where she lived now, but she didn't want to talk about that. Besides, right now, technically she didn't live anywhere. "Virginia Beach. I grew up just a block from the beach."

"That must have been great."

"It was. Have to admit I like the beach in the winter the best. All those tourists during the summer, the traffic—that's all too much. Give me a quiet morning at the north end any day. The feeling when you're walking at the edge where the surf is crashing, it's empowering." It had been too long since she'd taken the time to do that. Ron had never been much of a beach fan. "Making the only footprints—the feeling of the sand under my feet, the gulls singing above me. It's so . . . freeing. So fresh. So . . . I don't know . . . so honest."

He took a bite of the quinoa cake and nodded. "I think I'd like walking on the beach the way you just described."

Though she'd done it a million times by herself over the years, she and Ron had never taken the time to walk on the beach as the sun came up, pants rolled up, but damp nonetheless from the waves breaking at their ankles.

It was tempting to promise to take Derek for that first walk, but she stopped short. She'd just met the guy. She took another sip of wine to keep her mouth out of trouble.

She hadn't thought about the beach like that in such a long time.

Those were good memories. Maybe she'd spend some time there while she had the time off work. Soon.

Katy and Derek finished the meal and were both so full that they had to turn down dessert. They did opt for blackberry wine to go, however.

He got out of his chair and moved quickly around to her side, pulling her chair out as she stood. He peeled off some bills and dropped them on the table for the server, then led her to the register.

"Let me get my half of the bill," she said.

"No way. My treat. I insist." He paid and then opened the door for her.

The memory of Ron holding that door for that girl, her ducking under his arm made the blackberry treats she just consumed swim upstream a little. She shook it off.

That was then.

This is now.

Then they were swallowed into the crowd, walk-dancing through the streets.

Maybe she could get used to this kind of treatment.

Chapter Ten

Derek and Katy belted out the words to Poison's "Every Rose Has Its Thorn." Being equally out of key just made it more fun.

Four songs later they wandered down to an area fenced off for adults, so they could get a drink refill. A quick look at their driver's licenses and paper bracelets put them closer to the music and the bar. They stood to the side and sipped on blackberry wine slushies as a large group of people started line dancing.

A country tune filled the night. Katy swatted his arm playfully. "You got the boots. That your thing?"

She was teasing him, but he kind of liked it. "Nah. You've already enjoyed the extent of my dancing skills. How about you? You want to teach me?"

"No way. I might be pushing my luck with walking after the amount of wine we've had tonight."

"You aren't planning to drive anywhere tonight, are you?"

"No. I'm staying at a little inn. Out by the creek for a few days."

His hopes rose at those words. A few days. He didn't even know her, but he liked the idea of maybe bumping into her again. She was easy to be with. Down to earth. Not the type who tried too hard.

"They'll be closing things down here shortly. Could I talk you into coming back to my place? Just to chat." He raised two fingers. "Scout's honor. I'm just not ready to call it a night."

She looked relieved, but still hesitant.

A wrought iron table for two opened up near the railing. "Come on. Let's grab that."

They talked about pretty much nothing at all, but they did it for long enough that the DJ announced he was playing the last song. The crowd had diminished significantly since the last time Derek had even taken notice of what was going on around them.

Maybe it was the wine. Maybe it was the twinkling lights. Or maybe it was just the right time, but he surprised even himself when he leaned in and kissed Katy softly on the lips.

She seemed startled at first, her lashes tickling his cheek, but she'd kissed him back.

He pulled back and looked into her eyes.

She licked her lips and inhaled. "I might have had too much to drink."

"Are you ready to call it a night?"

Her brows pulled together. "I don't know."

He stood and held his hand out. "Come on. I promise I'll be a gentleman."

She started to say something, but then she didn't.

"We're less than fifty yards away."

"From what?"

"My truck." He took her hand and they walked up the sidewalk. Other couples, stragglers from the last call and vendors closing up shop, went by without a word, weary from the long day.

Katy looked across the street at the large church on the corner. He saw the flicker of recognition. If she'd parked where he'd suggested, she was probably parked there, but she didn't say a word.

She shouldn't drive after the amount of wine they'd had, but his desire to have her come home with him was not from reasons so pure.

He longed to feel her next to him. That familiar warmth of another body close. And that surprised him. Damn near scared him to death, really, because he hadn't yearned for that in a long time, and certainly not with anyone but Laney.

He brushed his thumb across the top of her hand as they approached his truck. He could just take her to Justin's place, but he wanted to take her home.

Derek opened the passenger door and helped her in.

They didn't talk on the short drive to his house. The landscape bulbs were the only light around as he pulled into his driveway.

He shut down the truck and they both got out.

"Wow. You can see every star in the galaxy from here."

"You watch long enough you'll see a falling star. Get your wish ready."

She looked at him with questions in her eyes. "I have one," she said, then let out a sigh.

He let her soak up the night. He'd gotten used to being in Boot Creek again, but he'd felt kind of the same way after first moving back. It was easy to forget how peaceful it was in this small town compared to the city, where stars were masked by the reflection from all the glowing electricity.

Derek held his hand out to her and she folded hers in his. He led her up the front porch stairs.

He could hear her breathe as he unlocked the door and turned on the soft lights on the fireplace wall. Even they seemed like a cop's flashlight beaming on them after being outside in the dark.

They stood in the foyer. "Your home is lovely," she said.

"Thanks. It's still a work in progress. I didn't move back all that long ago."

"Where did you live before?"

"Durham. My wife died." He hadn't meant to blurt that out, but there it was.

"I'm so sorry."

"Me, too. I stayed in Durham for a long time, but then I decided to move back here. This was my hometown."

"So you *can* come back home."

He laughed. "Yeah. I guess you can. You should have seen this place. I bought the place sight unseen, because I thought I knew it. I mean I'd lived in this town my whole life. Only what I didn't know was that Clancy Jennings's widow had gone hog wild for pink."

"The color pink?"

"Oh, yeah. I've spent the better part of the last six months with a paintbrush in my hand changing every darn Pepto-Dismal piece of wood and trim inside and out to the deep burgundy you see."

"That's hysterical. You really didn't know?"

"Not until the day I showed up to move in."

"That's so funny. I bet the town had a big laugh about that."

"Yeah, they still haven't let me live it down. In the daylight you'll notice that even all the flowers in the yard are pink, but they might just have to stay that way."

She chased a yawn. "Excuse me. I'm suddenly so tired," she said.

"The night air will do that." He took her hand and led her toward the stairs.

She hesitated for a split second, but she let him lead her upstairs.

When they got to the landing he pulled her into an embrace. Her heart was pounding so hard, and he didn't think it was from the walk up the stairs. She was nervous. Hell, he was too.

Don't rush things, he told himself.

"Maybe we should just call it a night. That okay?"

"Great." Relief ran through him that she agreed.

"You can have this room." He nodded toward the master suite. He'd sleep in the guest room. Alone. Not exactly how he'd hoped, but now with the sobering night air, it made more sense. He flipped on the light for her, glad he'd taken the time to make the bed this morning. That wasn't always the case. Living alone made a guy lazy sometimes.

She nodded and walked into the room. "No fire truck bed. That's a good sign."

He laughed. "Yeah. No fire truck bed. I outgrew it along with the race car bed."

She kicked off her shoes and crawled on top of the comforter fully dressed. "I definitely had a little too much to drink tonight," she said.

"Sleep well." He turned off the light, and started to walk across the hall.

"Wait."

He stepped back in the doorway.

She rolled over on her stomach. "Are you tired?"

"It's been a long day. I could sleep." The moon cast a hazy glow through the curtains.

"I'm wide awake. Maybe you could just lie here with me," she said. "And talk."

"You'll have to help me take my boots off first."

She bounced out of bed. "I can do that."

"Oh, you're an old pro at this?"

She sat on the floor at his feet. "No. Never done it, but how hard could it be?" She tugged on his boot but nothing was happening. Not even a slip or a wiggle. Finally she stood up with her hands on her hips. "You go sit on the edge of the bed," she ordered.

He did as he was told, wondering exactly how she was going to get his boots off. She walked over and lifted his foot in the air and pulled unsuccessfully. Then she spun around, straddled his leg, and with her well-rounded hind parts right at eye level, she reached between her legs and tugged on the heel of the boot. It came free, sending her stumbling forward.

"Easy there, girl."

She turned around laughing. "You weren't kidding. That's a job. Give me the other."

She used the same proven method to pull the other one off, only this time she'd centered her weight so she wouldn't go off balance.

"Thank you, ma'am," he said reaching for her hand and then pulling her down on the bed next to him. "So tell me what you're thinking."

"That you might be a little dangerous."

She seemed nervous, but he was too. "I'm harmless," he said trying to reassure her. Maybe himself too. "You don't really think I'm dangerous, do you?"

"I think . . . I'm glad I bumped into you this morning."

"Me too."

"And I really needed to laugh tonight."

"Laughter is good medicine." A doctor joke. A bad one, but then she didn't even know he was a doctor, so at least that one slid by.

"Then we should be pretty healthy for the next couple of weeks at least." She paused, and quietly said, "I'm more sleepy than I thought." Her voice drifted off and he liked that she was so easy to be with.

He closed his eyes. The way she lay in his arms didn't remind him of Laney at all. Laney would have had her butt to him. Spooning. They always spooned, but lying with Katy in the crook of his arm, her warm cheek on his chest, was nice.

Different. But nice. Really nice.

In just a few short minutes she was asleep—her breathing barely audible, her body warm against his. He pulled his arms around her and fell asleep feeling hope for the first time in as many nights as it had been since Laney got sick.

⁓

When Katy woke up she wasn't sure how long she'd slept since it was still dark, but it surprised her that she was in the exact same position she'd been in when she fell asleep. She was usually a wiggly sleeper. All over the bed. Ron accused her of chasing him in the dark. He'd spend his whole night dodging her. Maybe that should have been a warning flag. But she didn't want to think about him right now. He'd been her whole life. Her whole teenage and adult life. It was going to be hard to not weave him into every scenario, but she needed to make that break. Things would be different from now on.

"Are you awake?" Katy whispered.

"Barely," he breathed into the nape of her neck.

His body felt warm against hers. Ron always complained she was too hot, and sleeping in a king-sized bed may as well be like sleeping in another room if you're not going to snuggle. "I like this little bed," Katy said.

"Not a fan of a king-sized bed. I'm man enough to sleep in a queen," he teased.

I bet you are, she thought, but she kept it to herself. It was so quiet. No cars. Just the subdued sounds of a bird a little too happy in the middle of the night and random chirps and buzzes. Her mind wandered back to her situation. Life could change so fast. Maybe it wasn't meant to be in a steady state like a good software program. Maybe we were all fighting and resisting change that was supposed to happen. "Your wife. Had she been sick?"

"Mmm-hmmm. For a long time."

"That must have made you feel so helpless."

He pulled his arm around her. "You can't begin to imagine."

Pain tinged his voice. She lifted a hand and rubbed his well-defined bicep, then gave it a squeeze. "It feels good to snuggle."

"Yes, it does."

"Funny how something so simple can make you feel like everything is okay."

He shifted. "It's been a long time since I've felt like anything was okay."

"You must have loved her so much," she said.

"More than anything. We were soul mates. I knew it the first time I laid eyes on her." He looked up like there was a movie playing on the ceiling. "We were just kids. Friends first, then inseparable. I knew she'd be my wife someday. She was special."

"What was she like?"

"Kind. Positive. She could bring a smile to any situation. Supportive. Tireless. Creative. Perfect."

"It must feel amazing to be someone else's perfect." She'd thought for a long time she was Ron's, but then she didn't really have anything to compare it to. Had she been fooling herself? Or was it just that she'd rushed in to life with Ron before her soul mate found her? She wondered what his wife had died from.

He paused. The word came out quietly. "Cancer."

Like he read her mind. "I'm sorry."

"Me too."

Katy felt the hurt in his voice. It must be awful to lose your loved one like that.

"Cancer seems to touch all of us at some point. It's scary."

She felt him nod. "People marvel how we're all connected by six degrees of separation. If they considered cancer the connection point, I bet we're even closer than that."

"So unfair," she said.

She hugged his arm, snuggled back against his body, and slept until sunshine shot through a sliver between the curtain and the wall at just the right angle to swathe across her face. "Good morning," she said turning toward him.

"Good morning." He pulled his arm up under his head. "I slept well. Did you?"

"I did, but I probably should go. You probably have to work, and I—"

"I don't work on Sundays." Awkward. Morning after wasn't anything he'd ever had to deal with. He and Laney had been together their whole adult lives. "That's fine. You ready to get your car? Or you can hang out. I'm not trying to get rid of you."

"I'm ready to go get my car if you don't mind."

"Not at all. I can grab a shower when I get back." He slid out of bed. They were both still dressed, and a little wrinkled. "Only I hope I'll see you again while you're here." And did he just say that out loud?

She rolled over onto her stomach and watched him grab his boots and then sit down in a chair to put them on. "I'd like that."

He caught himself smiling. "Yeah, me too. About all that stuff I told you last night—I don't usually talk about it. I'm not sure why I did with you." And why had he? Maybe because she was going to be gone.

"I'm glad you did." She got up and ran her hands through her hair.

Once outside, he opened the passenger door for her and she climbed up into the truck. When they got to the church parking lot hers was the only car there. That wouldn't be the case in about another hour when the churchgoers started filling up the lot. That could have been embarrassing—especially when most of the town knew his truck, and would know this fancy red Mercedes wasn't local. He'd have been the talk of Sunday school, and not in a good way.

He pulled right next to her car and put the truck in park.

"I had a great time. So glad you stopped in Boot Creek to get gas yesterday."

"Me too."

"You're staying at Naomi's?"

"The Lonesome Pines Inn. Until Tuesday. Maybe longer. I'm playing it by ear."

"Do you know how to get back?"

The paper bag with the instructions was still on her seat, but it would be easy to find. "I'm good. I know the way."

"Can I give you a call over there?"

"That would be nice. Someone said I have to try the Blue Skies Cafe's fried chicken. Maybe we could grab some dinner one night." It was just dinner. That was innocent enough.

"It's my favorite place, and the chicken is great."

"Perfect. Thanks for being a gentleman all night."

"I'm a man of my word." His gaze held hers, with no hint of a snicker or laugh.

"You have no idea how much that means."

Her problems seemed so irrelevant in the scheme of things; maybe that was why this guy was put on her path, for her to keep perspective. Things could be a lot worse.

Katy put her sunglasses on and pulled out of the church parking lot with the big white truck right behind her.

Derek tooted his horn as he turned off to the right. She raised her hand and waved. "Thanks for a fun night." And she headed for the Lonesome Pines Inn unescorted.

When she passed the statue of Dillon Laumann, the thought crossed her mind that the last two days of her life made up a country song.

When she pulled into the parking area at the Lonesome Pines Inn, there were a few more cars than there'd been when she left. More guests probably.

She walked through the front door to the smell of sausage and coffee.

"Good morning, Katy. You were up and out early this morning."

It felt a little like getting caught sneaking back in your own window. "It's a beautiful day," she said.

"Oh, yes. I do love the mornings in June," Naomi said. "There's still plenty of breakfast. Get yourself some."

"I think I will."

Katy made a plate and took it outside to the smaller table on a brick patio. Her stomach welcomed the home cooking.

"You made it!"

Katy wondered if Naomi was losing it a little. They'd just spoken a few minutes ago. Bless her heart. "Yes." She forced a smile. Not quite sure what else to say.

The gray-haired woman busted out in a hearty laugh. "It's me, Nell. I know that look. You thought my sister went off her plumb rocker, didn't ya?"

How had she forgotten? "Nell? You two girls cannot be trusted. You even dress alike. That's no fair."

Nell held a hand to her mouth and laughed. "Guess we never grew out of it."

Oh yeah, the old gal was enjoying her little prank. One for the grannies. Katy could only guess how much fun those two had growing up. "Thank you so much for pointing me in the direction of this place. It's fabulous! More than I ever expected."

Nell looked around nodding. "Yep. Sis did pretty good for herself. Her husband, Marshall, could turn a dime into a dozen. Always had a knack for it."

"She's a great cook, too. Just like you said."

"I won't keep you. Just wanted to say hello before we zipped off to church. You're welcome to come along if you like."

"Thanks, but I'm going to hang close today."

"Enjoy," Nell said as she walked back inside.

Katy could hear the two sisters laughing. Apparently being a twin had lifelong benefits. She watched as they left. She and her sister had never had that kind of relationship.

Katy took her dishes to the kitchen and stopped in surprise. It was an enormous chef's kitchen. Her kitchen back home had been a real splurge, but this made that look like playtime. The granite sparkled with gorgeous veins of rust and black that really offset the cherry cabinetry. The subzero refrigerator and freezers were nicer than most restaurants had, and they were filled to the gills. Rows of canned goods filled one wall like a collage. Katy ogled the two-drawer dishwasher; she'd always wanted one, but opted to hand-wash her dishes and leave them on the drainer. What she wouldn't do to get to do a little cooking in here while she was visiting.

She was half-tempted to rustle through the pantry right now and bake some cookies, but she probably ought to at least ask permission from Naomi first.

Back in her room she scanned the floor-to-ceiling bookshelves for something relaxing to read.

The bookshelves held all kinds of books, and it wasn't until she really stopped and looked that she realized there was actually quite a meticulous order to how they were shelved. By genre, by author, and somehow they seemed to be by size too. Everything from fine literature in thick leather bindings to thin paperbacks and the whole Nancy Drew series. Current authors too. She scanned a row of paperbacks for a familiar name, then tugged out a bright yellow-and-pink book. It looked like it would be a light read.

She carried it out to the hammock on the adjoining patio. It took some balance to get in it without flipping over. For a minute she wondered if she should have brought her phone with her in case she got twisted up in a knot and couldn't get out. Hammock wrestling was never a skill she'd had to refine, but after a couple of tries she managed to finally steady herself. Getting out would probably be just as challenging, so she settled in for the long haul.

Lost in the words of the story, she had no idea how long she'd been outside, but the next thing she knew she was waking up in a sweat. The sun had risen high in the sky and the air had gone from warm to downright hot. And that peaceful, easy feeling she'd held on to earlier had been chased away by a bad dream. One where everyone was whispering and staring at her as she hosted a holiday party. The woman she saw Ron with was in every crowd across the room as she mingled, and she didn't even realize that it was the very same woman in every crowd. But everyone in the room did. The whispers as she walked by taunted her. Listen, Katherine. Look. She's right there, but in the dream she couldn't hear or see it. She wondered if the woman had ever been to their house. Was it a dream or a memory? It was possible. She'd been too naive to even suspect a thing.

This made her feel sick to her stomach.

She rolled out of the hammock to the ground. Not graceful, but effective.

Contacting Ron was still on her list of things to do. Before Monday. Dinner time already? She'd run out of ways to stall and there wasn't a whole lot of time left to Sunday now.

She sat contemplating whether she should call Ron now, or wait until later. "Get it over with." She dialed home, but got no answer. Her heart went cold. Sunday night, and he was out?

Confusing thoughts fought for her attention. Visions of Ron holding that woman, kissing her. Mom's face. The look of disappointment in her eyes at Katherine's marriage failing. Peggy trying to be strong.

"What a mess."

She thought through what her message should be carefully. Even wrote down notes. Planning. It was what she did best. Satisfied she had a script that would deliver the message she intended, she dialed Ron's office number.

"Ron. If you actually made it into the office this morning, then you've seen my message. The one I left after I saw you on Friday afternoon." Pause for effect. "With her. Was fidelity really too much to ask?" Pause again. No chance of him misunderstanding that. "Shaleigh will be in touch. Don't bother trying to contact me. Everything can go through her." She paused again, but this time it wasn't planned. Her anger was only matched by the sadness and disappointment of it all. Don't cry, damn it. There would be no more of those "Love ya, talk to ya later" goodbyes with him. "Goodbye, Ron."

She ended the call, feeling out of breath and a little afraid.

Pressing the contacts icon on her phone, she blocked his numbers. "Blocking my own home number. That's got to be a first."

No sense being tempted. It was over. Her heart was not going to go through this again. Ever.

Chapter Eleven

Katy stood on a craggy rock in Boot Creek hoping the sluice of cold water below would calm her. She stepped gingerly forward and swished her foot in the icy water. Even though it made her almost squeal, it was a welcome relief compared to the hot sun beating down.

Knowing that Ron would soon be getting his wakeup call had made her so anxious that she'd been unable to sleep. She'd unblocked the number on her phone sometime in the middle of the night . . . just so she would know when it happened.

She could ignore him when he called. She hoped.

But knowing was better than waiting and wondering. Not that it really changed anything, but she was a details girl. Sticking her head in the sand wasn't her style.

Rocks formed a random path across the creek. Although the ones along the creek's edge were sharp and ragged . . . those toward the center looked worn to a soft sheen.

How many years would it take to rub away the sharp edges with just the movement of water? Hundreds and hundreds for sure.

A large rock rose like an island out to her right.

She held her arms out to the sides like a tightrope walker keeping her balance. Nine well-executed hops and steps, and she'd made it to the big rock.

The chill from the water cooled the air out here in the middle. She sat down and watched the current sweep around her.

A school of minnows headed toward where she stood, then split as if choreographed. Half taking the left route and half swimming right. She spun around watching the two groups partner back up on the other side. A fish jumped somewhere nearby, and when she glanced across the creek, two turtles had crawled up onto the long felled tree that hung precariously from the bank to the water by its roots, its brown leaves clinging to dead limbs as it turned back into earth. One day it would let go and then where would those turtles sun?

Being one with nature had never once been something she'd entertained as a better way of life, but if anyplace could change her mind, it was this creek. The fast pace of her life with Ron didn't seem so attractive. For all that they'd compromised to earn more and buy more and climb the corporate ladder, they'd missed out on some of the simplest things in life, and she was beginning to regret that. Or maybe it wasn't so much regret as it was a new appreciation for something different. Something pure.

She pulled the phone from her pocket and checked the time, then tucked it away, once again navigating her way back to the creek bank.

Her phone rang in her back pocket, the buzz scaring her and nearly landing her in the water. She stepped up the pace and hopped over the last two rocks to the shore. She'd missed the call, but then she hadn't intended to answer anyway. Or had she?

No voice mail.

As she pressed buttons to see who had called, the signal for the voice mail came through. Must have been one heck of a long message.

She sat down on the ground and put her phone next to her while she put her shoes and socks back on. His picture was next to the icon. He knew. That's all she needed to know. Right?

Or she could listen.

Would he grovel? Beg her to come home? Say he was sorry?

Which might be true, but he wouldn't mean it the way she was thinking right now.

Shaleigh's words echoed, "Let me handle it."

She pulled her knees up in front of her and hugged them. Friday seemed eons ago, and her emotions were swinging like Tarzan.

She decided not to listen to the voice mail, but she didn't delete it either.

Katy walked back up to the house.

As she walked down the corridor to her room, a crash came from behind her. She turned and rushed back. "Naomi?"

But it wasn't Naomi.

A wisp of a woman lay in a heap of trinkets that had been on a table near the fireplace. She still clutched the heavy tablecloth.

"Are you okay?" Katy asked, almost afraid to help her up for fear she'd hurt her worse. The woman's skin was so pale. So light against the black velour robe. Velour in the middle of summer?

"I think so." Her voice was breathless.

"I'll call 911." Katy pulled her phone out of her pocket.

"No!"

Katy hesitated.

Kelly Jo, for this must be her, pleaded, "Please don't call an ambulance. I don't want to go to the hospital."

"I think you need some medical attention."

"Just help me to the couch."

Katy held out her arm for the girl and led her to the couch. "Are you hurt anywhere?" She was so frail.

"Aside from my pride? Just a bump on the shin. Really. It's okay." The woman sat quietly for a moment. "I'm Kelly Jo. I'm sorry I scared you."

"I know, please don't apologize. You took quite a fall."

"I'm Naomi's grandniece. I came downstairs to get something to drink. I lost my balance." She glanced over. "I sure made a mess."

"You just sit right there. I've got that." Katy rushed back over, collected the items from the floor, and righted the table. Just as she put the last item on the table, Naomi walked in and sang out a hello, but when she saw Katy huddled over the table and Kelly Jo on the couch, her expression fell.

"What were you doing up?" Naomi rushed to her niece's side.

"I'm sorry. I was just so thirsty. I got dizzy . . ." She didn't finish the sentence, but Naomi clearly got the gist of what had happened.

"Are you okay?"

Katy said, "She might be dehydrated. I wanted to call an ambulance."

"No." Naomi's answer was firm and nearly as fast as Kelly Jo's had been. "But Kelly Jo, we should go see the doctor. Just in case."

Kelly Jo's lips were paper-thin. "Can I get some water and just lie here for a minute?"

"Of course, sweetheart." Naomi swept Kelly Jo's fine wisps of hair to the side.

"Juice might be better," Katy said. "Want me to get it?"

"Yes. Thank you."

Katy rushed to get something for Kelly Jo. When she pushed through the doorway she stopped mid-step, spinning around in somewhat of a tizzy to find what she needed quickly. She pulled a cotton flour-sack towel off of a stack of them on the huge marble island and then grabbed ice from the freezer. She wrapped the towel into a knot, then filled a glass to the rim with some Gatorade she found in the pantry and raced back out to the living room.

"Here you go," Katy said. "It's Gatorade. If you're dehydrated, it will probably be better for you to drink, and here, put this on your leg."

"Thank you," she said, lifting the glass gingerly to her lips.

Even swallowing looked like an effort.

Kelly Jo closed her eyes and lay back.

Naomi lifted the robe and looked at her leg. "That's a goose egg."

Kelly Jo handed the ice to her aunt.

She placed it over the already bruising area, then turned to Katy. "Would you mind driving us into town to see the doctor after she rests a bit?"

"Not at all," Katy said. "We can go whenever you're ready."

She went to get her keys and purse, then moved her car up as close to the front porch as she could get. By the time she came back inside, Naomi was already trying to steady Kelly Jo. That looked like a disaster waiting to happen.

Katy grabbed the rolling desk chair from where Naomi had checked her in the other day and wheeled it over to them.

The young woman leaned against the wall and Naomi steadied her as she sat down in the chair. She was so thin the chair didn't even squeak or creak when she sat down.

"Hang on." Katy turned the chair around and headed for the front door, rolling it right out onto the porch and down the handicap ramp.

"I can stand to get in," Kelly Jo said.

"Okay. I'll be right here. Hang on to my arm if you need to."

Once Kelly Jo was in the car, Naomi hopped into the back seat and Katy wheeled the chair back in the inn before taking off.

"I don't know where we're going, so you're going to have to give me directions," Katy said.

"No problem. I've lived here all of my life." Naomi leaned forward between the two front seats. "Back out to the main road."

"I can do that," Katy said, negotiating the curves as fast as safely possible.

Naomi reached a hand over the seat to Kelly Jo. "Honey, we need to move you to one of the downstairs rooms. No sense you trying to climb those stairs by yourself. You'll just worry me."

Kelly Jo looked like she was going to argue, but then she didn't. "You're right. I'll do that."

Katy focused on the windy road, trying to stay calm. Kelly Jo looked like she was sweating, and Naomi looked nervous. "When I was coming in I saw a little sign that said FALLS on it. Is that someone's name or are there waterfalls nearby?"

Naomi's lips spread into a grin. "The waterfalls. I fell in love at the falls."

"Really?" She urged the conversation, trying to get Naomi's mind off of how bad Kelly Jo looked. Heck, trying to keep herself from panicking too.

A slip of a smile played across her lips.

"He must have been a pretty special man. I can see it on your face."

"A very kind and generous man. Marshall was my everything. He loved to entertain. That's why I live in that monstrosity of a house. I would have been perfectly happy with a little cottage on the creek. Those little nooks in the house became my way of making it feel cozy." She seemed to drift back to happier times. "We lived in some grandeur then. Remind me to show you some pictures."

"You still do. That place is lovely." Katy thought of the high-end touches she'd already noticed.

"It is. I love the memories there, but it's really too much for me. I couldn't possibly let it go to someone who wouldn't love it the way we did, though." She reached over and pointed to the street ahead. "Turn there, dear."

"He must have been very successful."

"I'll tell you all about him when we get back home. You can pull in the back lot. They usually have a wheelchair by that door."

"Perfect." Katy swung into the parking lot and pulled to a stop right at the base of the ramp. "I'll be right back."

She sprung from her seat and made her way up the ramp. Like Naomi had said, there was a wheelchair right by the door. She rolled it down to the bottom of the ramp where Naomi was already helping Kelly Jo get out of the car.

They easily moved Kelly Jo to the wheelchair. Even as little as Kelly Jo was, it was a bit of a workout to push that chair up the ramp, though.

Naomi walked ahead and pressed the handicap button, and the door opened. Inside, tiles shimmered white and sterile against the fluorescent lighting.

Naomi led the way. At the end of a long hallway they reached a glass door. The receptionist looked up when they came in.

"Miss Naomi. It's good to see you." She glanced down at her book. "Hon, you don't have an appointment today. Did you get mixed up?"

Naomi's eyes narrowed. "No. I didn't get mixed up."

Katy rolled Kelly Jo in just in time to hear that.

"That happened once," the receptionist whispered to Katy, then came around the desk in a hurry. "You don't look good, honey," she said.

"She took a fall," Katy said. "She was dizzy."

"I'll grab the doctor. Just wait right here and I'll get y'all in a room in one second."

A moment later the sound of a man's hurried footsteps came down the hall. "Kelly Jo?"

Katy leaned forward. The voice was familiar as he came into range, and so was the face when he cleared the door. Katy sucked in a breath.

He'd barely glanced in her direction, but it was Derek. She watched as he knelt at Kelly Jo's side, then jerked his head back up as if it just registered who was standing there.

"Hello again, Dr. Hansen. Didn't mean to be back so soon," Kelly Jo said.

He swung his head back to Kelly Jo, then looked to Naomi, and then back to Katy. *One of these things is not like the other,* Katy thought. "Katy?"

"Doctor?" Katy couldn't even believe she'd heard right. "You're a doctor?" He was a firefighter. She just saw him put on his firefighter gear in record time. You didn't do that without practice.

Who lies about being a firefighter?

Or a doctor for that matter?

Maybe the bigger question these days was who *didn't* lie?

Naomi didn't even give him a chance to respond. "He's a very well-known doctor," Naomi bragged. "He even got written up in a bunch of those journals for his work at Duke. Isn't that right, Derek?" Naomi pressed her lips in a tight line and then corrected herself, "Dr. Hansen?"

"It's true."

"We're lucky he's back here in Boot Creek," she said to Katy. Then turning to him, she said, "But that's not gonna change the fact that I can't get it through my head to call you doctor. You'll always be little Derek to me." Naomi's laugh tinkled like wind chimes on a spring day.

Kelly Jo managed a smile.

"At Duke?" Katy forced a smile, trying to keep her voice steady.

He nodded like it was no big deal. "That's a long story."

"Like the story about you being a firefighter? Who lies about being a firefighter?" Only she hadn't meant to utter that last part out loud.

"That was no story. I am a firefighter," he said.

Naomi's voice sliced through the banter. "Don't be too impressed with the firefighter stuff, Katy. Every man breathing in this town is a member of the Boot Creek Volunteer Fire Department."

"You're not helping here, Mrs. Laumann," Derek said with a heavy emphasis on the *Mrs.* "Kelly Jo, are you feeling dizzy right now?"

"Kind of," she said.

Derek glanced over at the nurse. "Let's get some fluids in her."

Naomi plunged on with her part of the conversation. "Even my dear husband was active duty on the fire department until the day he died, and he was too old to hold a match steady."

Kelly Jo piped up, "Uncle Marshall was a good man. Well-respected."

"I'm just telling it like it is," Naomi laughed. Katy took a step back and shoved her hands in her front pockets. Her fingers touched the small yellow ribbon. That felt like months ago . . . and it hadn't even been a week. She shoved it back in her pocket and took a breath.

He was the last person she expected to see here. The whole thing seemed like a weird, mixed-up dream. She wiped her sweating palms on her pants and then folded her arms.

Seeing him again made her heart race a little, which was unfair and very irritating in a way because it seemed like everyone she believed in was just a big fat liar.

———

Katy asked Naomi, "Where's the ladies' room?"

"Right down that hall to the left."

"Thank you." Katy practically jogged down the hall.

What was going on? Was there some kind of magnet in her outfit that just kept dragging the same guy back into her days in different roles like a whacked-out *Groundhog Day*? She went into the bathroom and stood there for a moment catching her breath. Her phone made that sound, the *buh-doop* of a text message coming in.

RON: Things are not always as they seem. I can explain.

Well, Lordy, didn't she know that. Unfortunately, his little scenario was exactly the way she saw it go down. She was so tempted to text him one of those pictures, but instead she copied his text and forwarded it to Shaleigh.

SHALEIGH: Don't engage with him.

SHALEIGH: Promise.

KATHERINE: Promise.

But it wasn't going to be easy. Right now she wanted to lash out at the world, and no one was playing fair. She walked back out to the waiting area, hoping Derek, the fireman-doctor-blackberry-festival-dancer, was gone.

A voice called her name from behind her. Had he been waiting in the hall for her?

He nodded toward the back hall. "I've . . . I've got a couple patients waiting. You're going to wait for Kelly Jo, right?"

She didn't answer.

"I can explain."

Of course, you can. You can all explain.

But when Kelly Jo was done getting the IV fluids, Katy whisked her and Naomi out to the car and got them back on the road. She didn't have the energy to have a discussion with Derek, or Ron for that matter. She should've just stayed in bed today.

<hr />

Katy kept her eyes on the road, but her mind was reeling. Fireman. Doctor. What was next? Indian chief?

Naomi had been rattling on since they left. "Derek has had a tough time of things. He's a good man. Came back to Boot Creek to help his father out, although I think it was really just an excuse for them to get Derek back home after Derek's wife died. They were really worried about him. What parent wouldn't be?"

Katy swallowed. She knew about his wife. At least that part had been true. Fine. So he wasn't a complete liar.

"She was so young. Cancer. That was his specialty, you know. Derek's."

"He was an oncologist?"

Kelly Jo shivered. "Yeah. He used to be one of the best cancer doctors in the state."

Katy cranked up the heat.

"Um-hmm. He'd made quite a name for himself too. He worked at Duke. Prominent in his field. Not being able to save his wife really tore him out of the frame."

Katy could hardly breathe. He'd said she'd been sick for a long time.

"His father has been the town doctor here for years, and his daddy before him. Kind of the Hansen family legacy around here, I guess."

Katy had a million questions, but they were bouncing around her head so fast she couldn't seem to get one to pop up like the next bingo ball to be called. So she just listened as Naomi rambled.

"He said your last name was Laumann. You were related to the singer?"

"Yes." She fidgeted with her seat belt. "I was married to Dillon's much better-looking and smarter brother, Marshall. Dillon is the Laumann everyone in the world remembers, though."

"Marshall and Dillon Laumann?" Katy couldn't help but smile. "Creative."

"Yes. I know. It is kind of funny. His mother was a little . . ." She held a finger to the side of her head and spun it in a circle as she whistled a coo-coo sound.

"Oh," Katy said. "Like really crazy?"

"Yeah. I'm sure Dillon got his crazies from his mother's side of the family. Most people never knew that Dillon Laumann was crazy."

Katy had her doubts that that was entirely true. It wasn't such a long shot for someone very talented to be a little eccentric.

"I'm not exaggerating. Their mother was flat-out paranoid—convinced every stranger that rolled into town was plotting her demise. And the woman could lie like no other. I don't really know if she even knew she was lying or she was delusional, but when she wasn't lying or hiding, she'd either be dancing on the street or pitching a random fit of crying somewhere. Everyone knew she was nuts." Naomi folded her hands in her lap. "Very few knew Dillon was a nutcase, though. Marshall kept that in check. He took care of his brother. His mom too until she died. Marshall got the smarts and business sense. Dillon got the . . . well, I don't know what that man got aside from the musical talent. He had a hard life, that one."

"Sorry to hear that. Did he spend a lot of time with y'all here? At the inn?"

"Well, it wasn't an inn back then. It was just our home, but yes, he stayed with us. He wasn't responsible enough to live alone, so Marshall would rein him back in and make him stay with us until he settled down and then put him back to work. In a way it was like Dillon was the monkey and Marshall was the organ grinder."

"That's kind of sad."

"In a way, yes. But it was that way always, so we didn't much even notice. He was fun. I'll give Dillon that. Life was never dull when that boy was in town. Everyone absolutely loved the Laumann boys."

"You sure did. I can see it in your eyes."

"I've had a very blessed life."

Katy drove back to the house without needing any directions. She helped Kelly Jo out at the front porch and then parked her car.

When Katy got back to the porch, a pretty dark-haired woman was helping Naomi get Kelly Jo inside.

Katy hung back as the two women helped Kelly Jo to the first room down the hall on the right.

When they came back out front a few minutes later, they were still talking. "I brought her some homemade tomato soup," the woman said. "I had just put it in the kitchen when you drove up. It's probably still warm."

"I don't think she'll be hungry for a while. She's getting weaker. I'm trying not to interfere, but I worry she's in too much pain and she still won't let us call in hospice."

"I wish like heck she'd call Todd," the woman said. "They need each other."

Katy stepped alongside Naomi and smiled at the woman, wondering who Todd was.

"She's still adamant about that." Naomi noticed Katy. "Where are my manners? Angie, this is Katy. Katy is staying with us."

"Nice to meet you. How long are you staying in Boot Creek?" Angie asked.

"Not sure yet. It wasn't really a planned trip."

"I work down at the Blue Skies Cafe. Drop in and I'll buy you a cup of coffee."

"Thank you. I just might do that."

"I've got to get back to work," Angie said. "Call if there's anything I can do. And let me know if she eats any of that soup, or I can try making something else."

Katy and Naomi waved as Angie walked out to a little smart car with a Blue Skies Cafe delivery sign on top.

Naomi pushed the front door closed and let out a sigh. "My goodness. What a day."

"How long has she been sick?"

"Longer than is fair. Bless her heart. I'm thankful she trusted me to come here, but the whole situation is really quite sad."

"Who's Todd?"

"Todd is her husband. A wonderful man. It's a long story."

Katy didn't want to pry, and Naomi seemed too exhausted to discuss it.

"So, young lady, I yapped the whole time you were driving. Are you going to tell me how you know our young Dr. Hansen?"

"I met him briefly at the blackberry festival." What else was she going to say? There really wasn't much to tell. And why did it irritate her so much that he was a doctor? Shouldn't that impress her?

They walked inside and Naomi paused at the desk near the front door. "I'm a little worried about how unsteady Kelly Jo is. I've got a walker in the back shed. I had to use it when I got my new hip last year. Would you mind terribly getting that for me? I think it might be a good idea for Kelly Jo to use that."

"Sure. Is there a lock on the shed?"

"No. There's no one around here who would ever steal anything from me except a couple squirrels and raccoons, and they don't use the doors anyway."

Katy went outside and took the path to what Naomi had called the shed, which was really more like a two-car garage. Inside everything was meticulously arranged. There on the right side was a bright red walker with hand brakes and a seat. The Cadillac of walkers. And it was pulled into a spot like it had its own reserved space between two bicycles and a lawn mower.

As she carried the lightweight walker back to the house, her phone buzzed.

She glanced at the display and then answered, "Hi, Shaleigh."

"How are you doing?"

"I'm doing okay." And that was true, because compared to what she'd been through today with Kelly Jo and her health state, her problems didn't seem nearly as bad.

Shaleigh, as usual, was all business. "Still ready to move forward with things?"

"Yes, ma'am."

"Okay. Well, he's already called me. He's hotter than a match head."

Katy ran her hands through her hair. "He left me a message. I haven't played it. You saw the text, though."

"I'll handle it. All that I need from you right now are a couple of signatures and we can get this separation under way. I'm forwarding them to you now. There will be a link that will take you to a signing website. Just follow the directions. Read everything carefully, but it's all pretty standard. Basically, we're just filing the official separation papers so he can't get you for abandonment if he decides to play dirty down the line."

Abandonment? "Okay. I can do that."

"Good. Read through them carefully. If you really don't want to fight for some of the specifics I've listed at this stage, just let me know.

The main thing is to get the separation filed. You can change your mind. Since y'all don't have children or anything complicated, it should be pretty quick, but there's no rush. Sometimes couples get through this stuff."

"And sometimes they don't," Katy added. She'd forgive Ron eventually. That was her nature, but it wouldn't be while she was married to him. He'd broken what they had. "Would you get over it if your husband cheated on you?"

"Oh, hell no."

"Yeah. Well, then, you know I'm not changing my mind."

"I hear you loud and clear."

"I'd love to have a picture of his face when he's served."

"That could be arranged."

She wondered if he'd be surprised or relieved that he could finally quit pretending. It seemed like it would be awfully hard to carry that around. "We might be on to a whole new reality show idea here."

"Maybe."

"Thanks for everything." Katy propped the walker against her hip and tucked the phone in her pocket as she opened the door. Naomi was sitting with her legs stretched out on the couch.

"You found it!"

"I did."

Naomi looked pleased. "I have to say I got pretty good with that thing. Should be like riding a bike." She waved her hand, motioning Katy to bring the red rolling walker closer.

Naomi swung her leg around and then positioned the walker right in front of her. She lifted herself up and put a knee on the seat of the walker. One push off with the other leg, and like a kid on one of those scooter things, Naomi was off and down the hall.

"Oh, Naomi. This has disaster written all over it. You're going to break your fool neck."

"Lighten up. It's fun, and it's safe." Naomi gave her an exaggerated wink and rolled up to the front desk and checked her book. "Let's take this down to Kelly Jo."

"I'll get a pitcher of water for her, and meet you back there."

Naomi drove that red walker like she was having a little too much fun. Katy had a feeling that long after Kelly Jo needed it, Naomi would keep that wheeled walker around just for kicks. She had to admit, she was a little tempted to try the thing out herself.

Chapter Twelve

Katy carried a tray with a pitcher of water, a cup, saltines, and a small mug of the tomato soup that Angie had brought over. Maybe Kelly Jo would be up to sipping a little of that.

"Knock, knock," Katy said as she walked in the room.

Kelly Jo was sitting up in bed, and Naomi had tucked the covers in around her, like a burrito baby, just like Katy's own mom used to do.

"This is a bright and cheery room," Katy commented. "I love the artwork." She walked closer to a set of two pictures of beautiful koi fish swimming with their fins fanning behind them. Almost like reverse sketches.

"All the rooms are all a little different," Naomi said. "I've had a lot of fun decorating, and redecorating them over the years. My Marshall was such a sweetheart about letting me have my way with the house."

"Aunt Naomi did those pictures."

"Really? It's like that scratchboard art, right? I noticed the sign out front is the same medium," Katy said. Not to mention half the town.

Naomi shrugged. "I was kind of known for that back in the day."

"Kind of," Kelly Jo said. "She's famous for it. Uncle Dillon wasn't the only famous Laumann."

"You did all the signs for Main Street too?" Katy asked.

"Most of them. Now they just have them made somewhere to look like the others. But yes, there was a time when I did all the signage for the town. It was fun."

"You are just full of little surprises. It's a great look. It's one of the first things I noticed when I drove through town." Katy pulled the nightstand away from the wall so Kelly Jo could reach everything more easily on the tray.

"Thanks, Katy. Sorry I was so much trouble this morning."

"Don't be silly. I'm glad I was here to help. What else can I do for you while I'm here?"

"Nothing." Kelly Jo took in a deep breath. "I'm just going to rest."

Naomi leaned over and pressed a kiss to Kelly Jo's forehead. "Love you, sweetheart."

She closed her eyes. "Love you, too." Her mouth moved but no sound came out.

Katy and Naomi walked back out of the room, and Naomi closed the door quietly behind them. "Bless her heart."

Katy wrapped an arm around her. "That's got to be so hard. Are you all the family she has left? You and Nell?"

"Well, and her husband, Todd. Remember. I mentioned him before."

"Where is he?"

Naomi shook her head. "Oh, don't get the wrong idea. He is an amazing young man. He loves that girl more than his own life. She just won't let him see her like this." Naomi raised a hand. "I know what you're thinking. Believe me. I've said my piece about it. The girl is determined that it will be easier on him if he's not here when she dies."

The breath caught in Katy's chest. She wasn't sure she could be that unselfish . . . heck, that brave, to go through what Kelly Jo was going through alone. How deep was a love that it would have you forge ahead alone to spare another. "She's trying to protect him."

"Yes, well, who am I to judge? I just want her to be at peace." Naomi's eyes glistened. "Things change when people die, leaving us to pick up the pieces and reshape our lives. It's not easy."

"When did Marshall pass away?"

They walked back out to the living room. Naomi sat in one of the large wing-back chairs, crossing her legs and looking rather demure. She'd probably been a beautiful young girl.

"Twelve years ago." Her mouth puckered a little. "Never has been the same without him."

"Had he been sick?"

She shook her silver-haired head. "No. He was older than me. He was resting in his lounger. He'd do that. Fall asleep in the chair watching CNN. One day, he just never woke up. I came in to share a cup of tea with him and he just didn't respond." Naomi stared off like she was reliving the moment. "I don't know how long I sat there, kind of knowing but not wanting to know."

"There's no easy way. Just before I came here one of my neighbors lost her husband. Same thing. No warning. Just didn't wake up one day."

"We had a good life. He left me in good shape financially. Nell always tells people I'm living off of my Social Security, but that's not true. I'd never be able to keep this place up on that pittance."

"I can imagine. The electricity bill alone has to be out of this world. You could rent the suite I'm staying in for so much more."

A gentle laugh filled the space. "It's not about the money. It's just nice to have someone to fuss over, to cook for once in a while. Really. It's my pleasure."

"I'm sure you get a lot of repeat customers. I know I'd come back."

"Thank you. I'd like that too. Marshall left me plenty of money to keep this place going without renting out the rooms, but he'd always had them filled with people staying for one thing or another and it just was so darn lonely here by myself."

She wanted to ask Naomi if the loneliness after Marshall died was why she'd named the inn Lonesome Pines, but that seemed too personal. "Why don't you sell this place and move to that little cabin on the creek you were talking about? Or build one on part of the land? It looks like you've got some acreage around here."

"I do. It's about eighty acres." She pointed to the bookshelf. "Bring those photo albums over. I'll show you some things."

Katy got up and retrieved a stack of four photo albums, all bound in cordovan leather with a gold-leaf border. Naomi got comfortable on the couch and then patted the cushion next to her for Katy to sit down. Katy joined her and they opened one of the albums up across both of their laps.

They spent the next hour with Naomi guiding Katy through pictures from her and Marshall's courtship, and their wedding. She'd been a lovely bride. Marshall was good-looking, too. Naomi hadn't exaggerated.

The parties were like nothing she'd ever imagined. Fancy outfits, people mugging for the camera, beautiful flowers—grand in every kind of way. Ron would have loved that life. She might have, too, if there had been a couple tiny ones to chase around the yard and pick up after between parties. On the outside Naomi's life looked perfect, but then she was renting rooms to strangers just to have company and someone to fuss over. Maybe her life would have been different had she and Marshall had children. That thought only made Katy yearn for children more. To hold that life in her arms. And Kelly Jo, so fragile. She ached to somehow help her.

Naomi pointed out a few celebrities in the grainy photographs. "That right there is a very young Loretta Lynn. She loved it out here. And look. Do you know who that is?"

Katy shook her head.

"Andy Griffith. He's from over Mount Airy way. I was always surprised he gave up singing to pursue the acting, but he was equally wonderful at both."

"So people like that came here all the time?"

"Not all the time, but any time. I never knew how many people we would be hosting. It was kind of like living on a party cruise."

"I can see why you wouldn't want to just walk away from these memories."

"The memories are in here," she said tapping the side of her head. "But I think this house isn't done with its work. I'd always thought I'd leave the place to Kelly Jo. She's the only one who ever loved it as much as I do. Marshall's niece was Kelly Jo's mother. She died very young. It was pneumonia."

"And you and Marshall never wanted children of your own?"

"Marshall was dead set against it. Afraid the crazy would be passed to our children." A wistful look cloaked Naomi. "I'd have given it a chance, but it wasn't meant to be."

"Kelly Jo is lucky to have you."

"I asked Derek, Dr. Hansen," Naomi corrected herself, "to come and talk to her. Not as a doctor, but as someone who has been through this. She's already been to doctors all over this country. But Derek, he's special. He knows what she's going through. I think if he shares his story with her, about his sweet Laney, that Kelly Jo will be able to let go. If nothing else, maybe she will let Todd back into her life."

Maybe Katy could pray for that. Peace for the sweet gal trying to navigate the end of her life. How does someone even emotionally wrap her head around that?

"Sometimes things seem so clear on the outside, but what's happening on the inside . . . it's a whole other story. I think sometimes people are just too brave for their own good these days. It's okay for things not to be perfect."

Perfect. Lord, Katy knew a few things about trying to be perfect. But then even perfect didn't last. Although Derek had described his wife as perfect, the short time they'd had together didn't seem fair and seemed pretty far from perfect.

"Love your life, my dear. I don't know what's going on with you, but I know it's something. I saw it in your eyes when you showed up. Don't let the past haunt your future. Just let the world take you in its arms and the journey will unfold."

Tears welled in Katy's eyes, blurring her line of vision. "I'm trying so hard to do that."

"Things happen for a reason. Though they sure aren't easy to see sometimes. Like Derek. Him losing Laney seemed to have derailed an amazing career, but I'm willing to bet there's something even better in his future. That's the way God works. It's kind of like me and my house. I know the right thing will happen at some point. Someone will come along who is going to carry this place forward in new and wonderful ways. I'll know when the right situation offers itself."

"I'm sure you will."

"I hope you'll stay for a while."

"Thank you. At least I can help while I'm here. I'm not used to sitting idle."

"My kind of girl."

"Good. Then, I'll stick around and give you a hand." And that honestly felt like the best thing she could do with her life right now. Make a little difference, ease a little burden, for people who needed her.

When Derek drove up to the house, Katy was sitting on the front porch.

She'd looked pretty upset at the clinic, but he wasn't sure why. It wasn't like he'd said he was a movie producer and tried to seduce her into an audition on his casting couch. They'd had a great night. Really great.

He hoped she'd say something that might give him a clue as to what was on her mind. He stood at the bottom of the stairs, waiting for some indication of what he was in for.

"You lied to me." Her jaw pulsed.

Was she mad or was she going to cry? Oh, he prayed she wasn't going to cry. "I didn't lie," he answered cautiously.

"You let me believe you worked for the fire department."

"And I do."

"Everyone does. Naomi said so."

"So, then it just corroborates my story. I'm on the volunteer fire department roster, and I'm a doctor." He shoved his hands in his pockets. "I told you about Laney. I left my oncology work behind after she died."

"It caught me off guard. You seemed so nice. Honest. And then nothing you said seemed real. I mean what little I did know about you wasn't what I knew at all. Or something. I don't know."

"Look. I've been out of this for a long time. When I saw you at the gas station . . . something just kind of clicked. It was nice. I'm sure I'm going to say or do something wrong, but are you really mad at me? I didn't lie to you. Do you think I was trying to be deceptive?"

"It sounds really stupid when you say it out loud." She shrugged. "Not exactly. But maybe."

"Well, everything I told you was true. Now add to that that I'm also a doctor filling in for his dad at his dad's busy practice so his mom can have company marking some stuff off of her bucket list; and I'm still practicing medicine to maintain some part of my career as I figure out what my future looks like."

The tension in her jaw relaxed a little.

"I really didn't mean to mislead you. We never talked about what we did. It just didn't come up. What do you do?"

"I work in the financial industry. A project manager." She laced her fingers. "This is so awkward. I don't do that kind of thing. I mean, the other night. Random get-togethers. With strangers." She groaned.

"I meant for a living, but the other night was fun. And I'm not that strange. Am I?" He walked up the steps and turned to sit next to her. "I haven't been out on a date since my wife died. I know what we had wasn't technically a date, but it turned into one. Didn't it? Kind of? Would you call it a date?"

"I'm so out of my comfort zone right now." Her laugh sounded nervous, and that was attractive, and the truth was . . . he was nervous too.

"Me, too, but I'd like to see you again while you're in town."

She held his gaze, but for the life of him he didn't know how to read her. He was almost afraid to continue. "If that's okay."

"I don't know, Derek. My life is really complicated."

"Whose isn't? I became a doctor to heal. To make a difference. And what good is that if you can't heal the ones that you love the most?"

"Her dying was not your fault."

"She'd been sick for a long time. Fought hard, but then I made her fight way longer than she wanted to. Every cutting-edge trial out there, I got her into it."

"Who wouldn't? You loved her. You wanted to save her. Don't apologize for that."

"In hindsight it was so selfish." He closed his eyes for a moment. He'd never even really talked about this with anyone. It had always been too hard. But then maybe since she didn't know Laney, it somehow made it easier, because here he was talking about her again with this woman he barely knew. "It was foolish to have believed that medicine could outdo what God had already planned." Not that God's plan made any sense in this case. Maybe it never did, but Laney was one of His biggest advocates. She shared the word. Lived it. A shining example.

And that just made Derek mad at God. Couldn't He have done something? If medicine wasn't enough, wasn't it His job to step in?

He shrugged, cutting off his own thoughts. "That's my story."

"You're right. It's complicated. And sad. I'm sorry you went through that."

"Thanks." He squeezed her hand briefly. "I liked being with you. It was easy." Not like that. "Wait. That didn't come out right. Not easy. You know what I mean."

She laughed. "Yeah, calling a girl easy is not the way to get a date."

"I told you I wasn't good at this. And it's not a date. It's just . . . a thing."

"A thing?"

"Dinner. In a public place?" He stood up. He was out of ideas. He'd been crazy to agree to see Kelly Jo. It was the last thing he wanted to do, but because it meant he might see Katy again, he'd agreed. And now here he was. His only chance. *Come on, Katy, give me a break.*

"Okay. Just dinner. Not a date. How about you take me to the Blue Skies Cafe?"

"You've got yourself a deal."

She stood up. "Okay then."

He nodded toward the door. "I promised Naomi that I'd talk to Kelly Jo."

"I feel sorry for her husband."

"You heard? Hell, I know exactly what that man is going through. Only, thank God, Laney never shut me out. He and I played ball in school years ago. I know this has to be tearing him apart."

"Why doesn't he just come?"

"I'm sure he's trying to give her what she wants."

"Wow. I don't know if I could do that," she said.

"Me, either. I admire him for it, though. I get it, too. I mean on one hand there's so little that you can do, that doing anything, like giving Kelly Jo her way on this request, is at least something. There are no right answers in this. Every single situation is different." He started toward the door. "I'm just going to . . ." He pointed to the door and then went inside.

As the screen door closed behind him, he turned to her. "Think we could go as soon as I'm done? I'll be ready for some good company."

She tossed her head back and laughed. "Are you serious?"

"Yeah."

"You don't waste any time."

"If there's one thing I've learned, it's that you can't waste a precious moment."

"I'll change. Take your time."

He had no idea what he was going to say to Kelly Jo, but he knew that he could do it a little better after talking to Katy. She gave him a lift. A spark. A something he hadn't thought he'd ever feel again. And even if it was temporary, it was a nice thing to know that it might exist again. And it didn't mean leaving those memories of Laney behind, either. There was room for both.

Chapter Thirteen

It had been over forty-five minutes by the time Derek came back down the hall from his visit with Kelly Jo.

Naomi had fallen asleep on the couch, and Katy sat rereading the same page in the novel she'd started. Why had she agreed to dinner?

Why hadn't she just moved on after she saw Derek this afternoon? That would have been the right thing to do. She could have gone on up to Virginia Beach and been walking on the beach by now. Not that the beach in June was anyplace she'd ever really wanted to be. Maybe Skyline Drive instead. The mountains were always nice in the summer.

There were plenty of people in this town to help Naomi around the inn. If she was trying to persuade herself that Naomi needed her, not that she wanted to stay, that reason wasn't all that convincing . . . even to herself.

When Derek came back down the hall from visiting with Kelly Jo, he had a pained look.

That visit must have been a tough one. It had to be hard to go back to that place that held such pain in the not-so-distant past, especially when the scars were still not healed. The look in his eyes made her heart ache for him. Do those scars ever heal? Would her own? Maybe all experiences are baggage of some sort.

She laid the novel down on the coffee table and met him halfway. "Are you sure you're still up to going to dinner tonight?"

He paused, then looked up for a moment. "Yes." He held out his hand for hers. "More than anything."

She placed her hand in his and let him lead the way outside to his truck.

Katy said, "She's very fragile physically *and* emotionally, isn't she?"

He nodded, and opened the truck door for her.

Katy got in and pulled her seat belt across her body and clicked it. Adrenaline pumped through her veins so hard that she could hear the thump-thump thumping in her head—the big bass kick-drum variety that seemed to vibrate all the way to her fingertips. Kind of like the last moments before you are locked into a big roller coaster at a Busch Gardens amusement park. She sure hoped tonight wasn't going to leave her with that sick, scary, screaming feeling you got afterward. She was more of a bumper car kind of girl, really.

He started the truck and pulled out to the main road.

Why the heck was she so nervous? He wasn't an ax murderer. Not if everyone in the town knew and loved him. She tried to relax. "I met someone who works at the Blue Skies Cafe the other day."

"Angie?"

"Yeah. How'd you guess?"

He pulled around the back of the restaurant. "Angie knows Naomi. This place has great food, but it's also a quick walk from the medical center. Beats cooking for one."

"I can understand that." Only she hadn't thought about just cooking for one. Until now. And now that he'd mentioned it, she realized she'd be figuring out a whole lot more about cooking for one soon. Popcorn for dinner every night if she wanted it. Take that, meat-and-potatoes guy!

She followed him inside and it seemed like everyone in the place turned and looked at them when they entered.

"We can sit right here," he said, motioning to the first booth they came to.

"It's nice. I love the stained glass." She sat with her back to the other customers. "I bet it's lovely in the afternoon."

"It is."

The woman that she'd met at the inn walked up to the table and her face lit up when she saw her. "Katy. So nice to see you here." Angie glanced over at Derek. "And you're here with one of my very favorite people."

"You really do know everyone in town," Katy said to Derek.

"Oh, yeah. Everyone knows everyone around here. Best part about living here." Angie tapped her pen on Derek's side of the table. "I know Derek wants sweet tea. What's your pleasure?"

"I'll have the same."

"Got it. Two sweet teas." Angie turned and grabbed two menus and put them on the table. "Special tonight is a bacon-wrapped fillet, baby red potatoes, and broccoli. There's always the fried chicken, and my personal favorite, the beefalo. Derek has had everything on the menu, more times than he'll probably admit. I'll be back in a jiff."

"Thanks, Angie," Derek said.

Katy opened the menu. "She's so nice."

"Good people, and she's right. I know the menu by heart. So what are you in the mood for?"

She scanned the menu and then closed it in front of her.

"You already know what you want?"

"Fried chicken. A no-brainer."

"Me too."

He was easy to be with, and a gentleman. She liked that. There was no pressure, but she had to be straight up with him right now. He'd confided in her, but she was still holding her situation close to the vest and that wasn't fair.

"You know, Derek . . ." She swallowed, willing the strength to say it without sounding crazy. "I need to tell you. To be sure you know." This wasn't easy. "I don't do what we did the other night—you know—going out on the town alone, because I—"

"Katy. I know you're a lady. Please don't worry about that. It was an unusual circumstance, but it worked out. You don't have to explain. Really."

And "nothing happened" seemed to be the unspoken words. Oh, but she did still need to tell him. Nothing sexual happened, but it was an intimate night. No husband would want to hear that his wife had lain in the arms of another man, even if they were fully clothed. The fact remained she was married and she couldn't keep that a secret from him.

Angie slid the two sweet teas onto the table, turned to the counter and swept a tray into her arm, and then whisked down to another table to serve the meals.

She made it look easy. Katy knew different. She'd tried her hand at waitressing during college and that had been one huge disaster. Instead she'd ended up taking a third-shift data-entry job processing donations for a huge online church network. They even had optical scanners; her job was simply to correct the letters the machine couldn't read. It had been tedious, but it had paid well and she couldn't spill anything or drop plates.

Derek leaned across the table. "Angie and I went to school together. She's a single mom. Her son, Billy, is great. Probably the only good thing she got out of her marriage. Her ex was a shit, always jumping from job to job and running around on her while she was trying to keep food on the table and raise Billy. I don't understand how anyone can be unfaithful."

She swallowed back a dose of her own medicine. How was she supposed to explain her situation after that? And did her behavior just sink her to Ron's level? Maybe nothing had happened, but still she hadn't been completely honest, either.

"I was so glad when she kicked him to the curb—she's the hardest-working girl I know."

Katy suddenly admired Angie. Not just for her work ethic, or that she was nice, but she'd been cheated on too, and she seemed to have all the confidence in the world. Katy wondered if she'd ever feel that way again.

Angie hustled over to their table.

"Are you the only one working the tables tonight?" Katy asked.

She tugged her ink pen and pad from the apron pocket and nodded. "Won't hear me complaining. Makes the night go by faster and I could use the double-tip night. My car broke down. That's why I was driving the restaurant car the other day." She smiled. "What'll y'all have?"

Katy gave Derek a nod. "Local's choice."

Angie raised a brow and kind of smiled. "Okay. So?"

Derek said, "We'll both do the fried chicken tonight."

Angie tapped her pen in the air like that was the winning choice. "Two fried chickens. But next time you come, Katy, you have got to get Ol' Man Johnson's CB&B." She leaned down and translated for Katy. "Carolina Beefalo and Browns."

"Beefalo? Browns? That sounds like football teams to me."

Angie laughed. "You're right! Hadn't thought of that before. But no, it's his cool twist on hash browns that will make it hard for you to ever order anything different." She raised her order pad into the air. "Hand to God, and the beefalo is grown local up the road. I'll take you out to Criss Cross Farm one day if you like," Angie said. "My boy loves going to see those animals."

Katy wondered if the high school chums were pulling her leg. "I've never heard of a beefalo. Are you serious?"

"Oh yeah. I'm off on Thursday. If that storm doesn't bring buckets of rain our way, I'll take you to see them."

Two weeks ago she probably wouldn't have even asked what a beefalo was, but here, closer to nature and the quiet, going to see them seemed like a really cool thing to do. Ron would die if he knew she was going to go to a farm. On purpose. And maybe that's what made it even more appealing. "Perfect. You're on."

Derek leaned back in the booth, watching the two of them talk. "Did you just steal my date, Angie?"

Date? Oh, God. That just sent red flags snapping in the wind. She couldn't date. She was married. Katy tried to hide the wave of anxiety that hit her behind a laugh that came out way too loud, and made her even more anxious.

Angie put her hand on her hip and leveled a stare at Derek. "You, my friend, can pray for rain and make your own plans with her."

"You can be my rain date," Katy said.

Derek pulled out his phone and studied the screen. Then he looked up and said, "Yeah. Okay. I'll take that." He turned his phone toward the girls. "Eighty percent chance of thunderstorms on Thursday. I think the odds are with me."

"Actually, I think the odds are with me," Katy said. "I win either way."

The restaurant was busy; it stayed that way all the way until closing time, and she and Derek were still sitting there when it did.

Angie locked the front door and turned off the OPEN sign in the front window. "I might have to ask y'all to come in every night. I think this was the best night we've had in a while," she said.

"I thought we'd stay and give you a ride home," Derek said.

Angie walked over to the table. "Y'all don't have to do that. I can walk."

"Don't be silly," Katy said. "It's no trouble at all."

"Well, then at least let me get y'all some dessert while I finish up here."

"Deal," Derek said.

Katy said, "We'll split one."

"I'll make it a big piece then." A few moments later she walked back out with a hunk of pie big enough for two, and two forks. She freshened their coffee and then went through the tasks to close down for the night.

Ol' Man Johnson came out and slid into the booth next to Katy. "Where'd you find this pretty thing, Derek?"

"At the Blackberry Festival."

The old man gave a doubtful look.

"True," Katy said.

"Well, I'm going to have to close up shop and go next year. Did you enjoy your dinner?"

"Very much," Katy said. "Everything was delicious."

"Good. Hope I'll see you back in here again then."

"Oh you will. I hear I have to try the beefalo and browns. I can't leave town without trying that."

"Not without being sorry." Ol' Man Johnson stood and bowed slightly. "Until next time."

He walked out the back door and Angie came around the corner with a wad of money in her hands. "This night was amazing."

Derek peeled off a twenty and stuck it on top of her pile. "Thanks for the dessert."

"Awww. You don't have to do that."

"I'm trying to impress my date," he said, and then he looked at Katy.

A part of her reveled in the attention. She didn't know if anything would ever come of it, but it was a sure sign that there were good men out there, and Ron's reputation wasn't holding up very well.

Angie locked up and they piled into Derek's truck. "Did Derek tell you all my bad habits?" she asked.

Katy laughed.

"No, but I did tell her you were pretty awesome and even better now that you kicked that cheating shit of a husband to the curb."

Katy's gut twisted, because even if Angie had already kicked her husband to the curb, it still had to hurt to revisit that betrayal.

"I think he thinks that's a compliment," Angie said. "Thanks for airing my dirty laundry to my new friend, Derek." She tapped Katy on the shoulder. "He's right, though. My ex was, is, a jerk. Gave me the best gift ever in my son, so I wouldn't undo the experience for anything, but for the life of me, I still don't know what went wrong."

"Don't waste your energy rationalizing what your ex did. There's never a reason to go outside of the relationship no matter what problems there are. It's not your fault." And as the words came out of her mouth, she suddenly realized that it was a lot easier to give advice than to take it, because doggone if she wasn't wondering exactly what could have driven Ron to do such a thing. "Give it time."

"It's been two years. I can say this—I don't think it matters how much time you give it. I think it's what you do with the time. That first year it was like I was in neutral. Maybe I was waiting for him to come back and tell me he couldn't live without us. I don't know. But once I quit waiting, letting time pass, things got better."

Neutral. That was a good way to explain it. Because although Katy wasn't a "stick your head in the sand" kind of a girl, not thinking about the situation and letting Shaleigh handle it had felt like a better way to go. But the advice was sound. She probably needed to be careful not to wait for something she knew she didn't want anyway.

"You're one of the strongest women I know, Angie," Derek said.

"Thanks, sweetie." She mussed a hand in his hair. "He has to say that. I know all of his secrets," she teased.

"We're here," Derek said. "Get out before you tell any of them."

Angie got out and Derek waited until she got inside the front door. "Thanks for letting me take the detour, Katy. It's a completely safe town, but that girl works so hard. I hate to think of her walking all the way home after a full day's work."

"No problem. I'm glad we did it."

He backtracked and took Katy back to the inn. There was no awkward almost-kiss. Instead, he walked her to the door, and gave her a hug and a kiss on the cheek with a pleasant "Let's do this again."

She watched his headlights disappear down the dark lane. Doing that again would be nice. And she could, but it was weird to go from married to not with no notice. But then she better at least let him know what was going on in her life. It was only going to get harder the more time that passed.

In her room, she undressed and got into bed. She toyed with her

phone before laying it on the nightstand. She lay there in the quiet. It
had been a nice evening. A busy day full of a lot of different emotions,
but good all the same.

She picked up her phone and clicked on the phone icon. The message from Ron still showed as unplayed.

She held her finger steady over the button, and then she pressed it.

"Katherine."

The way he said her name always had the same effect on her. Like
he'd been waiting all day to say it. The way he dragged the syllables
unrushed—kind of like the way he kissed her. Slow and wholly. Even
now . . . knowing what he'd done, that simple word—her name—made
her acutely aware of the increase in her heart rate. Damn him.

But what followed the sweet roll of her name from his lips was less
alluring.

"What the hell?" His voice sounded tight. "You think you can just
up and leave? Handle things without so much as a word to me? I'm not
one of your projects. I get a say in this, too." His voice held an edge as
sharp as a samurai sword.

"I know she's your friend, but you really called that bitch Shaleigh?
You know her reputation. She's a man-eater. She hates men. She'll ruin
my reputation. What are you thinking? If you weren't off flying around
the country half of the time, this would have never happened. It doesn't
mean anything. You need to come back home and we need to discuss
this. You can't ruin everything we've built. Although you did a pretty
damn good job ruining my birthday present, by the way. What the hell
is going on in that head of yours? Katherine. Listen, we have the perfect
life. You leaving is just f—. It's crazy."

Oh, yeah he was mad. Almost dropped the f-bomb on her right
there and he knew how she hated that.

"Katherine. Baby. You're upset. I get it. Let me explain. Come
home. Don't let Shaleigh turn this into something ugly. I love you. You
know that."

She replayed the message four times.

"Don't let Shaleigh turn this into something ugly?" She could barely repeat his words without a snicker of disgust. "You made it ugly, Ron. You."

———————

Katy got up early and accessed her online banking to make sure all of her bills were paid. Since she wouldn't have a paycheck the next few weeks, she needed to be sure she was careful with what she spent.

Feeling good about the early-hour accomplishment, she joined Naomi for coffee.

"Naomi, I was wondering if you wouldn't mind if I did a little of the cooking in that amazing kitchen of yours, as long as it's just you, me, and Kelly Jo."

"Don't be silly. You are a paying guest in this house. That wouldn't be right."

"But it would be fun for me, and quite honestly, you are not charging near enough for the hospitality and quality you provide."

"It's plenty enough," Naomi said.

"Please? Really. I'd enjoy it. Or we could cook some things together, maybe. That would be fun." And maybe that whole cooking-for-one thing had made her feel a little itchy. Cooking for others is what made cooking enjoyable.

"I do have some special recipes that someone needs to learn, especially now that Kelly Jo won't be the one to carry on that legacy." She looked away for a moment, and Katy, though sad, felt honored to be able to stand next to Naomi and be a surrogate in some small way.

"We have a deal then?"

Naomi looked a little hesitant, but said, "Yes. We have a deal. You're more like family than a guest already anyway. Make yourself at home in my kitchen."

Katy could hardly wait. "Do you like quiche? I make an amazing quiche."

"I do," Naomi said.

"Great." Katy jumped up from the table. "I'm going to make a list of what I need. Have you had breakfast?"

"No, but don't go running off to the grocery store. Look in the fridge and pantry first. I keep it stocked. If you're going to cook, at least use my groceries."

It turned out Naomi was not exaggerating about the grocery situation. If there was ever a famine, this was the place to be stuck. No one would go hungry for months.

While the quiche baked, Katy cut fresh fruit into a bowl. It was fun to cook in a kitchen like this. She felt a little like a contestant on one of those fancy food competition shows. There'd been a time when Katy cooked every night. She used to be a pretty good cook, in fact, but over the years, as Ron's and her careers had advanced, their schedules just got too hectic and her specialty had turned into reservations and takeout.

Katy went ahead and set the table for the three of them, hoping Kelly Jo would feel up to coming into the dining room with the help of the walker. Maybe with a nice setting, the ladies would feel a little perkier.

She walked out the back door of the kitchen to the garden, where fresh herbs and flowers abounded. She plucked some basil, and then a cluster of small colorful flowers that kind of looked like daisies, only these had a lot more leaves. Didn't matter. They were pretty.

She took them inside and pulled the quiche out of the oven. She garnished the plates with the fresh basil and a slice of orange and placed a perfect wedge of quiche on each plate.

Just as she was getting ready to go check on Kelly Jo and Naomi, Kelly Jo came through the door alone, steadied by the bright red walker on wheels.

"I'm so glad you decided to stay." Her voice sounded weak.

"You look like you feel better today." Katy tucked the flowers into a white milk vase. "I made some brunch. Maybe you can eat a little something."

"That was so nice of you. Thank you."

Katy motioned her to the table. "I'm going to go round up Naomi."

Kelly Jo sat down. "I think she's on her way. I heard her singing down the hall. She loves to sing."

Naomi came through the doorway. "I thought I heard voices in here." Her mouth dropped open. "Katy? This is way more extravagant than I'd ever expected."

A sense of pride washed over her. "Just trying to keep up with you, Naomi."

"I think you're going to give me a run for my money, dear." Naomi sat down next to her, then reached over and took Katy's hand in one hand and Kelly Jo's hand in the other. "I'll bless the food real quick."

"Thank you," Kelly Jo said.

Katy bowed her head.

Naomi closed her eyes. "Lord, we are so grateful to be here together on this beautiful day. Lord bless this food to our use that we might better serve you. And thank you for bringing Derek into our lives at a time when all of us need his guidance and fellowship. Amen."

Katy had a feeling each one of them at the table needed that blessing right now, and she'd give a big amen to that.

After brunch, Katy insisted on cleaning up while Kelly Jo and Naomi talked. Katy had a feeling they were discussing something of a personal nature and she didn't want to intrude, so afterward she grabbed her phone and went outside.

Angie was walking up the stairs when Katy stepped out on the porch.

"Good to see you again," Angie said.

"We just finished up brunch, but there's quiche in the kitchen if you're hungry," Katy said.

"I'm good. I just have a few minutes. I wanted to check in on you girls."

"That's really nice of you."

She shrugged it off. "Nothing any of you wouldn't do for me or anyone else in this town."

Katy nodded. The sincerity of those words touched her deeply. Just a few weeks ago she'd have said that about Preakness Heights, but the truth was this was a whole new level of community.

Angie headed inside and Katy walked outside and sat in one of the rocking chairs.

She was so disappointed in Ron. She'd have never broken that trust. And yet, maybe she was just as guilty for what had happened. Work kept them both busy. They were tired when they got home. Well, maybe she'd been the only one tired.

If she extended her leave of absence, she'd have three months to figure things out. Where she would live. Whether she'd go back to work at the bank or find something new to do. But time wasn't going to fix this alone. She had to use her hiatus wisely.

Even her job, which she'd loved, just didn't seem to have the kind of purpose her contribution to this world should. Certainly there was something different she could do that would matter. Would make a difference.

She dialed Peggy, who answered with a cheerful "Hello."

"I was just thinking about you," Peggy said. "How are you doing?"

"I'm doing okay. How are things with you and Tucker?"

Peggy made a sound like she was coughing up phlegm. "I don't know. I think he'd rather I have to live in a tent than work out something with me. What is wrong with him? Doesn't the fact I put up with him all this time amount to anything? He even took my dealer car and gave me a minivan. Me. A minivan. Are you believing that? Shaleigh says he can do that too. Just has to be sure I have wheels. For now. Once the divorce is over, it will be different though. I guaran-damn-tee that."

Well, she'd certainly caught Peggy in a mood. That fiery redhead temper was rolling hot.

Now, none of it seemed important. The big house. The fancy car. The expensive dinners and fancy parties where she'd spend nearly a mortgage payment on a dress for one night.

For what?

She realized that all the stuff, and making a fair split of it, didn't even really matter much to her. She just wanted to be out of the lie.

"I'm sorry things aren't going the way you'd like," she said to her friend.

"Yeah. Me too. I thought it would be way easier than this. I mean it's not like I ever did anything wrong."

"Do you think it might have been any easier if you'd talked to Tucker yourself? I mean instead of going the lawyer route?"

"Who knows? Somehow I doubt it. You know Shaleigh's reputation. If Tucker is going to be a jerk, I darn sure want her fighting my fight for me. Better to know now than be tricked out of it later. Who knows if it really does make a difference who your lawyer is?"

And that was the question of the century. Who decided right from wrong anymore? The lines sure did seem gray.

Maybe all of this was her chance to find a new direction.

Things could certainly be worse.

Chapter Fourteen

Katy needed a plan. Despite the residual negative feelings from her talk with Peggy, Angie's comments about using her time wisely had really resonated with her. Ron had screwed up plain and simple, and she had no intention of trying to repair the damage.

There *was* no good reason for someone to go outside of the marriage for attention, ever. So how she used this time she had off of work was up to her. She could sit idle wondering what was going to happen next, or move the heck on.

After ten years of marriage, there was no reason to try to start brand-new. What he'd done was unforgivable in her eyes and she didn't need to hide behind Shaleigh or anyone else. She was in the right here.

Peggy had meant well, and Katy getting out of town while she was stunned and hurt had absolutely been the right thing. Putting some distance between what she'd seen in that bistro and Ron had given her time to catch her breath, regain her sensibilities.

Katy made two pretty fruit parfaits for Kelly Jo and Naomi and left them on the top shelf in the refrigerator.

Satisfied with this, she was determined to make today meaningful.

She'd head to Atlanta for a night or two. Sync up with Ron and set things straight. They could be adults about this. There was no reason they couldn't be amicable. He could have his little girlfriend and half the stuff. At this point she just wanted to move on. And from that visit, she could at least have a feeling for whether her life would be in Atlanta or somewhere else.

Did he want the house, or like Peggy, would she still reside in Preakness Heights? And if he wanted the house, where would her life be?

Even if she decided that her life was back in Atlanta, she thought she might come back and help Naomi and Kelly Jo for a little while. She left a quick note for Naomi about the parfaits and explained that she'd had to run back down to Atlanta for work, but that she'd be back.

Then she grabbed her purse and headed out. Navigating the twisting back roads was becoming easier. She was able to get from the inn to the interstate in nearly half the time it had taken her to find the inn that first day.

She dropped in behind a trucker on the interstate and let him push the speed limit, following in his draft.

At this pace she'd be in Atlanta before Ron even got off of work; then she could visit with Peggy and that would be good, too. She'd give her a quick call when she got closer to see if they could swing a short visit.

By three-thirty she was off the interstate. It felt like her car was poking along in the city traffic after hours of interstate driving.

Her hands shook a little as she reached for the radio button. She knew better than to go all day without eating, but it wouldn't be the first time that she had her mind set on something and didn't bother to stop for the basic necessities. Since she was early, she swung by her favorite frozen yogurt place and grabbed a snack.

She sat at an outdoor table under a bright pink-and-green umbrella eating her yogurt.

Katy texted Peggy to see if she was home.

PEGGY: Sure am. How are you? I was getting ready to text you.

KATHERINE: OK. In town. Thought I'd stop by and see you.

Her phone rang. It was Peggy.
"Too much trouble to type?" Katy asked.
"Too hard to type."
"What? You just get your nails done? This is Tuesday. You get your nails done on Wednesday."
"I'm texting you a picture. Hang on," Peggy said. "Where are you?"
"Just around the corner. At the yogurt place."
"Get over here. I'm home."
Katy threw her trash away and got into the car. As she pulled up to the stoplight, *bah-doop*. Peggy's picture must have come through.
The light turned so Katy held the phone in her hand as she drove, waiting to check the text until she took the turn into her neighborhood. She slowed to a stop at the first stop sign.
The picture was of a light-greenish Prius.

KATHERINE: New car?

PEGGY: No. It's in front of your house.

Katy's fingers folded into her own palm.
"My house?" Ron would never drive a car like that. She tossed her phone on the passenger seat and gunned the engine toward her house. When she came around the corner, sure enough, that little car was parked right in front of her side of the garage.
She slowly drove by, jotting down the license plate number, not sure even why. Then she pulled into Peggy's driveway.

Peggy raised the electric garage door and waved Katy inside.

She clamped her jaw tight, got out of her car, and peered out of the glass windows of the carriage house garage doors at that car. She spun around and faced Peggy.

"It's been there all night. I saw her get out of the car last night. Ron had her put the car in the garage overnight. I saw the whole thing."

"She?"

Peggy folded her arms. "Oh yeah. Definitely a she." She walked over and stood next to Katy. She punched some buttons on her phone and then handed it to Katy.

Katy flipped through the pictures.

"Is it the same girl that you saw him with? I know the pictures aren't that clear. I did the best I could."

The little dark-haired girl could rock a pair of skinny jeans. "It's her." Saliva pooled in Katy's mouth.

"Katherine, I'm so sorry." Peggy wrapped her arms around her. "I wasn't sure if she'd left sometime during the night, but then I saw her pull the car out of the garage a little while ago and go somewhere. She's only been back about a half an hour."

"Do you think he's there, too?" Katy bit down on her lip.

"I don't know, honey."

Katy stared at the pictures. Oh, it was the same girl all right. Had she been there when Ron was leaving her messages? She handed the phone back to Peggy, and then went and got her purse out of the car. She dug through it and then walked to the garage's side door. "Wait here. I'll be right back."

"What are you going to do?"

"Just wait."

Katy stepped outside, and then ran across the yard to her own house. On the passenger side of the car, in the same magenta lipstick that she'd used to leave the note for Ron, she scrawled *S L U T* across the side of the car. The *T* scratched into the paint a little as the lipstick tube hit bottom.

She turned and walked back over to Peggy's.

"I can't believe you just did that. Sweet Katherine Barclift just broke bad."

"Believe it." She tossed the empty tube of lipstick into her purse and got her phone. She dialed Ron.

"Hey, Ron. It's me. I wasn't sure if you'd take my call."

"Well, thank God you've come to your senses. What the hell were you thinking siccing Shaleigh on me? Were you serious or were just trying to scare me?"

"I wasn't playing games, Ron. You brought this on yourself."

"It's not what you think it is."

Katy shook her head and held the phone away from her ear. "Unbelievable," she mouthed to Peggy. "So if it's not what I think it is, what is it?"

"Take a picture of that car," she mouthed to Peggy.

Peggy ran to the side door and stepped outside, clicking off several, and then came back inside and sat on the stoop with a front-row seat.

"Uh-huh, so it doesn't mean anything? You haven't seen her since?"

"Of course not, babe. It was innocent. She kissed me. You know how pushy some women can be these days when they smell a successful guy. I told her I was totally off-limits. I swear."

"Really." It took all she had not to scream "Liar" into the phone at him. Man, she wished she had this conversation recorded. "Well, isn't she just a little slut to take advantage of you like that. She could have ruined our marriage."

"I would never let that happen."

"Of course not."

"People don't throw away the success we have together, Katherine. We have the perfect life."

And there it was. The bottom line. Not that it was a surprise. Not exactly her kind of perfect. If this was the perfect life, then what would life after perfect be like?

He'd miss her paycheck. He had champagne taste, and it wasn't the cheap stuff. They both made good money, but cutting their income by half would put a dent in his preferred lifestyle.

She wondered what he'd have done if she'd become ill. Like Laney. What if he'd been put in that position? Would he have made sacrifices? Or maybe he'd have just left right then. Replace her with someone else with a decent income. Was he doing that now?

"Tell you what. I'll come talk to you about it. You're right. We shouldn't let Shaleigh make this into something it's not."

Peggy's brow wrinkled.

Katy shook her head, hoping Peggy would realize she didn't need to worry.

Oh, this was going to be good.

She waved Peggy to follow her and she walked back outside and stood at the edge of Peggy's yard with her back to the little car, the word SLUT screaming in magenta across the passenger side, and her beautiful home in the background.

"Actually, honey, I'm on my way there. I should be home any minute. I can't wait to talk this out."

"You're on the way? You'll be here tonight?"

"No. I left this morning. I had time last night to think it through and, of course, you were right. You'd never do anything to put our life together at risk. I mean it was perfect. You said so yourself."

"Okay. Yeah. Well, then I'll see you in just a little while."

"I'll be home waiting for you."

She pressed END before he could answer, and then said to Peggy, "Start videotaping, girl."

Katy held her phone up and put it on video too. In selfie mode, she had half of her own face and the car in view.

Just as she predicted, little Miss Carpe Diem came hot-stepping it out of the house. She didn't even seem to notice that not just one, but two women were videotaping the whole thing . . . or that she had a banner scrawled down the side of her car.

Katy and Peggy kept videotaping as the green Prius cruised out of the neighborhood.

"Oh. My. God." Peggy was laughing hysterically. "That is too much. They say timing is everything and damn if you didn't just prove it."

Katy was so mad she was tempted to go in and ransack her own house, but if Shaleigh was going to be pissed that she'd contacted Ron, she'd be double-pissed if she did something like that. And if Ron was inside and trying to hide the fact, she wasn't up for a confrontation either. No. She couldn't stoop to that level. Karma had a way of keeping the score even and she just as soon be on the positive side of that pendulum.

Katy spun around and faced Peggy. "Do you have wine?"

"Do bears shit in the woods?" They walked inside and Peggy broke open a bottle of the good stuff from Tucker's collection.

"I have a toast for us," Katy said.

Peggy held up her glass and Katy did too.

Katy said, "To new beginnings. May all the yellow ribbons of hope and opportunity bring us all the good things we deserve. Thank you for being my friend, Peggy."

"I love being your friend," she said. "And I really am heartbroken this is happening to you."

They walked into the living room and sat down.

"How are things going with Tucker?"

"Slow. He's going to make this as laborious and as painful as he can. I think he's hoping he'll wear me down and I'll let him come back." Peggy pulled her feet up into the chair. "He's staying in a hotel near the dealership. For now."

"Is that good? Is that what you want?"

"He wants to give me some time." Peggy refilled their glasses. "Were you really coming back to try to make things right?"

Katy shrugged. "No, but I thought we might be able to be adults about it and just come to an agreement on how things were going to be split up. I definitely had myself convinced we could be civil. I mean ten years of marriage should mean something."

"One would think. Mine isn't any easier. At least you don't need his income to stay afloat. I feel so trapped."

There was no doubt that she was sitting in a pretty good position. She wondered if Ron was dashing around the house in an attempt to hide all the evidence of his little visitor, or was he sitting in traffic heading for home, thinking he was in the clear since he'd run little Miss Carpe Diem out of the house? Didn't really matter one way or the other.

She looked at her watch. She'd give him another fifteen minutes and then burn all his happy little thoughts to a crisp. Would serve him right.

"Are you driving back tonight?" Peggy asked.

"I was just thinking about that. It only took me six hours to get here. It's not a bad drive. I think after all of this, I'll be plenty charged up for the drive."

"He'll know you're over here."

"I was thinking about that too. I don't want you stuck in the middle of it." Katy took another sip of wine and then picked up her phone again. "Can you send me the video you took?"

Peggy pressed keys and then went and sat next to Katy on the couch. "Which do you think is better?" Katy played the one Peggy took and the one she'd taken.

"Oh, the one with your face just in the frame is priceless! That girl was booking. Talk about looking guilty. And she looked pissed too."

"Good. Serves her right."

"He sure dug his own grave."

Katy brought up the text to Ron and then added the video. "Here goes nothing." She pressed SEND. Then she typed. "Looks like we're back to working through Shaleigh. Thanks for making this so much easier."

Then she blocked his number.

"You blocked him?"

"Yep."

"Aren't you curious what he's going to say?"

She took in a deep breath. "You know, I'm not. I'm just over it. Numb. I'm better than this." Katy forwarded the video to Shaleigh too. "I just forwarded it to Shaleigh. I'll probably get a vandalism ticket for the lipstick. Hope she knows a good attorney for that."

"You can probably plead insanity."

"You'd think, right?"

Peggy hugged her. "You are better than this. Better than this plus so much more."

"I'm going to head out. I'll make sure he sees my car leaving the neighborhood, so he won't bother you."

"Don't worry about me. He isn't going to bother me at all. Do you want a soda or snack to take on the road?"

"No. I'm good."

———

They walked back out to the garage and Katy got in her car as Peggy hit the button to open the garage door.

She had a sick feeling as she drove by her house this time. Was Ron inside? Was he watching her drive by?

An hour into the ride back to Boot Creek, Shaleigh rang Katy's phone.

Katy put it on speaker.

"I'm in the car. I've got you on speaker."

"Are you alone?"

"Of course."

"I can't believe you came back to town. What were you thinking?" Shaleigh's voice held an edge that made it quite clear she wasn't overly impressed with what Katy had done.

"I wasn't. I guess I had a weak moment, but that'll teach me."

"I'm sorry you had to go through that, but great video. You might make some money on one of those video shows with that one."

"Am I in trouble over the lipstick?"

"Only if Ron gives her the video and she presses charges. Just lay low and see what happens."

"That'll be easy."

"Look. He's mad. I got a call from his attorney a few minutes ago. He's threatening to file for alimony since you make more money than he does."

"What? Are you kidding me?"

"Not kidding. I told you these things could get ugly. Look. Until we get it all settled, no need in making it look like you're trying to take advantage of anything, so don't use the checking accounts or credit cards. You can open a new account and have your paycheck deposited in it."

"But I took an unpaid leave of absence. I don't have any money coming in."

"That might actually work to your favor."

"But I don't have any money. Well, I have that cashier's check from our savings account."

"If you have to, use that. It's rightfully yours anyway."

"If I don't go back to work, it might be all the security I have left."

"Well, then take a little part-time job in that little town of yours. He can't get alimony off of you if you're making minimum wage. At least not for a while."

"Why am I the one that just seems to keep getting screwed here?"

"Sorry, honey. I told you to let me handle it."

"Point noted."

She pressed END.

It was time for a change.

So tonight, when she was back safe and sound at Lonesome Pines Inn, she'd dream of new beginnings and better days ahead, whatever those looked like.

———

Derek woke up in a great mood. When he'd left Katy at the door last night, he'd wanted to kiss her so badly, but instead he'd given her a hug and a gentle kiss on the cheek. He was wading into new territory, and he liked the way she made him feel. Just to feel anything was a start.

He'd lain in bed for hours, unable to shake the feeling that there could have been more, but slow was probably better. At least what was keeping him awake was a good feeling for a change. He'd had his share of miserable sleepless nights.

Finally the night faded away and he got up and took a white dress shirt from his closet and pulled a tie off the rack. He hadn't bought a new tie since the last one Laney had picked out for him. She had a knack for picking out a good-looking tie.

He pulled the next one in line. Rotating them had seemed like the easiest way to not wear the same ones too often, so he'd hung them up in rows and just wore whatever was next. He pulled the fine silk around his neck and tied a perfect knot.

Sometimes he could still feel Laney peeking over his shoulder on tiptoe and kissing his neck. Telling him how sexy he was all dressed up in a tie.

Normally he was up with the sun and had already checked a few things off of his list, but this morning he was moving more slowly. He wasn't quite sure why except that he'd been a little sidetracked thinking about Katy.

He got in his truck and drove over to the clinic.

Wendy was already there, looking concerned.

"Good morning," he said.

"I was beginning to wonder if you were going to show up," she said, a little on the snippy side.

"Patients don't start for another fifteen minutes. I've got time to spare."

"Yeah, but you're always here early."

Her attitude struck him as funny. "Not always. Apparently." She'd probably been worried that she was going to have to reschedule all of the patients.

"Everything okay?" he asked, looking her dead in the eye, challenging her to say anything else in that tone.

"Yes, sir."

"Good. What do we have today?"

She handed him the printout of the schedule.

He scanned it. "Good. Busy morning and a light afternoon." It always seemed that the walk-ins happened late in the day—people need more time to get into trouble. He walked down to his office, put on his coat, and grabbed his stethoscope off the hook where he kept it.

Derek was tempted to give Katy a call. He looked up the number to the inn and jotted it on a notepad on his desk. But just as he began to dial her, he was called out of his office for an emergency.

The whole day turned into a string of back-to-back emergencies, and by five o'clock he hadn't even taken a lunch break and still had three more patients to work in. He walked out to the reception area. There were two more patients sitting there too.

"Can I see tomorrow's schedule?" Derek asked Wendy.

She turned her computer screen toward him. "I haven't printed one out yet. It's been so busy."

"Don't I know it? This is fine." He scanned the schedule for Wednesday. "I'd like you to schedule Mr. Peters for a follow-up tomorrow in this slot at eleven. And then I need you to mark out this hour and a half at one o'clock where we don't have anything. I have something I need to do."

"Yes, sir."

Now that he knew there was a window of opportunity tomorrow when he could slip out and go see Katy, he didn't really care if he worked all night. Hopefully, she'd be available too.

"I have some messages here for you," Wendy said.

"Thank you," he said, sifting through them as he walked back down the hall. Only one in the bunch actually was important. Laney's mom had called. He was overdue to talk to her. They usually talked every couple of weeks, but with the extra work that went into the Blackberry Festival, he'd gotten off schedule. Maybe that was a part of moving on, too.

His workday didn't end until close to seven. A summer cold was running through the area and everyone was pretty miserable.

When he finished up with his patients he dropped off the messages that Wendy could complete by calling in refills, then went to his office to call Laney's mom, Terri.

He sat in his chair and then got up and carried the picture of Laney back to his desk. Her mom wasn't one of those pain-in-the-butt mother-in-laws like the ones men complained about. She and Laney were a lot alike, and Laney's death had been just as hard on her parents as it had been on him. They'd always been close, but they'd made an extra effort since Laney was gone to be sure they stayed connected.

It had been hard for him to come to grips with burying Laney in Adams Grove, but since the two of them had met there and it was in the middle between Boot Creek and her parents' home in southern Virginia, it had seemed the right thing to do. A good compromise. Besides, since Ted Hardy, the florist there in Adams Grove, had done all of the flowers for their wedding, he knew exactly what to put together to adorn her headstone. He always did a great job.

As the months had gone by, it got easier and easier to not feel like he had to be at the graveside to get that closeness with Laney. For a while there, he was driving down to Adams Grove practically every day. Now, he didn't have to be at her grave site to feel like she was with him all the time. No matter where he was, she was there.

Talking to Laney's mom was always hard. Her voice sounded just like Laney's, especially her laugh, and sometimes that was more than he could bear.

Slumping in his chair, he stared at the picture of Laney. She'd been his whole life for so long, figuring out how to move on while still carrying the good memories was no easy task. He wanted to push away the bad ones, except there were good bits and pieces in those too.

Wendy knocked on the door. "Need anything else from me tonight?"

"No, Wendy. Thanks for everything today. It was a busy one."

"I'll see you in the morning."

"Yeah. I'll see you."

He pulled his hands behind his head and leaned back in his chair. He sat there with Laney's picture for nearly an hour. By then it was too late to visit the inn just for a social call. He'd just have to take his chances on stopping by tomorrow.

It was too late to call his mother-in-law back too. He wasn't really up for that tonight anyway. The longer the time between calls, the harder they were to make. Derek forced himself to get up and go home.

Chapter Fifteen

As Derek drove down Main Street the next day, he was half tempted to stop in Bootsy's Bouquets and pick up some flowers before heading to Naomi's, but that seemed a little too presumptuous. Besides, Bootsy was his mom's best friend and she'd have twenty questions for him, wasting time he could spend at the inn.

He drove on past. When he got to the bridge, the water had risen so high in the creek already that the road crew had put out the high-water sign. It wasn't unusual for this stretch of road to close down when the tides got high, and with the storms they'd been calling for tomorrow, the road would probably be washed over by noon. He'd spent a night or two at the office because of that in the past. But for now it was still passable.

The weather continued to be unpredictable as the first tropical storms of the season continued to pop up off the coast and drive warm, then cooler, air into their area. They'd already sped through the first few letters of the alphabet and it was early yet. The rain last night had come in buckets. A frog strangler, Laney would have called it.

He took the turn toward the inn. When he pulled into the driveway, he realized that he'd been hoping Katy would be out on the porch again. That wasn't the case today, though her car was there.

When he walked inside, the whole house smelled of something sweet.

Naomi greeted him in the front room. "Angie was here earlier. She said you were coming by again today. I thought maybe she was confused."

"Nope. She was right, and I told you I'd stop in every couple days."

"Thank you, Derek. Kelly Jo seemed so much more at peace after your talk."

"I felt more at peace after our talk too." He'd been surprised. He had to admit that it had felt good to talk to Kelly Jo and hear what her thoughts were about the treatments and when to stop. It was like getting to air his concerns with Laney almost, like when Kelly Jo looked him in the eye and said, "Do you mean to tell me that you don't have any problem pushing aside the way Laney looked those last few months from your mind? That you can see her beautiful and happy without that interfering?"

He'd had to be honest, though he knew she probably wished he could tell her it wasn't so. "You're right," he'd said. "Those images haunt me sometimes." Laney had gotten so thin that a skeleton looked sturdier, and her skin looked like it could tear. She'd aged. There was barely a hint of her youthful, vibrant self. "But I wouldn't have left her side for anything. I wanted to be with her for every single breath of her life. Kelly Jo, you have to know that love isn't about what someone looks like. We even commit before God for sicker and for poorer."

He'd seen the struggle in her yes, in the way she clenched her fists. "Yeah, and I'm leaving Todd in debt too. It's awful, and so unfair to him. On one hand I wish he could find someone else right now and move on, and on the other hand I hope he pines for me every day."

"He will." Derek knew that feeling. You couldn't pray or wish that loneliness away, but hearing her internal struggle opened his eyes to something new. He'd never really considered that there was an emotional tug-of-war along with the physical one for Laney.

"Right, and then that makes me feel guilty for wishing it was already over and I was gone. I don't want him to be sad. See. There's no way to win."

"You're right. It's not a win-lose game though, Kelly Jo. This is life. We don't have any control over it." He caught himself choking on the word *control.* "God knows I sure thought I had some control for a while there. But even medicine, for all the advances we've made, cannot change God's plan."

Derek forced himself to let that conversation drift back into his memory. Today was a new day.

"Is she still in the room downstairs?" he asked Naomi.

"Yes. I told her she should stay down here. Family has always stayed upstairs, but that is just silly. If she took another tumble, I don't know what I'd do. Thank goodness Katy was here the other day."

"I'm just going to . . ." He lost his train of thought when he saw Katy walk out with a tray of something that appeared to be baked goods. Pushing the side of his white lab coat back, he shoved a hand in his pocket trying to look casual, but just the sight of her made his heart two-step. He looked back at Naomi, and then at Katy with a grin. "Hi, Katy."

"Derek? Hi. I didn't know you were coming today." She set the dish on the sideboard and walked toward him. "Here to see Kelly Jo?"

Tendrils of hair softened the line of her face, loose from the warmth of the kitchen. It became her. "Yeah. I'm . . . I was just going to see her."

"I just made little carrot cake cupcakes. Be sure to take one when you leave."

"I smelled them when I came in. I'll be sure to do that," he said. He made an awkward departure down the hall, cursing himself for always bumbling when he was around her.

Kelly Jo was sitting in a chair staring out the window. He tapped lightly on the door and walked in. "How are you today?"

She turned toward him, pulling her feet up tighter underneath her. "I'm good. You came back."

"Told you I would."

She nodded. "I did something this morning."

"Care to share?"

She nodded. "It's thanks to you and our conversation that I called Todd." Tears streamed down her face.

"You did?" He leaned against the dresser near the chair. A huge feeling of relief rose from his chest. He could only imagine what Todd was feeling. "I'm glad." He glanced out the window, trying to maintain control of his own emotions. From here she had a lovely view of the creek.

"Me too."

He waited. It was tough work for her . . . talking. He'd learned that early on in his career. In some cases, it was a choice between breathing or talking; in others just the effort to talk was too much. He gave her plenty of runway to finish her thoughts. He had the time.

Her lips moved uncomfortably, and finally she uttered the words. "I was being selfish, and there's no time for that."

"Time." He took her hands. She knew she was running out of time. "You need him too. Let him be there for you."

"He's coming," she said. "Soon." She ran her tongue across her lips. Her eyes teared up. "Thank you so much."

"You are welcome. And thank you." He laid his hand on top of hers. "Kelly Jo, you helped me too. You brought up some new things. We needed each other."

"I'm glad." She nodded and forced a weak smile. "I can hardly wait to see him now."

"Good. You can bet he's just as excited as you are."

"Can you help me to the bed? I'm so tired."

"Sure." He stepped over and held out his arm, and then rather than let her struggle, he lifted her into his arms. She was so light. She barely weighed as much as his turnout gear bag. He moved slowly, gently placing her on the mattress.

She let out a breath, and he pulled the sheet and blankets up over her.

Kelly Jo snuggled under the covers, drawing them up high against her chin.

"Laney was very blessed," she said, and then she closed her eyes.

He sat in the chair near the bed and watched her sleep for he wasn't sure how long. Her tiny frame barely made an outline under the heavy quilt. The soft yellow pattern looked pale compared to her skin. Her liver was failing. She was right. There wasn't time for much of anything anymore.

———

When he walked back out to the front of the house, Naomi was sitting on the couch, but he didn't see Katy anywhere.

"Thanks, ladies," he said anyway, raising a hand.

Katy swung through the kitchen door. "I thought I heard your voice." She came toward him. "I wrapped up a couple of those cupcakes for you. They're right there on the desk."

He reached for the small plate with a piece of plastic wrap across the top. Toothpicks tented the plastic from the frosting.

"Thanks." He lifted it and gave her a nod. "Didn't know you could cook."

"I think anyone can be a good cook in this kitchen. Have you ever seen it?" Her eyes were wide, like a kid who had just spotted Santa at the mall.

Derek shook his head. "Can't say that I have."

"Naomi, do you mind if I show him the kitchen? It's amazing."

Naomi shook her head. "Sure, honey. Grab me a cup of tea while you're in there, would you?"

Katy waved Derek back, and then picked up Naomi's teacup and headed through the swinging door to the kitchen. She held the door wide. "Look at this!"

Derek had heard the stories of this place, of course, but even though Marshall and Dillon Laumann threw a lot of parties and had quite a public following, few of the locals had actually ever been on the grounds of the huge estate until after Marshall died and Naomi had turned their home into an inn.

"I'm glad I didn't have to repaint a pink kitchen this size."

"I used to love being in the kitchen, but I'll admit I'm a little out of practice. I sure am enjoying rattling around in here. I can't seem to keep myself from cooking. You might have to put Naomi on a diet when I leave here."

"I think she could do with a few pounds. Probably with the help too."

Katy nodded thoughtfully. "You know, I'd had the same thought. Maybe that's why I landed in Boot Creek. I mean they say everything happens for a reason."

"Right." That made him think about his own project. "Maybe you'd like to come over to my house. I've got this thing I've been thinking about. I wouldn't mind bouncing it off you. It's not fully fleshed out, but maybe you could let me know what you think. With your project background, you might even have some suggestions."

She didn't answer right away, and that caught him off guard. In his head, this conversation had gone a lot more smoothly. She'd answer with a big smile and notable excitement in her eyes. Instead, she sucked in a breath like she was going to make a wish and blow out a candle. He wasn't quite sure if she was going to say yes or no.

"Yeah. Sure. That sounds good."

He tried to hold back the obvious relief he was feeling. "I'll pick you up when I finish up at the clinic today."

"Okay. I'll see you later then." She poured Naomi's tea and then headed for the door, holding it for Derek.

But he put his hand above her head and scooted her through first. His mom raised a gentleman and he wasn't about to compromise on that.

Naomi poked her head up over the couch like a meerkat. "I'd heard you bought Clancy Jennings's old place after their kids shipped his wife down to Florida." She started laughing, a raucous you-got-stuck kind of belly laugh. She had to catch her breath. "Oh, Lordy, when Clancy died, she was so mad at him for letting things get in such disrepair. She'd been hounding him to paint forever. You'll love this, Katy. When the old fart died, just for spite, his wife hired a bunch of college kids over the summer and had them paint it pink. And I'm not talking some peach pink or burgundy pink. I'm talking fluorescent highlighter pink!"

"Very John Cougar Mellencampish," Katy said trying to make light of the fact that she'd already been to his house.

"Tonight at six-thirty?"

Naomi was nodding her head, as if encouraging the words out of Katy's mouth.

"See you then."

"Great." He wanted to run out the door before she could change her mind. "Good." He shoved his hands in his pocket and backed out. "Looking forward to it." He started to walk away, but then turned around. "Got your phone?"

She pulled it out of her pocket and held it in the air.

"Hand it over."

Katy typed in her security code and then thrust it in his direction.

He typed his phone number in her phone and called himself. His phone rang. Now he had hers too. "There you go. In case anything comes up."

He walked out of the house with his confidence spiraling upward.

In the truck, he typed in her name on the contact entry and saved it.

True to his word, Derek picked Katy up at six-thirty. He helped her into the truck and they made the short drive from the inn to his house.

When they got to his house, Katy could see what he meant about all the plants being pink, too. Every flowering plant on the property was pink. Pink crepe myrtles and pink petunias. She could guess that the azaleas that filled the flower bed following the fence line probably bloomed in a hot pink or magenta in the spring too. At least it played nicely in the sunshine with the new wine color he'd painted the shutters. She could only imagine his reaction when he'd first rolled up to this house only to find it painted pink.

Probably enough to make just about any grown man cry.

Derek wasn't wearing his lab coat, but he still had on his crisp dress shirt, and had lost the tie, opened the top buttons, and turned up the cuffs. He looked some kind of good no matter how he was dressed, and her heart made it hard to play it cool.

He parked in front of his house and led her inside. "I've got some pork chops we can throw on the grill if you're hungry."

He looked a little nervous too, and that made her feel a little less so. Thank goodness because those first few minutes her heart felt like it was pa-pow-pow-pounding. At least now it wasn't echoing in her own ears.

"If you're not too hungry yet, I thought I might show you around the property before we eat."

"I'd like that."

He held the door open and they walked outside. Out back there were at least a dozen dwarf fruit trees. "If you like baking, you ought to come get some of these apples. I drop as many as I can into buckets and take them over to the hog farmer in Level Green a couple times a week just so they don't go to waste. Can you make an apple pie?"

"Best apple pie you've ever had." She raised her hand into the leaves of the tree.

"Are you bragging?" he asked.

"Totally," she said.

He led her down the path through the tiny orchard and then out to the clearing. He'd marked off what he hoped would be the future site of the retreat weeks ago. It was very preliminary with all he had to get done on the house first, but it kept him motivated.

She turned and looked curious, pointing to the stakes with bright yellow tape hanging from them. "What's that?"

"That's part of the project I wanted to tell you about. My future. Well, maybe. It's still in the idea phase."

"You mean in case the doctor and firefighter gigs don't work out?"

He liked her quick wit. "No. I've been thinking about maybe building a retreat here one day. This would be the building site. At least I think so."

"What kind of retreat?"

He took her hand and walked toward the markers. She hadn't noticed the bench beneath a curved area where a half dozen river birch trees stood until now. It blended right in with the surroundings. He let her sit first and then sat down next to her. The wooden slider chair moved back and forth.

He lifted his arm up over the back of the chair. "I still want to make a difference in this world. Somehow. But after Laney, it changed how I felt about cancer and treating it. So, I'm thinking about building a retreat of sorts. Somewhere to get away and rebalance."

"So, a retreat? For cancer patients?"

He shook his head. "No. Not for the patients. For the doctors. Creating a place where medical professionals can renew themselves and keep themselves balanced. It just might be my way of giving back."

Her eyes widened. "I see. So treat those that heal. Keep them healthy and they can heal more people."

"Exactly."

"Neat. So tell me about it. How many rooms? What's it like? Do you have a style in mind?"

"Picture casual elegance. Two stories. Plenty of privacy. Lots of windows. Sunlight is good. Lots of it."

She watched as he described the setting. If she had to guess, he could probably describe every room. He'd given this more than just a little thought. She admired his passion—he could look past his pain to find a way to give back. How long would it take before she could look past what had happened to really see a different future?

He pointed off to where a thin stand of trees seemed to mark the entry to deeper foliage. "Hiking trails over there."

"That sounds beautiful."

"Honestly I don't think it matters what it looks like. I think it will be the attitude of the place that will make it work. I want it to have a relaxing feeling to it. Simple, but comfortable."

"How's this different from the inn?"

He nodded. "You're a smart lady."

"Yeah. I know." She could tell he had a lot more going on in that brain of his.

"Can I tell you over dinner?"

"Absolutely, but I'm not going to forget."

"I don't want you to."

Derek stood, then took her hand and they walked back up to the house without much conversation. When they got to the back deck, he raised the top of the grill and pressed the button. The flame danced beneath the grates as they went inside.

He went straight over to the refrigerator and retrieved a covered plate.

"Is there something I can do?"

"I've got some salad. We'll just do a salad and pork chops, if that works for you."

"Works for me." She followed him outside.

He put the chops on the grill and just as she walked over to sit down on one of the chairs on the deck, the sky opened up.

She raced inside, but Derek was already soaked to the bone.

He closed the lid on the grill and ran into the house for cover.

"That is the coldest rain!" He was laughing and wet. When he saw that she was laughing, he grabbed her in a hug, soaking her too.

She wiggled free from his grip. "Hey. No fair."

He glanced outside. "Maybe we don't need those pork chops."

The rain came down in buckets.

"Don't you have an umbrella?" she asked, and a roll of thunder shook the house.

"That doesn't seem like a very good idea. You have a death wish? Because I'm pretty sure even when things get bad, I still want to live."

"Oh, stop that. There's no lightning."

"Yet," he said. "Besides it'll be a little hard to hold an umbrella and turn the meat and hold the plate and . . . we might just be eating salad."

"You have to have protein. A balanced diet. Aren't you a doctor? You should know that."

"I get paid to say that."

They exchanged a subtle look of amusement. "Where's the umbrella?"

"There's one by the door."

She got it and they stood at the door watching for lightning. "I don't see any lightning. Do you?"

"No, and those pork chops are smoking." He looked at her as if challenging her. "It's now or never."

She twisted the knob in her hand and swung the door open. She pushed the umbrella out first and opened it. The huge blue golf umbrella was big enough to cover both of them and a friend. The Duke Cancer Center logo showed more proof of the life this man had once lived, and that he hadn't let go of it completely. She wondered if he'd ever find his way back. Maybe Naomi was right and there was something even bigger in the future for him.

"No sense risking bad luck," she explained. "Come on," she said as she stepped outside under the umbrella.

"I'm already wet." He stepped outside, too, and walked alongside her.

"Get under here. You're going to catch a cold."

He gave her his serious doctor look. "That's not how you catch a cold."

"It could happen, and then it would be my fault." Okay, so maybe that was stretching it.

He dipped his head and got under the large dome with her. "Happy now?"

"Yes."

He leaned forward and kissed her.

The rain pounding on the umbrella was loud, and it was probably a good thing because she was pretty sure when he moved in deeper with that kiss that she'd just moaned. His mouth on hers made her want to drop the umbrella and clamor for higher ground, for air, or maybe really what she wanted was more. The assault of emotion was dizzying.

And then as quickly as he'd surprised her with that kiss, he stepped out from under the umbrella back into the pouring rain and lifted the lid of the grill to rescue the pork chops from the rising flames.

"They're on fire!" she said, and she knew exactly what it was like because every nerve in her body felt like it had just sparked. "Break out those fireman skills. Want me to go get your cute suit?"

He gave her an exaggerated glare.

"Too much?"

"Yeah."

He quickly moved the meat off to the side of the grill, away from the flames, and then opened the drawer below the cooking space to get a small basting mop. He swished the mop into a sauce on the top rack and worked it over the pork chops and then settled them back on the grill top.

"What is that?"

"Chef's secret."

"Really now?"

"Okay, it's just butter and garlic with a little barbecue sauce mixed in."

"Garlic butter?"

"Yeah."

"Guess it's a good thing you already kissed me." And she'd liked it. A lot.

"You look disappointed."

She opened her mouth, but nothing witty came to mind, and she wasn't about to say what was on her mind . . . which was, "Yes, I'm disappointed." She closed her mouth and shrugged. Seemed like the only safe response at the moment.

He dropped the top of the grill down with a loud clank and turned to face her, taking the umbrella from her hand and tossing it over the side of the deck.

"Hey—" she started.

But suddenly his mouth was on hers and she couldn't care less that they were getting soaking wet, or if those pork chops got burned to smithereens.

Lost in the kiss, Derek didn't seem to notice the smoke pouring from the grill, but she could see it floating up behind him. The rain sizzled against the hot metal.

He turned around and glanced at the grill. "Damn." He fished the meat off the grill onto a plate.

She laughed. "I'm sure they'll taste fine."

"I wanted to impress you."

"You did. It was those firefighting skills." And so many other things about him that she'd needed right now. Like someone who wanted to share. Wanted to hear her opinion. Who seemed interested. She hadn't even realized how much she'd missed that . . . until she had it again.

He ran his finger down her rain-soaked top.

She shivered at his touch.

"The temperature has dropped," he said, looking to the sky.

"That wasn't that kind of chill." She barely recognized the deep, soft tone of her own voice.

"Is that okay?" he asked.

"Oh yeah. Amazing."

"Good. I like that," he said, dropping kisses into the nape of her neck with each word. "It'll be even more amazing if I didn't completely ruin our dinner. Let's get these inside and see what we've got."

Katy walked inside behind him. "I promised Naomi a doggie bag if we ate."

"She might be going hungry."

But the chops were fine. A little charred on one side, and Derek played it off as a way to settle their stomachs and overeat at the same time—giving her a little Medicine 101 on the benefits of charcoal for intestinal discomfort and heartburn.

She stayed away from the garlicky mushrooms.

"I'm eating those, so you better," he said pointing to the mushrooms.

"What? You gonna withhold my dessert if I don't eat my veggies?"

"Hey! If I have garlic breath . . . you should have it too. Unless you don't plan on letting me kiss you again."

She stared into his eyes, enjoying the playful banter. She lifted her fork and, without ever breaking the lock with his gaze, she stabbed a mushroom and stuck it in her mouth.

"That's my girl."

She licked a finger seductively.

"Yeah, and that." He pointed at her. "That's just not fair."

"You're good for my ego."

"I don't know why someone as beautiful as you would have any problem in that department."

If he only knew.

That Friday afternoon when she saw Ron with that girl everything had changed. In that one moment she'd lost her sense of self. She'd felt small, and ugly, and unworthy. And then again when she watched the same girl walk right out of her very own house. It was unforgivable. She wondered how long it took the girl to realize she had graffiti on the side of her car. It didn't matter now.

Here with Derek, she felt special and desirable.

Chapter Sixteen

He'd promised an early night and he made good on the promise. And although part of her really respected him for it, part of her wished he'd gone totally Neanderthal on her and picked her up and carried her off to his bedroom.

When she had been nestled in the crook of his arm that first night, it had been the best head prop of her life. If they sold a pillow that fit like that, she'd buy one for sure.

Derek negotiated the winding road. "Power must be out," he said. "It's dark, but you can usually see lights from a couple of the houses along this road at night."

The rain had stopped, but the water sloshed beneath the tires at each curve. He slowed near the turn into the gravel lane. Little frogs hopped across the lane. So many there was no way there weren't going to be some casualties. "Where did those all come from? It's like a horror movie."

"There are always a ton of frogs out here near the creek." He pulled in front of Lonesome Pines and just as he'd predicted, the power was out. The yard lights weren't on and there wasn't even a hint of one of the fifty night-lights Naomi had in the sockets around the house to make getting around at night safe.

"Let me get a flashlight," he said.

She sat tight while he got out of the truck. It was only partly because of the dark that she was almost afraid to move. In the daytime, the grounds were lovely and peaceful, but now every sound was amplified and that deluge of frog traffic had her skin crawling.

The dome light came on when he opened the door and she let out the breath she hadn't even realized she was holding.

He opened her door and held out his hand to help her down, using a large lantern-type flashlight in his other hand to light up a wide area in front of them. He led her to the porch and helped her inside.

Naomi must have already turned in for the night, but she'd left jar candles burning in the first-floor rooms with a note. Katy trained Derek's light on the note so she could read it. It told her where there were more candles if she needed them, and Naomi had left a flashlight out for her to help her get around. At the very bottom of the note she had scrawled, "PS—I hope you didn't make it home to read this note tonight. Xo"

She laid her hand over the paper so Derek wouldn't see that.

"She's the sweetest lady," Katy said trying to play it off lightly. "Point the light over here so I can put Naomi's dinner in the refrigerator."

He followed her through the space, and they both laughed as they bumped into things in the shadowy darkness. She slid the dinner into the refrigerator and closed it quickly.

"Do you think the power will be out long?"

He shrugged. "They'll probably get it up in the morning. It just depends on how big of an outage it is."

"At least she was prepared with all of the candles."

Derek frowned. "She shouldn't have left them burning unattended."

"They're attended now."

"So they are." He flashed the light toward the note again. "What'd it say?"

"The note?" She shrugged. "She's in bed. Candles. Flashlight. That's it."

He turned off the flashlight, and in the soft flicker of the seven candles around the room, he pulled her into his arms and kissed her.

A rumble of thunder rolled across the sky.

"Mother Nature doesn't seem to approve," he said.

"Or," she said, pulling in closer, "she doesn't think it's safe for you to leave."

He raised an eyebrow.

She nodded her head.

"Where's our room?" he asked.

She turned and crooked a finger toward him. "Follow me."

"One second. Hold that thought." He went around and blew out all of the candles, then caught up with Katy and let her lead him down the hall.

Feeling like a kid sneaking back in after curfew, she motioned for him to follow her.

He held the flashlight steady, lighting a path in front of her.

With each step down the hall, she became more aware of him right behind her.

They stepped inside her room and Derek turned off the flashlight.

She sucked in a deep breath, the darkness a welcome relief from the insecurities that were taunting her, but she didn't want to resist.

He pulled her into his arms.

She ached for his touch and his moves as intense and volatile as the storm had been outside.

He laid her down on the bed and undressed her.

Part of her wished for at least the moonlight to see the outline of his form, but the darkness played on her senses like a wicked masquerade. Somehow freeing, yet dangerous at the same time.

He was awakening feelings that were foreign to her. The sound, the warmth, even the taste of him filling her with desire for even more.

The connection was more powerful than it had been the night they'd met. They'd been able to resist going too far then, but not tonight. There was no holding back now.

They lay in the darkness, breathing so heavily that even the storm seemed to have quieted.

"I could stay." His hand ran the length of her arm.

"I'm not sure that's a good idea." She had explaining to do, but she couldn't do it now. How would that look? "What would Naomi think?"

"That the bridge was closed?"

"Let's take it slow, Derek." They were both taking steps on shaky ground. And she didn't need a rebound guy to make things even more confusing than they already were. Besides, he had roots here, and she'd just been uprooted.

He kissed her on the forehead and then pulled her into his arms. "I can't wait to see you again."

But those words tempted her like she'd never expected they would.

She walked him out to his car with the light, and reluctantly waved as he left. It might have been nice to have him stay, but it wasn't the right time. She regretted not telling him about her situation. Maybe once she had the separation papers in hand, it would be easier to tell him. And it would be more final. Then again, the right time might never come.

She needed to stand on her own two feet right now. At least she'd earned back a little self-esteem in the process tonight.

Using the flashlight to find her way back to her room, she undressed and crawled into bed in the silent house. One didn't really realize there was such a hum from all those electronics until it wasn't there anymore.

Katy's phone woke her from a dead sleep. She rushed around the room trying to find where she'd put her purse in the dark last night and finally put her hand on her ringing phone.

Shaleigh's voice came across the line. "Have you looked at Facebook today?"

"No. Why?"

"Seems the little Prius driver has tagged you. In a video."

"Uh-oh."

"Yeah. No charges have been filed yet, but I guess Ron gave her his phone or sent her the video. Not your best move, Katherine."

"It was spontaneous."

"Like combustion. Never leave a trail. Haven't I taught you anything?"

"Sorry." She turned on her computer, waiting for it to boot up while she talked. "I'm kind of surprised she'd post it. Doesn't she know that video is not flattering of her behavior?"

"I don't think she sees it that way. But then consider the source. She was sleeping with your husband."

Even though she knew it, hearing the words roll right off of Shaleigh's tongue like that resulted in a painful stab.

Katy had only seen the video on her phone. At least here she could go full screen. "Hmm. Well, there are already over two hundred likes. I wonder if they like what I did, or what she did?"

"Don't think it matters. It's only nine in the morning. I'm sure it will become clear later on."

"Great. Maybe I'll repost it with hash tag slut on it."

"Please don't," Shaleigh said.

"How about #RonBarcliftIsACheater?"

"Same."

"You're no fun." She closed the Facebook screen. "What else is going on?"

"Just wondering if you thought any more about taking a simple little job in that town."

"Not really. I thought about going back to work now. Ending the leave of absence, but then I'd have to rent a place to stay, and quite honestly, I'm not ready to go back to that job."

"So don't. Just get a little job at a restaurant or in an office or something. I'll say you're too distraught to go back to the pressure of your career and this is all you can do for now. Get this turned back to Ron doing you wrong."

"I could do that. As long as it's not with a financial institution, there won't be a conflict."

Shaleigh's voice didn't hold an ounce of amusement. "And please quit acting like a Power Ranger and taking matters into your own hands. You're supposed to look hurt and fragile."

"I am."

"Well, act it." Shaleigh laughed, finally. "Even your 'hurt and fragile' is more put-together than anyone I know. Why am I surprised?"

"Sorry. It's just the way I operate. Plan what you're going to do, and do what you plan."

"I'll send you the t-shirt. Just lay low for a little while. Deal?"

"Deal."

Katy hung up the phone and turned on the light. The electricity had come back on sometime during the night. It was probably time to get that cashier's check cashed so she'd have some money. Without Ron pushing his agenda on her, she could open an account at one of the big banks with lots of branches.

She got dressed. Naomi must have gone somewhere because she wasn't anywhere to be seen. Kelly Jo's door was pulled shut, too.

She went to the desk and looked in the phone book for a list of banks. A quick look in the tiny phone book showed there was a national bank right on Main Street.

She got a cup of coffee from the kitchen and then went with her coffee in one hand to her car and headed to town.

With the cashier's check safely tucked into her purse, she went into the big fancy building. It looked out of place with its shiny, glass exterior. Inside everything was electronic. Not that old hometown feel. She waited for her turn to speak to a teller.

Finally she stepped to the counter and handed over the cashier's check and her driver's license.

"Are you a customer here, Mrs. Barclift?"

"No. I'm just here on vacation. I live down in Atlanta."

"Not this branch. Our bank."

"Oh. Well, no. Not that either. I bank with them. See there on the cashier's check."

The woman's mouth took on an unpleasant twist. "I'm so sorry. We can't cash this for you. We only cash these for our customers."

"I need the money. Can you just put a hold on it, or charge me a fee or something?"

"I'm sorry. Maybe you can find a branch close by."

"You've got to be kidding me."

"I'm afraid not. You'd be surprised how many fraudulent cashier's checks we run into. We really have to be careful."

Katy snagged the check and her license back and stalked out of the bank. Great. Well, that would have been nice to know before she'd left Atlanta for the second time. She'd always thought a cashier's check was as good as cash. When did that change?

She left feeling aggravated and madder than ever at Ron for making things so difficult. If he could have just been faithful, none of this would be happening.

Leaving her car at the curb in front of the bank, she walked down the block to the Blue Skies Cafe.

When she walked in, Angie was the first person she saw.

"Hey, girl!"

"Hi. I had some errands to run. Thought I'd drop in for some breakfast. What do you recommend?"

"Omelet. The best."

"I'll take it. With orange juice, please."

"Coming right up."

Katy checked her messages and the weather forecast on her phone. Angie brought her juice and slid across from her in the booth.

"So you and Derek had a little date last night?"

Katy laughed. "I don't know if I'd call it a date."

"It was a date. He hasn't done anything with anyone since Laney died. You're the best thing that's happened to him . . . in way too long."

"Well, I could probably say the same thing. He makes me feel pretty good too."

"Naomi stopped in earlier. She was driving to the airport to pick up Kelly Jo's husband."

Katy couldn't hold back the tears. "I don't know why I'm crying like this. I just feel so relieved. Happy. Something for her. She needs him with her through this."

"I know." Angie swept tears from her own cheeks. "Aren't we just a couple of girly messes?"

"For sure."

"Eat—before it gets cold." Angie walked away, but then came back. "And I just want you to know that whatever it is you've been through, Derek is a good guy. He would never hurt you."

"How? Why do you think—"

"When we talked about my ex, I saw your pain." She smiled. "You have to trust again. It's different for me. I've got Billy. When he's older, then I'll take a chance again. But you've got the chance now."

Katy sat dumbfounded for a moment. She wasn't even sure if she was looking for anything, but then isn't that always when the biggest opportunities came your way?

Maybe that was her problem. She was looking too darn hard. Katy felt more at home in this little town every day. "Hey, Angie, when you get a second."

Angie waved to her and then stopped to take someone's order.

After Angie put the order in, she came back over to Katy. "What else can I get you?"

Katy bit down on her lip. "Nothing from the menu. I was kind of thinking of sticking around for a little while, but I need work. Do you know of anything locally?"

She grinned. "You're gonna stick around a while. Really? I'm so excited. Between Derek and me, we know everyone in this town. We'll find something for you." She did a little wiggle dance. "It'll be great to have you around."

"Thanks. I appreciate anything you can do to help point me in the right direction."

"Absolutely. We can talk about it when we go over to the farm this afternoon. You're still up for that, right?"

"Been looking forward to it all week."

"Me too. I don't get to do stuff just for fun much anymore."

Katy sucked in a deep breath. A stream of golden light cast a glow through the back of the stained-glass divider onto the table.

The color of hope and opportunity.

She left money for her bill and a tip on the table, and took the back door out of the cafe, heading for the medical center.

She walked inside, and before she even got halfway down the hall, Derek stepped into the hallway.

"Katy? I wasn't expecting you. Everything's okay, right?"

"Oh, yeah. Everything's fine."

He looked relieved. "Good. I was just going to my office. Come with me."

She followed him down the hall and into his office. "Nice." Katy walked over to the certificates on the wall. "Looks like a lot of studying."

"It was."

She turned back toward him and then took a seat across from him, as he sat behind the desk. "I was just over talking to Angie. Naomi went to pick up Todd at the airport. I was wondering if there was anything I could do to help her be more comfortable while he's here. You know, anything she could eat or do?"

"There's not much you can do for her. Make sure she stays hydrated. Todd will be the one who will need comfort. I'm sure anything you make will be appreciated."

She nodded. "It's thanks to you that he's coming."

"It was time. I think Kelly Jo knew it. She just needed a reason to change her mind."

She noticed the picture on the bookshelf. Hesitating for just a moment, she picked it up. "This is Laney, isn't it?"

He nodded.

"She's beautiful."

"Thank you." He walked to her side and looked at the picture with her. "She had a beautiful soul. Even when the cancer stripped her of her outer beauty, she still had that spirit. Angelic."

"She was lucky to have you," she said, looking up at him.

"It worked both ways." His lips quirked.

"You miss her."

"Every day." He cleared his throat. "That will never change."

She put the picture back on the shelf. Some things scarred you for life. Like tattoos. Some with better stories than others.

His voice shook just a little. "I know I have to move on. To live. I want Laney's memory to live on and bring positive things to the world . . . somehow . . . even though she is gone." He placed his hand on her arm. "I think the retreat could be the thing that does that and helps me move on. And you. You coming here, and all. I haven't felt this alive in a long time. I'm really thankful that you stopped in town when you did."

"Timing is everything." If he only knew. "I'm sure you'll find the right way to pay homage to her memory. I think you have more gifts to bring to the world too."

"Maybe we all do."

"I hope you're right." She stood. "I'm headed back over to the cafe. Angie and I are going to go to that farm this afternoon."

"That's right. I forgot. Y'all have fun."

"We will. Thanks for your time."

"Any time."

She could feel him watching her as she walked down the hallway.

Katy got up from the bench outside the diner when Angie walked out. She'd been checking email while she waited. "I'll drive. My car is just up the block."

Angie nodded and fell in step behind Katy. "You are about to be introduced to some real live beefalo."

They hopped in her car and Angie gave her directions as she fidgeted with the air vent. "Just keep following this road."

Katy nodded. "I saw a picture of Laney in Derek's office earlier. She was really pretty." But it wasn't how pretty Laney was that worried her. It was the history. How clear it was that she would always be his first love. Could anyone ever compete with that? And it was too early to even be thinking stuff like that, but she couldn't help herself.

"It was sad that it ended the way it did. They'd wanted children, but they'd waited until he was out of medical school, and then he had to intern, and then the research kept him so busy . . . it was when they'd finally decided to start a family that she found out she was sick."

"Waiting to have children." Sounded a little too familiar. "I guess waiting for the perfect time isn't always easy to predict."

"Yeah. Talk about a surprise." Angie dug in her purse, took out some gum, and offered a piece to Katy.

"No thanks."

"Laney was the picture of health. Her getting sick was a shock to everyone. When he lost Laney, it was bad enough that he was losing his wife, but he was losing everything he believed in. All those years in school, the internship, practicing medicine had been turned upside down."

Katy's heart weighed heavy at the thought of all he'd been through. Why did it always seem worse when it happened to good people?

"I have to admit though, now taking care of Billy on my own, that I'm kind of glad Derek is not trying to raise a child while finding his way through all of this."

Katy drove the car through the big gates at Criss Cross Farm.

"Or focusing on their child might have been," Katy reasoned, "the one thing he could still believe in." She clung to the steering wheel, her hands sweating. She felt on the verge of tears. Life was so fragile. Laney. Kelly Jo. And then all of those marriages that got tossed aside like they meant nothing. A tough pill to swallow.

Chapter Seventeen

Katy and Angie spent three hours at Criss Cross Farm, and when they walked back into Lonesome Pines Inn just after five o'clock, with their arms full of grocery bags, they felt like they'd been friends forever.

Naomi pulled her hands up on her hips, looking a bit like a miniature soldier—probably more like a mom catching her daughters up to no good.

"We're cooking beefalo tonight," Katy explained.

"Katy's never had it, and we thought with Todd just getting into town, we'd bake up a big double batch of comfort food to help out."

"You girls are too sweet. I know Todd will appreciate the thought. I'm not sure he'll ever come back out of that room though." Naomi gulped air and pulled her arms around herself. "Both of them just collapsed into tears when he walked in her room. He crawled right into that bed with her and held her." She placed her hand to her heart, her voice quivering as she tried to speak again. "I swear, I can't even say it without crying." She swept at the tears that streamed down her face. "Thank you, God, for bringing those two back together."

Angie walked over and hugged Naomi. "It needed to happen. He needed to be here."

"She needs him too," Naomi said. She sniffed back the tears and shook her head like she was pushing away the sorrow. "Beefalo? I guess those guys over at Criss Cross Farm have turned into quite the salesmen."

Angie nodded. "I wouldn't know. They gave it to us for free."

Katy interjected, "Plus Angie has a date with the best-looking cowboy on the ranch."

Angie blushed. "It's true, Naomi. Can you believe it? I'm going out with Jackson. Thanks to Katy."

"I'm one heck of a wing woman. Besides it's about time you gave yourself a second chance at love. All men are not like your ex," Katy said breezing past them and heading to the kitchen.

Naomi raised a brow and fell in step behind Angie. "Now, who the heck is Jackson, and is that a first or a last name? I always did like a man with two last names for a name."

Angie put her bag on the kitchen counter and then pointed an accusing finger toward Katy. "I was just showing this one around and she gets to talking to the guys about their marketing and supply and demand—all kinds of business stuff. I swear, after a few minutes every single guy working that farm was over there talking to us."

Katy felt a blush rise in her cheeks. "It was not like that."

"Was too. Looked like a danged parade of cowboys."

Katy shook her head. "She's exaggerating, but they did invite us in for some sweet tea, and I accepted. It was totally innocent." But it wasn't really completely innocent. Katy had been plotting to hook Angie up the moment she laid eyes on that group of men, and it had been fun.

Angie pursed her lips. "Then she played matchmaker."

"Oh, don't act like you weren't happy about it," Katy teased, pulling things out of the paper sack and placing them on the center island in the kitchen.

Angie laughed. "No. I can't lie. Actually, I am thrilled. Do you know when the last time I had a real date was?"

Naomi piped up. "Probably too long. Well, good for you two. This is what living is all about. Laughing and sharing the good times."

Naomi pulled down an apron and put it on. "Let me at least help."

"Of course. This will be so fun," Angie said, and then winced. "Only I need to pick up Billy at the bus stop. Naomi, would having a kid around here for a couple hours make you half nuts?"

"No. I love that little boy of yours. Are you kidding? Go get him."

"We'll be right back, then," Katy said. "Come on, Angie."

They left the bags right on the counter and started for the door. The phone rang, distracting Naomi from their departure.

Katy headed for her car. "I'll drive."

"Okay." Angie hopped into the front seat and gave Katy directions to Billy's bus stop.

They pulled up just as the school bus did.

Angie got out of Katy's car and walked over to where the kids were hopping down to the street one at a time. When Billy got off of the bus, he gave his mom a hug. Even if he hadn't, Katy would have known the boy was Billy. He looked just like his mom with that dark, thick head of hair. Katy watched as they spoke. Billy grinned and nodded, then he took his mother's hand and they headed to the car.

She thought of her little niece, Chloe. That last hug they'd shared and Chloe asking her if she was running away. That tugged at her heart. She yearned to have that in her life. There should be more to life than keeping up with the neighbors and climbing the corporate ladder. There had to be a bigger payoff . . . and not a monetary one like Ron had been chasing after, but rather an emotional one.

"Hi, Billy," Katy said when he climbed into the car. "I'm Katy."

"Hello, Miss Katy."

Katy held her hand to her heart and gave Angie an approving look. "So sweet," she mouthed.

"I like your car," he said. "Red is my favorite color."

"Mine too," Katy said.

When they got back to the house, Naomi had all of the groceries unpacked and was waiting for them. She had pulled out a pudding cup and a glass of milk for Billy.

"Hey, Sport. I got you a little after-school snack. Figure everyone loves pudding."

"Yes, ma'am," he answered as he jumped up on the stool at the end of the island and dug right in.

"So what is it you girls want to create tonight? I was going to start slicing or dicing or something, but with all these ingredients I wasn't sure what you had up your sleeves."

"We're going to make a shepherd's pie with the beefalo," Angie said. "It's my specialty and Katy here says she's never had it."

"You're in for a treat, dear," Naomi said.

Billy chimed in. "My mom is an awesome cook. She cooks as good as Mr. Johnson at the cafe. He even said so."

"I'm not *that* good a cook, but I do enjoy it."

"Do you ever help your mom in the kitchen?" Katy asked Billy.

"Sometimes I do."

Angie gave everyone something to do, even Billy, who was in charge of smashing the potatoes that would go on top of the pies, and it made short work of the preparation.

Naomi held the oven door open as Angie set one of the heavy ceramic pie plates of shepherd's pie on the rack to bake, and Katy followed with the other.

"Now all we have to do is set the timer."

"And this place is going to smell so good," Billy added. "Just wait."

"He's not biased," Angie teased.

They were sitting around the island in the kitchen when Todd walked in. He was tall and athletic, and looked as though his heart had been tugged from his chest. His sandy hair curled over his shirt collar, like he'd missed a few haircuts, probably a lot of sleep after all he'd been through, too. He held an empty pitcher. "Can I get some water?"

Naomi motioned toward the refrigerator. "Of course, Todd. Make yourself completely at home. Anything at all."

"Hi," he said with a nod to Katy. "Angie. It's great to see you, girl."

Angie walked over to him and gave him a hug. "I'm so glad she let you come."

"It's been so hard to be apart. I love her more than anything. She agreed to let me call in hospice to help with the pain too."

"Thank goodness," Naomi said, glancing to heaven with a little silent thank-you.

Todd nodded. "They said they'll be out this evening. I just got off the phone."

There wasn't one word any of them could say that seemed right . . . or enough.

Todd refilled the pitcher and Naomi walked out of the room for a moment. When she came back, her eyes were suspiciously redder, but her face was composed. "We're making some shepherd's pie—Angie's famous recipe. You promise me you'll eat something, Todd. I'll bring it to you in her room if you like, but son, you have to keep your strength."

"Yes, ma'am. Thanks for taking care of her all this time. It's the only thing that's kept me the least bit sane the last few months . . . knowing she was with you." He took the pitcher and headed back to Kelly Jo's room.

"We're here if you need anything." Naomi didn't take her eyes off of him until he turned to go back down the hall. "I'll say this. There is not a stronger love than what he has for Kelly Jo. I can't even imagine what it took for him to honor her wishes, but boy am I thankful he's here and he was able to talk her into help from hospice."

A pang of regret hit Katy. Life wasn't about bomber jacket leather desk sets or scrawling trashy comments across the side of cars. It wasn't even about getting her fair share of a big savings account. That was stuff. Stuff could be replaced.

She excused herself and went back to her room. Closing the door, she crawled onto the bed and let the tears she'd been trying so carefully to control go.

Being worried about the money and Ron playing dirty didn't even seem important now. Even without the cashier's check she had other options. She was healthy and able. She had transferable skills. A good project manager could manage just about any kind of business. She'd always be able to take care of herself, and with that high-dollar car of hers paid off, she could sell it and live just fine the rest of the year. She would find a way to help make a difference.

Freshening up before leaving the room, she paused. Why should it matter if the others knew she'd been crying? They were all feeling fragile today.

She went back out to the living area where Billy sat on the floor in front of the coffee table playing Old Maid with his mom and Naomi.

"Got room for one more?"

"Yes, ma'am," Billy said. His crooked smile looked cute now, but Katy knew orthodontia would be another thing Angie would have to worry about in a few years.

One more hand of Old Maid and the buzzer in the kitchen sounded. The house smelled of fresh herbs and home cooking.

Todd joined them at the table in the dining room while Kelly Jo slept.

"May I say grace?" he asked.

Naomi patted his hand. "Of course."

"Heavenly Father, we are grateful as we pause before this meal, for all the blessings of life that You give to us. Daily, we are fed, nourished by friendship and care, feasted with forgiveness and understanding. And so mindful of Your continuous care, we pause to be grateful for the blessings of this table this evening. For the love and family and friendship You've given us, bringing us strength through times we don't always understand.

"And Lord, please bring comfort to Kelly Jo. We are thankful for these precious moments You are giving us no matter how short the time might be. Let all of us be grateful and live as You would have us. In the name of Your Son, Jesus. Amen."

The conversation was quiet and thoughtful. Todd's exhaustion was apparent and Katy wondered if he'd get any sleep at all.

After dinner, Angie had to get Billy home so they could get through his homework before bed, and Todd was retreating back to Kelly Jo's room.

Katy gave Billy and Angie a ride home.

Billy tumbled out of the car like the Energizer bunny, and came around to her side of the car and opened her door. He reached in and clung to her neck. "I had fun, Miss Katy. Come over on Tuesday. Mom lets me make homemade pizza for us on Tuesday. I'll share mine with you."

Katy turned and flashed a "no fair, he is so darn adorable" glance at Angie. "I'd love that, Billy."

Then she drove back to the inn. Rather than going inside right away, she chose to sit under the moonlight near the creek's edge.

There, she tried to empty her mind of everything and just enjoy the sounds of nature. She reminded herself of the affirmations she'd practiced as a young girl, even in college. When had she stopped doing that?

Had Ron been the one to take her off track, or had she just been too quick to follow rather than lead? She couldn't place blame on someone else. She had options. Choices. It was time she take back that control.

Tomorrow would be a new day. With a new focus. Seeing Kelly Jo, the same age as her, limited now to a very small window of life made her want to make the most of her own.

When she walked inside, Naomi was standing at the desk near the door. "You okay, Katy?"

"Yes, ma'am."

"I know there's a lot to take in around here right now. You won't hurt my feelings if you feel you can't stay. I completely understand."

"Would you rather I left? I mean, I know this is personal, and I—"

"No." Naomi came around and glanced down the hall. "I love what you bring to this house. I don't want you to leave and you are welcome here as long as you like. I just didn't want you to feel obligated."

Katy's heart fluttered. "Naomi, I want to help. More than anything, in any little way, I want to be here."

"I was so hoping you felt that way."

"Thank you."

"Hospice will be here shortly. They'll be setting up equipment and stuff. I don't know how long they'll be or how much of a ruckus they'll make."

"That's fine. I'm going to be in my room. Let me know if you need my help."

"I will."

Katy walked down the hall feeling a part of something that seemed bigger than her own life. She should call and check on Peggy, and see how Bertie was doing too. Now that the funeral was in the past, people would start fading away. She couldn't imagine what it would be like to lose a husband after so many years of marriage.

Before Katy could dial Peggy, her phone rang. It was Shaleigh calling.

"How are things going?" she asked.

"I'm doing fine." Katy glanced around at the beautiful room, and thought about the new friends she'd made in the short time since she'd been in Boot Creek. "Things are good here."

"Well, good, because I'm getting ready to throw a wrench in your relaxation."

"Great. Should have known it was too good to last. I tried to cash that cashier's check from the savings account this morning. They won't cash it since I don't bank with them."

"Well, then maybe this won't be as inconvenient as it sounds."

"What?"

"Ron is insisting you come and talk to him. You can cash that check while you're here in Atlanta."

"Can he do that?"

"He can ask for it. You can say no, but it probably wouldn't be a bad idea for you to come and we'll meet with him and his lawyer. I'll do all the talking."

"Are they going to arrest me for vandalizing that woman's car?"

"I think they are going to try to use it for leverage, though, Katherine, he admitted to the affair. Of course, he says it's over."

Katy closed her eyes. Just the thought of it made her cringe. "It wasn't too darned over for him to share the video with her."

"Yes, Melissa sure did take that and run with it," Shaleigh said.

"Melissa?" The name came out like a hiss. "That's her name?" A warm, sour taste rose in her throat, and her lips became numb. She'd just been "that woman" until right now. A nameless person who had interrupted her life. There was something less threatening about a woman with no name. But Melissa? Did he call her Missy for short? Of course not. Ron would never do that. Just like he would never call her Katy. Oh, no. He'd call her Melissa even if her parents had named her Missy, and he'd expect her to act as prim and proper as a Melissa should. Like she had, as Katherine, for so long. The perfect wife.

"Yes. He's admitting to the affair. Says it was a mistake, that he loves you and wants to reconcile. He and his lawyer want to meet tomorrow."

"Tomorrow?"

"Yeah. Two o'clock. My office."

The last thing she wanted was to be in the same room as Ron, but it was going to have to happen eventually and at least Shaleigh would do all the talking. Besides, back home she could at least cash that cashier's check. And if she sold her car on the way, all the better. Especially if she could figure out a way for Ron to notice it. He sure did love that car. "She won't be there, will she?"

"The girlfriend. Good lord, no. His lawyer would never allow it. It'll be you and me and Ron and his lawyer."

"I'll be there."

How were you supposed to sleep when you had thoughts racing through your mind as fast as one of those high-performance cars lapping an oval track?

Katy sat in the bed, her laptop on her lap, at four o'clock in the morning. Her stomach twirled and her mind bobbed back and forth between anger and hurt feelings.

It had been a long day. Well, not longer than last Friday. Lately that whole TGIF thing was losing its luster. Last Friday, when she saw Ron with that woman, felt so long ago. And now this Friday she'd be sitting in her lawyer's office facing him, with his lawyer. Step one toward dissolving their marriage.

She googled MotorCar Nation, and used the locator tool to see which locations would be on her way to Atlanta.

Ron would be shocked when he found out, but the car was in her name, and she'd spent her own bonus on it. This was completely her right to do.

He loved that car. Probably more than he loved her, if the remaining picture in his office proved anything. It was such a symbol to him. She'd never really cared one way or the other. It was pretty, but she'd been happy with her other car. Besides, this was money she could put to better use.

The dealership opened at eight-thirty.

An online price estimate showed they were paying the same no matter which location she went to, so she picked the one in Charlotte. She could be done before lunchtime, and then get down to Atlanta no problem. Finally, with a plan in mind she thought she might actually be able to get some rest before the long drive. She set the alarm on her phone and closed her eyes.

When her alarm went off, she'd actually gotten a little sleep. She turned off the alarm, got dressed, grabbed her purse and the folio of her important papers, and went into town.

Angie was just flipping on the open light at the Blue Skies Cafe when Katy parked at the curb. Angie leaned out the front door. "What are you doing out and about this early?"

"I have some errands to run today. Thought I'd stop and grab a cup of coffee and a muffin for the road."

Angie waved her in. "Come on. I've got the coffee ready."

A few minutes later, Katy was armed with a brown paper sack containing a blackberry streusel muffin and a large cup of coffee already tanned and cooled to her liking. "I'm hoping to be back this afternoon and starting that job hunt. So be thinking about where I might start."

"Of course."

Katy gave Angie a hug. "Thanks for everything, Angie." When Angie turned to put the coffeepot back on the warmer, Katy took an envelope from her purse and slid it on the counter next to the cash register. "I'm out of here." She knew Angie would refuse the help if she offered, but this way the few hundred dollars Katy'd set aside for emergencies would help Angie out in some small way. It would at least cover the repairs on her car.

"Drive careful."

"I will," Katy said waving as she walked out.

She sipped the coffee as she got on the interstate and made it to MotorCar Nation just a little after they'd opened.

She'd seen the commercials on television a million times. It had never occurred to her that she might actually need the service someday. While she'd been online this morning, she'd submitted all the details on her car and gotten an instant cash quote. She'd taken a screenshot of the quote. It was good for four days. But she only needed it for one.

She didn't want to stand out. She didn't want to spend her days trying to get one step ahead of everyone else anymore. She just wanted to stop and enjoy things. To blend in for a while. You couldn't blend in anywhere in a bright red Mercedes.

She cruised up on the lot just after the dealership opened.

By the looks of the giant neon numbers plastered across the windshields on the cars filling the front of the lot, she'd be able to have the pick of the litter and still have money left over to live for the next few months without bothering any of the joint accounts she and Ron had. Things would be settled and she'd be single before she could spend the money from that check and the sale of the car.

With her purse on her shoulder, she walked across the line of shiny used cars to the front door of the huge dealership. A young man with shaggy hair wearing a polo shirt with the MotorCar Nation logo embroidered across the pocket raced to her side as soon as she walked in. "How can I help you today?"

"I submitted an online quote for my car."

The sales guy glanced out to the lot and then back at her. "That one?"

She nodded.

He looked puzzled, but then he lifted his chin and nodded along with her. "Trying to get out from under a payment, aren't ya? Happening a lot these days. We can pay the lien holder directly."

"No. It's paid for. I've got the title right here."

"You trading it in? I'm not sure we have something on this lot that is going to be . . ." He looked out to the lot then lowered his voice. "Ma'am. Our cars are more for the economically minded, if you get my drift."

She was so tempted to go for the minivan. That would totally kill Ron, but she did have to drive whatever it was she bought. "I'm interested in the black Chevy Malibu. Says it's this year's model. How many miles are on it?"

"Um. Yeah, well." He looked totally flabbergasted. "Guy who brought it in had bought it for his daughter to take to college, but the girl ran off and got married instead. He traded it for a pickup truck."

"How many miles on it?"

"Just over three thousand. It's like brand-new. It's clean. When we got it detailed, I got to take it up to the street to our other location. She has some get-up-and-go."

"Sounds perfect. Can I drive it?"

He patted his pockets and pulled out a key. "Sure. Let me get the key." He turned to walk away. "Oh, and if you want to give me your keys, I'll have my manager take your car out for a test ride and then he can work up the final quote."

She pulled her keys from her purse and tossed them across the aisle to him. "Let's do it."

A few minutes later the shaggy-haired salesman walked out with his manager. Clearly the manager wasn't buying the story the kid was selling. She remembered fighting for respect at his age in business. It always sucked.

The manager repeated pretty much everything that had already transpired between her and the young salesman. "Yes. What he's told you is exactly as we discussed."

"Excellent. Well, I can take care of you from here."

"No." She countered icily. Maybe this was more about just changing her life. Maybe she could do a little something to help here too. "I'm pretty happy with . . ." She glanced at his name tag that hung crooked from his shirt. "Marcus."

Marcus straightened, clearly proud that he'd just gotten kudos from his best chance at a commission all month.

"Well, ma'am, I was just thinking since you were considering trading in the Mercedes . . . What year is it?"

"Last year's model."

"Yes, well that perhaps we could put you in something a little nicer than the Malibu that Marcus was telling you about."

"Marcus and I have already discussed, and pinned down, exactly what I'd like. I don't really see any need in wasting your time. Why don't you work up that price for me while Marcus and I take a test-drive?"

The manager's lips thinned in anger, but he kept his mouth shut. Good, because no matter what he said from here on out, she had no intention of letting him steamroll that kid out of the commission. It had turned into a cat-and-mouse game and she felt like winning.

His voice was curt. "I'll need your license and information for a credit check."

Of course you will. Now he thought she was a big fat fraud. She pulled her driver's license out of her wallet. "What do you need me to fill out?"

The manager put her in a small office where she could fill out the form. Marcus stood just outside the door, flipping the keys in his hand.

She filled in the blanks and then walked out, handing the form off to the manager, then nodding to Marcus as she headed for the door. "Let's test-drive this cute little car."

By the time they got back, the manager appeared to have cooled down. The flush of his skin had returned to normal and he was treating both her and Marcus with a bit more respect.

An hour later she was walking out of MotorCar Nation with a big fat check and a clean, sensible ride. She hadn't let them take the time to tidy it further. A little dust on it would just make Ron go that much more crazy, and that was fine by her.

Marcus had pulled the Chevy up next to her Mercedes and was going to help her transfer all of her things from one car to the other while the lot boy put on the thirty-day tags.

She'd just popped the trunk when she got the text from Shaleigh.

SHALEIGH: Ron's rescheduling until Monday at 2.

Auuggghhh. Could he have waited any longer? Seriously? She breathed through her nose because she knew if she opened her mouth she just might scream.

She took a couple steps away from the car and texted Shaleigh back.

KATHERINE: Seriously? I'm in Charlotte.

SHALEIGH: I think he was planning that. Said you could stay at the house for the weekend. He'll be back in late Sunday night.

KATHERINE: Not on his life. No wait. Maybe his life would be worth it.

SHALEIGH: Don't talk crazy. I'm not that kind of lawyer ;) Monday?

KATHERINE: Yes. Damn him. Tell him if he doesn't show Monday, I want the house.

SHALEIGH: Now we're talking.

KATHERINE: Don't tell them I want the house. I don't want that big mortgage. He can have it. But tell him 2:30 just so he doesn't get his way.

Katy shoved her phone into her purse and rubbed her left hand along her temple. He was exhausting. She could go around and around with him like this forever if she wasn't careful. She knew how he operated. Of course, she'd always admired how he could manipulate things to get his way, but then that was when she wasn't on the other end of that game.

Her phone rang and she checked the number. It was Derek. *I definitely can't talk to you right now.* She pushed the button on the top of the phone to shut it down, then got behind the wheel of her new car and headed back north toward Boot Creek.

Chapter Eighteen

Derek didn't know if he was happy for Todd Keefer or not. Angie had said he made it into town yesterday to be with Kelly Jo. Part of him knew he should go over there and offer his support, but things were moving forward. He'd received the call from the hospice team to get all of Kelly Jo's medications and things transferred to them for her final care.

No one else knew what hell it was to watch the person you loved die, except someone who'd been through it. But he wasn't sure that mattered when you were going through it. Mostly he'd just wanted to be left alone with Laney. Todd probably felt the same way.

The transfer of Kelly Jo to hospice had made those old demons kick back at him again. That dark hole in his chest that he'd thought was finally lightening up had grown heavy once more. He was a little afraid, hell, terrified, that being too close to Kelly Jo and Todd's situation would land him right back at the brink of the darkness he was just now getting past.

He wasn't sure he could put himself through that again.

In the past week, he'd seemed to have found a new normal. Rather than staying so busy that he'd fall into bed at the end of a day, he'd looked forward to finding pockets of time where he might stop and enjoy doing something. And suddenly, he wasn't feeling as lonely. Maybe it wasn't a new normal. Maybe it was more like his old normal. Whatever the case, he hoped it would stick around. Well, not it, so much as her. Because this new normal was a much better place to be than where he'd been the last couple of years.

He'd be lying if he didn't admit that even if it weren't Friday and his normal French toast morning at the Blue Skies Cafe, he'd be sitting right here waiting for a chance to talk to Angie anyway. She and Katy had planned to spend the previous day together, and he was curious to see what she had to say.

He finished his breakfast, pushed his empty plate to the side, and opened the newspaper, biding his time until Angie had a chance to walk over. She would. She always did, but they'd been friends for so long, she wouldn't bother until she caught a break in the morning flow of customers. Angie walked through the cafe topping off coffee, giving and getting her usual round of good mornings and hellos. She wasn't working his booth today, though.

"Hey, handsome," she said to him as she came back over near his booth to start a fresh pot of coffee.

"You're in a good mood today."

"I'm always in a good mood in the morning."

He narrowed his eyes, feeling pretty certain she was hiding something. "True. But there's something a little springier about you this morning. You and Katy must have had a good time on your afternoon off." Okay, it wasn't a subtle lead-in. Katy was on his mind and Angie would know he was digging.

"We did. The guys at Criss Cross flocked around her like seagulls over a fat guy on the beach with French fries."

Jealousy surged through Derek. He never did have a good poker face.

She knew him so well; her reaction told him that she knew exactly what he was thinking. "But don't you worry; she is crazy about you," she said pointing an accusatory finger in his direction. "Not that I think you mind that one bit. Oh, but she did land me a date."

"Really? With who? Anyone I know over there?"

"Jackson."

He'd met Jackson. "He's a good guy. I could see you two together."

"Well, you just might if you happen to be in Level Green for the antique car club thing tomorrow night. It's Vette night and the Night Crawlers are playing. He's taking me."

He was glad she was getting out. She worked hard. She needed a little playtime. Of course, everyone was always telling him that too.

When Laney died, he'd made sure he was too busy even to miss the thought of romance ever again, but that had been shattered the moment he set eyes on Katy at the gas station that day.

She's so different from Laney. Maybe that's what was so perfect about it. A different kind of perfect for a different time in his life.

"You're thinking about Katy, aren't you?"

Ol' Man Johnson called out, "Order up."

Angie shrugged. "It's good. Don't go trying to dissect it." She started to walk away, but then came back and leaned over his table. "Seriously, Derek. I think this is really good for you."

"I do too." He repeated those words to himself. And he believed them.

He left the money for his tab and a generous tip on the table and headed out the back door. The short walk over to the clinic wasn't short enough when the air was thick and swampy like it was this morning. The constant rain and heat cycle they'd been experiencing had been downright tropical, and not in the nice "lie on the beach" way, but more in the "sweat your ass off in the rain forest" kind of way.

At five-thirty Derek drove over to the firehouse for the weekly meeting and a check-in before the storm that was expected arrived to cause trouble in their area. The captain shared the final numbers from the Blackberry Festival and they'd beat their target. Someone had even taken the time to analyze which parts of their efforts brought in the most profit. The carved bears brought in the most money, but after the artists were paid their portion, it wasn't the most profitable.

The captain raised his hand in the air. "Big firehouse shout-out to our own Derek Hansen for rocking the Turnout Gear Challenge with a record-winning heat and retaining his title, and for being the most profitable gig on the ticket."

The guys cheered. "Could have been more if you'd have done those stripper moves Patrick put on," one man shouted.

"That'll never happen. I may have won, but Patrick was the star of that show," Derek said. Although he'd walked away with Katy that night, so he considered himself the real winner.

Derek's mind remained on Katy as the captain reviewed the calls from the last two weeks and discussed lessons learned and concerns. The meetings were always short and productive. Derek liked that about the captain. The last captain they'd had would keep them there for over an hour just to hear himself talk.

The team talked through the drills, contingency planning for power outages, and communications during the time of the storm.

When they wrapped up, Derek decided to skip the dinner. He walked out to his car and dialed Katy's number. If he didn't catch her, at least he could leave her a message. But when she didn't answer, he hung up. He'd try again later.

At home, he heated up some leftovers in the microwave, and then he tried her number again.

"Hey there. Was hoping I'd catch you. Angie said you had to go out of town."

Katy's words came at a clip. "I'm on my way back to Naomi's now."

"You sound a little frustrated. Are you okay?"

He heard her let out a sigh. "I'm fine. Tired. What's up?"

"I was going to see if you wanted to go to the movie tonight. They have one of those big blow-up screens out at the park. Since you're back, you up for it?"

She paused, then said in an apologetic tone, "Not really. I'm kind of beat. I was up early. Maybe another time."

"Sure. They'll probably do it a few more times before the weather changes."

She didn't say anything.

"Okay, well I'll let you go."

"Talk to you soon," she said.

He hung up the phone, sorry that he'd called. He'd had his hopes pinned on a date or at least some conversation. Maybe she'd just had a bad day.

While he was washing his dish, he noticed the shock of pink flowers outside, and a thought occurred to him.

He took the scissors from the knife block on the counter and walked outside. He must have snipped twenty-five flowers, forming a big bouquet that would cheer up just about anyone. He cut a piece of cotton twine from the ball he'd used to tie the tomato plant stems to their stakes.

Not bad.

He went inside and grabbed his keys and headed for his truck.

When he got to Lonesome Pines, Katy's car wasn't there. He must have beat her home, which was good because he hoped the flowers might cheer her up after a long day on the road. He went to the front door, knocked, and let himself inside through the open front door.

Naomi stopped mid-sentence, and Katy was standing right across from her.

He knew her car hadn't been out front, but it was most certainly her. "Hey, Naomi. Katy. I . . . I." He glanced back toward the door. Confused. "I didn't think you were back yet. I was just going to leave these for you."

Naomi looked as impressed as if she'd been the one to raise him.

"Thank you," Katy said.

"We just got done with our meeting at the firehouse. The storm is expected to cause some trouble. Looks like you just barely beat the rain."

"I ran through some showers on the way in," she said.

"If the creek starts to rise, I want y'all to know that you can come stay at my house. Just call and I'll come get you."

Naomi didn't look worried. "That's sweet of you, Derek, but that creek has never risen high enough to cause a problem here. We'll be just fine. If worse comes to worst, we'll take to the second floor."

Katy gave him a half smile. "I'll just go put these in a vase."

She left the room and now what had seemed like such a fun and romantic gesture felt awkward as hell with Naomi standing there smiling that knowing smile at him.

Thank goodness it only took Katy a minute to grab a vase and fill it with water. She returned, put it on the table in the front room, and started fussing with the flowers.

"I'm just going to go check on Kelly Jo and I've got some . . ." Naomi spoke as she headed out of the room. "I've got stuff to do upstairs."

"That was subtle," he said with a laugh as Naomi hotfooted it out of the room.

"Yeah," she said pushing her hair behind her ear. "Look, Derek. This is really nice. Sweet, really, but I think we need to slow things down. I—"

"No pressure. I know you're tired. I just wanted to stop by. You sounded kind of stressed after the drive. I thought the flowers might make you smile."

"You sure know how to do that," she said, then stepped around to the other side of the table fussing with the flowers, only he had a feeling it was more to put space between them.

"So?" He wasn't quite sure what had changed, but the signals were clearly different.

"It's complicated," she said.

"No. What Todd and Kelly Jo are going through, that's complicated."

She pulled her arms up and crossed them tight at her chest. "Okay, so it's not life-and-death complicated, but it's complex. I have to go back to Atlanta on Monday."

"Okay. So, what is in Atlanta? I thought you lived in Virginia Beach."

She shook her head. "I grew up in Virginia Beach, but I live on the outskirts of Atlanta."

"Oh?" Only he wasn't really understanding. He was falling for this girl. Not even a week. It was ridiculous. Crazy. He knew it was. Even his hopeless romantic of a mother would say so, but it was true. She'd awakened feelings that he thought he would never feel again. And he liked it. And now she seemed afraid.

"I'm sorry I know I'm not making sense. I'm so tired."

"I didn't see your car when I pulled in."

She looked puzzled, then nodded. "That's because I got rid of the Mercedes this morning."

"Is it the money? Do you need money? I could help—"

Katy's face flooded a soft pink. "No, it's not. Money isn't a problem. I can get a job. I'm just a grump. I'm sorry. I'm never like this."

"Why don't you come with me? I'll put you in a better mood."

Naomi poked her head around the corner. "Go on, Katy. We'll be fine here."

Derek and Katy shared a smile. Had Naomi been hanging right there around the corner the whole time?

"I won't even make you go outside in the rain."

She laughed. "You were the one who didn't want to go out in the rain. Not me. You almost sacrificed our pork chops because of a little rain."

"How about popcorn and a movie? We'll veg out in front of the television and just relax."

"I'll probably fall asleep."

"I happen to be a pretty good cuddle," he said. "Come on. The rain sounds great under the tin roof."

***

The pounding of the rain on the roof of the truck somehow relaxed her. Plus it was so loud there was no way they could talk. She didn't feel like talking. Ron's manipulations had drained her. She'd be glad when all of this was behind her. And being with Derek was so easy. So nice, but she needed to figure out what her own priorities were. It had been so long since she'd even tried to parcel out what were hers versus theirs as a couple that she wasn't sure where to start.

But here she was. In his truck. Letting him lead the way. Tomorrow. Maybe tomorrow she could focus on her next steps.

Derek pulled up to the house, and then pressed a button for the garage door.

Katy winced as he drove into the garage, like maybe she thought the truck wasn't going to clear the opening, though that wasn't really it. The truck was big. No question about that, but her being here with Derek was more nerve-wracking.

"I've parked in here a time or two," he said with a wink.

"Sorry," she said. "That is some crazy rain."

"Yeah. Hope the satellite hasn't gone out, or we might have to watch a DVD."

"That's fine with me."

He got out and by the time she opened her door, he was at her side, helping her down.

Inside the rain pounded the roof.

"It's peaceful. The tin roof."

"It takes some getting used to." He hit the button on the remote, but all they got was the satellite searching for a connection. He flashed her an apologetic look. "I was afraid of that."

"It's okay," she said.

"You really are out of sorts today. Do you want to talk about it?"

Tears welled, one slipping down her cheek.

He caught it with the back of his hand, his knuckle sweeping it away, and then his thumb brushing across her lower lip.

"Don't cry. What is going on?"

"I'm sorry." She shook her head. "I can't. I shouldn't have come."

"Hey. Calm down."

She liked the way his lips moved when he talked. She lifted a hand and touched his cheek. She'd been dying to do that and it was as soft as she'd imagined. She pulled her hand away, but he caught it and held it close to his chest.

His heart pounded under her touch. If his hand were on her chest, he'd feel the same.

"Come with me," he said pulling her up.

She stood there for a moment, and he reached for her hand.

He placed her hand in his and she followed him upstairs. He sat down on the edge of the bed, and tugged her down next to him.

"Don't say a word." He leaned back and guided her next to him, stretching out next to her. The heat of her tears dampened his shoulder. "It's hard, what's going on with Todd and Kelly Jo. I know it's heartbreaking. It's okay to be sad."

"It is heartbreaking. I feel so ungrateful and lonely and I can't even explain it. I am so sad for them that I can barely stand it."

"I know. It makes you feel like you've suddenly lost your way, doesn't it?"

"Yes. It does."

He ran his hand through her hair, letting the long tendrils wrap around his finger as he held her in his arms in the dark. Holding her closer. His breathing slowing to match hers. "I'm here. We'll get through all of this."

"Thank you," she whispered, then scooted up, nearly nose to nose with him, and initiated a kiss.

The quick inhale on his part proved she'd caught him off guard. She'd expected to surprise him, but her own soft moan sent an unexpected, eager intensity through her. She released all control like someone would when a wave crashes around her and pulls, wanting to drag her deep into the undertow.

The intensity of their kisses grew and she pulled his t-shirt up, dropping kisses in a path along his chest.

His breath hitched and she could feel the well-defined muscles of his stomach under her fingers and lips as she traced his torso.

He lifted up just enough to pull his shirt off over his head. The soft cotton landed in a heap on the floor near the bed.

When she kissed his neck, he ran a finger in between the buttons of her blouse, sending a shiver through her and she knew if she said no, things would stop. If she didn't, there was no turning back.

Her mind clung to that as his hands deftly worked the front of her blouse.

She wanted this.

She needed it. When he pushed her shirt back over her shoulders, she sat up and let it slide to the floor near his.

He got up and stood next to the bed. He stepped out of his jeans, and then leaned forward kissing her. She sat up, letting her fingers dance across his strong arms, and then he laid her back and kissed a trail from between her breasts to her tummy.

She pulled the sheet into her hands and closed her eyes. The images of his face, at dinner, smiling, laughing, different times and places over the past week, were all good. She opened her eyes. He was watching her.

He rested his chin at the waistband of her skirt. He swept his tongue across the spot where her skirt met her stomach and then he slid his hands under the fabric.

She closed her legs around his hand, and then parted them. He paused, just long enough to give her a chance to stop him, but she didn't.

He slid his hands to the top of her skirt, and in one move, swept it and her panties over her hips and to the ground.

Her breathing came in short breaths, but his was just as uneven. He climbed back onto the bed and stretched out alongside her.

"I want you tonight, Katy."

She closed her eyes and nuzzled her face into his shoulder.

Cupping his hands on each side of her head, he tilted her face to his. He kissed the side of her face, slowly. Then her mouth, and she felt the growing urgency of something sensual and wonderful and she let herself ride that thought.

She couldn't deny herself his touch. He made no attempt to hide that he was watching her. Enjoying every moment that she shivered or tensed until there was no holding back, and she pushed her fingers into the flesh of his arms and the world fell away.

For a moment there was nothing but that passion—their breathing a well-practiced melody that even drowned out the rain against the tin roof.

His skin was hot, moist from the dance. The sound of their skin touching, moving together, was only heightened by the soft moans of pleasure that can't be re-created on command.

She knew this moment, this night, would replay in her mind forever. She would cling to it. Relive the joy she was feeling right now, and it would take her through another day and many to follow.

In the darkness, Katy ran her hand along Derek's chest. She had no idea what time it was but it was still dark out, and the light in the yard cast a soft glow across their entwined bodies under the crisp, white sheets. She'd slept for a little while, but now she was half awake. The rain wasn't falling as hard now.

Stillness had replaced their movements, as they lay next to each other. He brushed her damp bangs back from her face, but never said a word. Words would only clutter what they'd just shared.

Chapter Nineteen

Derek wished he didn't have to work this morning, so he could stay in bed all day long with Katy, but the last thing he could do was break a promise to his father, or embarrass him in front of his patients. So, when the sun peeked through the curtain, he'd carefully slid out of bed.

It was awkward to just steal away.

He started to write her a note, but his handwriting was typical doctor scribble, and he kind of doubted she'd be able to read it. Instead he grabbed another sheet of paper off the table. He simply drew a big smiley face and printed CALL YOU LATER across the bottom. He laid it on the pillow next to her, and then slowly walked out of the room.

The door creaked as he pulled it closed behind him. He quietly made his way down the hall.

Outside, the rain had stopped, but the sky still cast an angry glance over the town.

With everyone still watching Tropical Storm Eva, it was anybody's guess what they were in for the next three days. They would either be blasted with heavy, damaging wind and rain for the next three days, or if she chose to do-si-do back offshore, they could have clear sailing all weekend.

Being this far inland, the town rarely saw these kinds of storms. They hadn't had a bad flood since 1967, but that year the flood was so bad they'd had a state of emergency.

He couldn't recall how Naomi's house had been affected in the past, but being that it was right on the creek, it didn't seem like the best place to be if the rain didn't give them a break.

When he got to the office, he checked his schedule. He'd have to get back to his house before noon so he could take Katy back to the inn. He certainly couldn't leave her stranded at his house all day. It wasn't like you could just hail a cab in a town like this. Besides, he'd want to talk to Naomi again about a contingency plan if the storm came this way and the creek flooded.

An hour later his schedule freed up and he texted Katy to let her know he was on his way to pick her up and take her back to Naomi's.

She met him at the truck and climbed in.

"Good morning."

"Back at ya," she said. "How's your day going?"

"I wish I'd had the day off."

She smiled and turned to look out the window. She wished he'd had the day off too.

He pulled into the parking spot next to the front porch and shut down the truck.

"Are you coming in?"

He nodded. "Yeah, thought I'd check on Kelly Jo and check on things."

Derek and Katy walked inside together.

"Have a fun night?" Naomi sang out.

Katy felt three shades of pink brighter than the flowers in Derek's front yard. It was like getting caught doing it in your parents' house or something. "It was nice."

"Nice?"

Oh, yeah. She knew. Great.

"There are ham biscuits in the kitchen."

"Thanks," Katy said, quickly making a beeline for the kitchen to escape further questioning and for some much-needed coffee.

When Katy walked back out into the dining room, Naomi was sitting there alone. "How's Kelly Jo feeling this morning?"

"I don't know. She and Todd have had the door closed all morning." Naomi looked worried.

"It's heartbreaking."

"It is. At least he's here now." She leveled a loving look at Katy. "You're a good woman, Katy. You deserve happiness too."

Katy's phone rang. She glanced at the display, and then leapt to her feet. "I've got to take this. Excuse me." She gave a half-grin and jetted out the back French doors since that was the closest exit. "Hello," she answered.

"I just got off of the phone with Ron," said Shaleigh.

Katy's throat felt thick. "And?"

"I don't think he'll try changing dates again on us. We had quite the little conversation. He tried to play it all off—the whole thing—but when I told him I'd seen pictures of him kissing his little friend, he was off-balance." She laughed in a haughty way. "I described that kiss quite nicely if I do say so myself. I should take up writing erotic novels. I did so well that I left him a little speechless, in fact."

"That's a first."

Shaleigh continued. "He was only speechless for a moment. Then he went into grovel mode."

But what did that even mean from someone who would lie?

"He says he wants you back home. Says it was a mistake."

"What is going on with him? He can't keep pushing and pulling me like this. He should have kept our meeting if he was so hell-bent on seeing me." Katy's hand balled into a fist. "I'll tell you what he thinks is a mistake—that he got caught. Well, too bad, because he *did* get caught." He probably was starting to realize just what half of everything was and that it was going to make him half as happy.

"Any amount of groveling going to change your mind? He says he'll do anything."

Katy hated that question.

"He should have thought about all of that before he went traipsing off with Miss Melissa." She'd waited to have children. Given in to everything he'd ever wanted. Put her own desires on hold. She'd done it all willingly. All she'd expected in return was fidelity. Even that had been just too much to ask of him.

"Why is he doing this?" Her voice rose, sounding unfamiliar to herself, and instead of feeling sick, anger grew inside her. "I don't care what he says. What he did was wrong. Unfair. Cruel. The damage is irreparable." She turned and saw Naomi watching from inside on the couch. She stepped out of view. She'd gotten loud. So mad she'd forgotten where she was for a moment there. "Sorry? He probably doesn't even know how to spell the word."

"Don't kill the messenger," Shaleigh said.

"I know, but don't they always say that?"

Shaleigh's laugh broke up the tension Katy was feeling.

Katy looked toward the sky. Her mood was as gray as the clouds that continued to threaten the area. "Is that all for now? Until Monday?"

"Yes. It is. Sorry to ruin your day."

Shaleigh hung up and Katy put her phone in her lap, and just as she did, it rang back.

"Yes?" she answered, expecting that Shaleigh had forgotten something.

"Katherine. It's your mother. I've tried to stay out of this, but I'm your mother and this is crazy. I was just talking to Ron. What is going on with you?"

"Me?"

"I thought you were going to go back and work things out with him. You've been gone a week?"

"I never said I was going back."

"I told you—"

"And I appreciate your advice, but that was not the direction I chose to take."

"You are better with him than without him," her mother said.

The words played in her mind—actually an interesting thing to ponder. "The truth is, Mom, he is better with me at his side. I'm just fine alone."

"Oh, Katherine, don't be ridiculous."

"Ridiculous? Mom, I make more money than he does. I was faithful. I'm a smart woman and I don't know why any smart woman would stay with a man who thought so little of her that he'd run around with another woman. And by the way. That woman. The one he was seeing. She has a name. Melissa. He admitted to it. And I saw her at my house when I tried to give him a chance to discuss things. Would you like the video? I can send it to you."

"Honey." Her mother's voice actually sounded sorry.

"Mom, I know you're trying to help, and I'm sure Ron is trying to build up his side of the story in a way that makes me look like the bad guy. But, Mom, you raised me better than that. Why can't you just support me on this? You support Jacquie on everything. Every stupid screw-up and half-baked idea."

"I'm sorry, Katy-bug. I'm truly sorry." Her mom let out a long sigh.

Mom hadn't called her that in forever. Not since Katy had come home from college with Ron's big theory on successful names and demanded everyone call her Katherine.

"You know, you've always been the one who could get things done. Always excelled. Made good decisions. Your daddy and I, we're so proud of you. You've never needed us for a thing."

"I just need you to believe in me, Mom."

"And I screwed that up. I'm sorry. You're always so perfect that I guess I just think you always will be."

And getting a divorce makes me somehow imperfect? Was this little chat supposed to make me feel better?

"You didn't screw it up. I know your intentions are good, but you have to believe that a good marriage is not about money, or things. It's about sharing the good times and the tough times, being honest, faithful, and exploring life together. I should have seen the red flags, Mom. You're right. I worked a lot, but it was what we did. I thought he and I were a team and we were achieving goals together."

"You will land on your feet. You always do."

She hung up the phone feeling her mother's love. When she went back inside, Derek was talking to Todd and Naomi on the couch.

"Am I interrupting?" Katy asked. "I can just go to my room."

"No," Naomi said patting the seat cushion next to her. "Come here. We were just talking about doctors and stress and stuff. Hmmm . . . come to think of it, maybe you should run! It doesn't sound like too happy of a topic, does it?"

"I was telling them about the retreat idea," Derek said.

Todd looked worn out. "I don't know how you can be around this kind of stuff and stay sane."

"Well, that was kind of my point. To help the doctors who help the patients. Help them balance their lives. Make it easier for them to take the time off that they so desperately need. You'd be surprised at the number of hours doctors put in, and how little time off they take. It's hard to balance it all."

Naomi rocked forward. "I think it's a wonderful idea. You know it's not so different from what my Marshall did here in our home over the years. With singers, band members—they needed that break to reenergize, get their heads on straight. It sounds so simple, but it really is a big deal. That's why we ended up with a house with eighteen guest rooms."

"You can hire me to manage it," Katy said.

Naomi looked surprised. "Well, you know, I don't think I ever even asked what it is you do for a living. You said you were on vacation, but I never even wondered from what."

That was what Katy had kind of liked about this place. That she didn't have to meet any expectations or answer questions.

"I manage multimillion-dollar projects for one of the biggest banks in the nation."

Naomi's brow lifted. "Impressive."

"I'm very good at it, too."

Todd chimed in. "Oh, a great project manager is a real gift. Hard to find, and hard to hang on to because those headhunters are always trying to steal the good ones."

Katy nodded. "I'm on leave. I'm thinking about picking up a little temporary work while I'm here though. I'm in a pretty good position to do just about anything except physical labor or mechanical work, but you know what I mean. I'm flexible. So, y'all let me know if you know anyone who needs some help."

Naomi rummaged through a newspaper sitting on the end table. "Actually, they are already looking for someone to fill the position overseeing all of the tourism stuff for Boot Creek—the Blackberry Festival and some watershed projects. Things like that. Look." Naomi pointed to a big square ad in the lower left-hand corner. "This sounds exactly like you. I happen to have some connections in this town still."

Katy took the paper and read through the employment ad. She had every qualification they requested, and then some. It wouldn't be a temporary job, but that suddenly held even more appeal. "I have to go out of town on Monday, but when I get back, I might just call these folks."

Derek reached for the paper. "I like the idea of you sticking around."

"Me, too," Naomi said. "You could even stay here for a while. Rent-free. I'm really enjoying your company."

Derek read silently then looked up. "This sounds like a good opportunity, Katy. The festival and tourism coordinator position takes experience, and it sounds like you have that."

"Okay. Yeah. Maybe that's a good idea."

Todd got up. "I'm going to go slide into bed with my bride. It was good chatting with y'all. I'll talk to you in the morning."

"G'night, Todd," Katy said, and Naomi echoed her.

"I've got to run, too," Derek said. "You two sit tight. I'll let myself out."

Katy watched Derek leave. Naomi got up and brought back a pair of scissors from the front desk and set to cutting out the employment ad. Her hands were unsteady and Katy thought maybe she'd have done a better job just ripping it out.

"Here you go. If you'd like a good word from me, it might help. I'd be happy to do it."

"Thank you, Naomi."

Chapter Twenty

Monday morning Katy got in her car and headed back to Atlanta. She'd been a little anxious the whole ride, but it wasn't until she drove past the Carpe Diem Bistro that her mood dipped.

Shaleigh's office was just a few more blocks up the street. She shouldn't have been surprised by the plush, high-end look of the offices when she walked in, but it made the super-high hourly rate make even more sense. If location was everything, Shaleigh had picked the right spot. Even from where she was, standing at the receptionist's desk, she had a clear view of some of the nicest parts of the city.

"I have a two-thirty with Shaleigh. Katy." She stopped herself short. "Katherine Barclift."

The receptionist wore a designer suit that probably cost an easy five hundred bucks, and Katy had treated herself to the same necklace earlier this year. She wondered if it was a coincidence that the receptionist's outfit coordinated perfectly with the fine leather chairs and metal sculptures in the room.

The woman announced her arrival.

A moment later the door to the waiting area opened and in walked Ron and his attorney.

Katy turned back to the receptionist wishing she'd been just a couple minutes earlier and could have missed this awkward moment.

"Katherine. You look beautiful," Ron said.

"Thank you." She'd actually stopped at the outlet and picked up a new little black dress and heels. A much sexier one than she'd been wearing, with the thought that it wouldn't hurt to just make him wish she was still his. Childish, she knew. But the look in his eyes right now told her all she needed to know. It had been worth it.

Shaleigh poked her head out into the waiting area. "Hi, Katherine. Will you come with me?" She glanced over at Ron and his attorney. "We'll be with you in just a few minutes."

Katy walked past them and she could feel Ron's eyes on her all the way to the door. She slipped behind the door and Shaleigh wrapped her into a big hug. "You look dynamite, girl! I think this separation becomes you."

"Thank you."

"You doing okay?"

"I am."

Shaleigh shuttled her down the hall to a large fish bowl of a conference room. "You and I will sit here. They can face the sun . . . I mean the view, of course."

"Tricky."

"Yeah. Whatever. Sometimes you have to take pleasure in the tiniest things. He's asking for counseling."

"Good. He should get some. Cheater."

"No, couples counseling," Shaleigh explained. "He wants you to move back into the family home and maintain your half of the bills, as you've established over your ten years of marriage. He wants the two of you to go to couples counseling, and he wants you to pay to have the young lady's car repainted."

Katy's eyes felt like the ones on springs that boogeyed out of a cartoon character's head. "You cannot be serious. It was lipstick. Tell the tramp to go to the Wishy Washy. I am not paying to have her little car repainted."

"Well, you might end up having to do that, just because it's on video and there's no question you did it. We'll ask our own body shop to do an estimate."

"I'm not doing it as part of my separation, and what the hell kind of separation order is that? It sounds like a together order."

"Umm-hmmm. What are you thinking?"

Katy's tongue felt so thick that she could barely spit the words out. "That the guy has lost his ever-loving mind."

"You're not going back?"

"No. I absolutely am not," Katy said.

"No counseling? What if he gets counseling?"

"No." Katy couldn't even believe Shaleigh was asking this. Hadn't they had this conversation? *Is she second-guessing my decision?* But she knew what she was doing was right. This was the right path for this point in her life. She was taking her life back. "Whose side are you on?"

"Hey. I'm on your side. I'm just asking you these questions so you and I are on the same page before we all get in the room together."

"Fine."

"Here's what I've drawn up. It's a split right down the middle of all of your funds. You keep your own 401(k) and IRA, he keeps his. You each keep your cars."

"I sold mine."

"The Mercedes?"

She nodded. "Traded it in for a Chevy Malibu."

Shaleigh started laughing. "He doesn't need to know, but you know it will frost his balls. Can I mention it? Please let me roll it out there."

"Sure. Have a ball. I'll be sitting here watching him die a thousand deaths over that. Might be the best part of it all." Was there any chance she could videotape that?

"This'll be great." Shaleigh focused back on the papers she'd drawn up. "I have him getting the house and he pays you half of the equity that's in it. No alimony."

"Sounds fine to me."

"Okay, well, let me get our boys."

Katy's hands shook under the table as she sat there waiting for Ron and his lawyer to come to the conference room with Shaleigh. Katy fought the nervous twitch in her eye, hoping it wasn't a sign she was going to cry, because she was done crying over Ron or the past.

She was even done being bitter. It was what it was, and some of those years had been awesome. She was no worse off because of those years; now, she'd take her experience and live a new life. One where she chose the priorities and the pace, and if she didn't find a new partner in life, maybe she'd just adopt a child and raise the child on her own. Women did it all the time.

Ron and his lawyer sat down.

"We can work this out, honey," Ron said.

She didn't respond, just turned her attention to Shaleigh. She let Ron's attorney speak first. He didn't say anything new, just pretty much what Shaleigh had outlined to her earlier. Then Shaleigh kicked into high gear and Katy saw firsthand why her friend was the best divorce lawyer in the business. She was amazing to watch. In thirty minutes, she had rolled out the pictures of Melissa and Ron, the video of the girl leaving their home, and gotten in the little mention of her Chevy Malibu, after which Ron spoke up and asked about the Mercedes.

It took everything Katy had not to laugh.

"You can't just get rid of that car. How much did you get for it?"

Shaleigh handled it all like the pro she was, and Ron stammered like a skipping record.

By the end of the meeting, Katy had a signed separation agreement, leaving the divorce papers as the next and last step.

She left Shaleigh's office feeling on top of the world. She called Peggy as she pulled out of the lot.

"Hey, Peggy," she said.

"Katherine. How are you?"

"Great. Just got my signed separation agreement and divorce is the next step. I thought I'd stop by before I headed back out of town. You free?"

"I'd love to see you. Come on over."

There were no cars in the driveway at her old house when she drove up to Peggy's. She felt like celebrating and she had a feeling Ron wasn't feeling quite as much the winner right now. Served him right.

She gave a double-knock on the door and Peggy answered.

"You look great!" Peggy stepped back. "Come in. Let me look at you."

"How have you been?"

"Good. That little town looks like it's treating you right."

"It's great. You should come visit me in Boot Creek. It's a charming little place. I even danced in the streets at a blackberry festival with a very good-looking doctor one night. Can you picture me dancing in the streets? We're talking conga line."

"No. I absolutely cannot imagine that. Hysterical." Peggy laughed. "I'm happy for you, girl. No surprise you'd find someone else so fast."

"It's not like that, Peggy. I'm not trying to replace Ron. I'm just trying to figure out who I really am without him. You should come visit. It would do you good."

"Oh, you know me. I'm a city girl, through and through. I like it right here close to the action, but enough about me. Is the separation official?"

"Yes. I can hardly believe it." Katy clapped her hands. "How's yours going?"

"Well," Peggy paused. "Tucker moved back in."

Katy's jaw almost dropped. "What?"

"I'm going to give him another chance."

"Oh." Lordy. What do you say to that? It was the last thing she expected to hear. What happened to making him pay for it the rest of his life?

"We're going to go to some counseling. He's working on himself. He's so outgoing, it's hard to realize that his confidence was suffering, but he promises it will never happen again."

Katy reached out and held Peggy's hand. "Is that what you want?"

"It is. I think it will work out this time."

"Well, then I hope it does."

"Tell me about you. How's it going in that little town? What was it called again?"

"Boot Creek. Oh, and the inn where I'm staying belongs to the sister-in-law of that country singer Dillon Laumann. You know who I'm talking about, right?"

"Yes." Peggy started singing one of his hits.

"Yes. That one!" Katy hummed along. "His sister-in-law, Naomi, is such a darling. Her inn is right on a creek. So peaceful. I never thought I'd enjoy the whole back-to-nature thing, but it's been a good place to tune out the old noise and get my head on straight."

"I'm so glad for you, Katherine. It sounds like things are going to work out perfectly for both of us."

Katy couldn't imagine Tucker could change that much. And with that in mind, it was hard to even have small talk. Besides now that she had those separation papers in hand, she had every intention of going back and clearing everything up with Derek. It was long overdue, but at least now she could completely let go of the past.

She looked at her watch. "Gosh, I've got to get on the road or I'll hit all the traffic heading back." She hugged Peggy. "I'm so happy for you. Keep me posted on how it's going, okay?" Only she knew that she'd probably never hear from Peggy again.

Peggy wouldn't want the reminder of the other path.

Chapter Twenty-One

Derek stopped by Angie's house on his way home. She was sitting on her front porch, still wearing her waitress uniform, watching Billy play kickball in the yard with some friends.

He parked along the curb and walked up to the house. "Hey, girl." Derek sat down next to her on the stoop.

Angie leaned her elbows on her knees. "I got a call from the garage. They finally figured out what was wrong with my car and it's to the tune of five hundred dollars."

"Need a loan?"

"Real funny." Her lips pursed.

"What?"

"I know that was you who left that envelope on the counter. You know I won't borrow money from you, Derek. Is that why you've been scarce lately?" She dug into the pocket of her apron and handed him the envelope.

He looked inside. A stack of twenties. "I didn't do this."

"Stop."

"No. I didn't. Maybe I should have, but I didn't."

"Well, then who . . ." A look of realization crept across Angie's face.

Nancy Naigle

"What?"

"I found this right after Katy left the other day. Do you think she did this?"

"Maybe. I don't know, but it's good timing. Maybe it was just a happy customer. Don't look a gift horse in the mouth, but do let me know if you need me to watch Billy for you."

"That would be great. So much is going on, it's a little overwhelming." Angie laid her head on Derek's shoulder. "How long have we been friends?"

"Forever. You were the first girl I kissed."

"In first grade. A girl never forgets her first love, and man, I've been so proud of you. You've done big stuff, man. Thanks for talking to Kelly Jo the way you did. I know it wasn't easy for you, and I know it's tough on Todd. On her too, but there is some joy in them being together. You did the right thing."

"It wasn't easy, but she shared some things with me that were eye-opening too."

Angie reached for his hand. "I'm sorry this is still so hard for you, but Derek," her hefty sigh seemed endless, and then her voice softened, "it's been eating you alive for two years now. You have to move on. You have to forgive yourself one day. I think your meeting Katy has been a good step for that."

He couldn't disagree.

After Billy went to work on his homework, Derek and Angie talked on the porch. It was close to eight by the time he left.

He drove over to the inn hoping he might catch Katy there.

When he walked in, he was delighted to see Katy standing there talking to Naomi.

She looked beautiful in a black dress and heels. And happy. Her smile absolutely radiated.

"How're you doing?"

260

Derek smiled at Katy. Her caring way endeared her. "Want to go walk down by the creek with me?"

"Sure." She waved to Naomi, not even hiding her grin. "Let me change into jeans and tennis shoes real quick."

"I'll wait for you on the porch."

"Okay."

A few minutes later she rushed outside wearing a faded pair of jeans and a blue t-shirt. She had her shoes and socks in her hand. "Ready?"

"Let's go." He took her hand and they walked down to the water.

She dipped her foot into the water. "It's amazing to me how cold this water can be when the air is so hot. It's not that deep. You'd think it would be like bathwater."

He steered toward the dock. They stepped over a thin cable meant to keep people off of it. "It's sturdy."

She followed him and they sat on the edge with their feet dangling.

"I like spending time with you, Katy."

"Derek, I need to tell you something."

"Sure. Anything."

Anything? He might not really feel that way when he heard what she had to say. Her throat felt dry. "I tried to tell you before, but the situation just never seemed right, and then when you asked me about selling my car and if I needed money, I should have told you then."

"Do you need a loan?"

"No. I'm good." She pulled her hands into her lap and picked at the polish on her thumbnail. "That car was paid for. I had a really high-paying job. I bought it with my bonus. Technically, I still have that job. I'm on a leave of absence."

"So, you're trying to tell me you'll have to go back."

"No, I'm trying to tell you something else." She dropped her head back. "This is not easy. You see, I never even wanted to buy that car in the first place. I'm not that kind of gal. I like nice things, sure, but that whole status symbol thing, it just isn't so important."

"Okay."

"I didn't pick it out. I don't know how to explain this." She closed her eyes. "This is harder than I thought."

"It's just a car, Katy."

"I know that, but it's not just about the car, but everything it stands for."

"You don't owe me any explanations about your car. I'm sorry I brought it up."

"No. It's good you did. I need to do this."

"Is this going somewhere?" he asked.

She looked up and their eyes locked. "My husband picked out that car."

"Your—?" Where the heck did that come from?

Her breathing became heavier and her voice lowered. "My husband."

She absently stroked her ring finger. She's married? What do you even say after that kind of news?

"I left him. He'd cheated on me."

"Okay. So, you're divorced." That was a whole different story. A better one.

"No. Not divorced. But I will be. Actually, we just signed separation papers in Atlanta."

"You mean 'just,' like today?"

"Yes. Today. I told you this is all so complicated."

His mind reeled. "How long has this been going on?"

"I saw him." She took in a breath. "With her. The day before the Blackberry Festival."

"Two weeks ago?"

Her gaze pleaded. She shifted in the seat, moving toward him. Tears welled in her eyes. "I know. I should have told you. I'm so sorry."

What could he say?

"It's over. When I saw Ron with her I thought I was going to die right there on the spot. I wasn't sure what to do, and then I left town and I ended up here. He didn't even realize I was gone until Monday."

"My God, Katy." He lowered his gaze. "You're married?"

"I'm getting divorced."

"You just up and left. Without a word?"

Tears fell down her cheeks, but this wasn't something he had the least bit of interest in being in the middle of. "I saw him. I left him a message . . . and . . ."

"Oh man. I never expected this. Not in a million years. There's a lot more to marriage than that."

She straightened. "Don't tell me that. Tell him! I have always been faithful."

"You don't just leave." He looked at her like she was crazy. "When the going gets tough, and it will, believe me no marriage is so perfect they never have a problem . . . but you work it out. Together."

"But this was—"

"No." He raised his hand to stop her from saying anything else. "I trusted you. Do you have any idea what it meant for me to open up to someone again? Shit."

"I'm so sorry."

"You got all bent out of shape because I was a doctor and didn't mention it, but you had a husband at home who didn't even know where you were?"

"I know. It sounds horrible."

"Yeah. It does." He blew out a breath and scrubbed his hand across his chin. "It is."

"The separation papers are signed. I was leaving him before I met you, and then I met you and you made me feel so . . ."

"What? You thought a one-night stand would be a good way to get back at him? Thanks a lot."

"It wasn't like that. I promise you." She clutched her hands to her face. "Please. You have to understand."

He got up and walked back to his truck, then started it and spun tires down the lane.

———

Katy watched him leave. Watched all she'd hoped was good news turn into her being as bad as Ron. A liar. A cheater.

Naomi came running to the front porch. "What was that? Is everything okay?"

Katy was crying so hard she couldn't even answer.

"What's the matter, Katy? What did he do?" The old woman looked like she was ready to grab the heaviest cast-iron pan in the kitchen and go to war.

"No. He didn't do anything. It's me. I messed up." There was no way she could tell Naomi. She'd be as upset as Derek. "Excuse me," she said and went straight to her bedroom, leaving a wide-eyed Naomi standing there with her mouth dropped wide open.

I have to find a way to make it up to him. Will he ever forgive me?

She hung the DO NOT DISTURB sign over the handle and closed the door behind her.

Pacing the room, she fielded conflicting thoughts—more anger at Ron, which she knew was misdirected, but had he never done what he'd done, then all of these dominoes would have never been lined up, or toppled over.

Derek had trusted her. He'd put himself out there, vulnerable and barely prepared for a perfect run, much less one that was going to create chaos in his life.

Was there something there? Something real? Or were they just two broken hearts finding temporary comfort? She had baggage. A lot of it, and it didn't matter if your baggage was being dragged behind you in designer-labeled bags or trash bags—when you got right down to it, baggage was baggage.

Chapter Twenty-Two

Before Katy could dry the tears streaming down her face, Angie knocked and walked in. She tossed the Do Not Disturb sign on the bed. "You know real friends ignore this kind of stuff, right?"

"What are you doing here?" She dropped her face into her hands. "Oh, Angie. I have let everyone down."

"Naomi called me. She doesn't know what's going on but she's worried sick. I called Derek. He filled me in."

"I messed everything up. I'm so sorry."

"You should have told—" Angie stopped mid-sentence. "It doesn't matter. It is what it is. Should-haves won't put things on a better path. Quit looking back. Look ahead. You'll figure it all out."

"There's no fixing this."

"Yes, there is and I'll be right here with you no matter what."

Katy closed her eyes, more tears finding their way down her cheeks. "Will you ever be able to forgive me?"

Angie patted her friend's arm. "Nothing for me to forgive. I love you just the same. You are a good friend. I would have understood had you told me, but it's okay, Katy. Really."

"Sorry," she whispered.

"Sometimes life seems way more complicated than it really is. I remember when I was going through that stuff with Billy's dad. I thought I'd never get through it."

"You are stronger than I am."

"No, I am not." Angie sat down next to her. "But I'll share my strength with you."

Angie handed Katy a tissue.

"Derek's another story. He's hurt. Real hurt." Angie cocked her head. "Your husband, ex, whatever . . . that came as a real blow to him."

Katy drew in a ragged breath. "This is crazy. I know it. But I felt such a connection with Derek that first day. I made some poor decisions."

"That's how love is. It just comes out of nowhere." Angie smiled. "Plus he's a hot doctor. And a fireman. And kind of perfect. A triple threat."

"Derek thinks it was revenge. Me getting back at Ron." She looked into Angie's eyes, praying she understood. "It wasn't."

"Katy, don't worry about that right now."

Pain shot through her chest. "I've ruined any chance I had with him. Even as friends."

"No. He cares for you. I can see it in his eyes. He hasn't looked this alive in . . . well, way too long."

"He will never forgive me," she said. "I won't forgive me."

"Stop it." Angie walked over to the window and pulled open the drapes. "First, we need to concentrate on getting you back on your feet and getting you a job interview for that great job. You can't be good with anyone until you can be good on your own. I think you might have even said something like that to me after you wrangled that date for me with Jackson. Thank you by the way. Second. You will forgive yourself, and Derek will forgive you too. It'll all work out."

"I wanted to tell him, but I waited too long . . . and it . . . got complicated."

"Calm down, Katy. Everything will fall into place the way it should. We're going to take this one step at a time."

Someone tapped at the door.

Naomi poked her head inside. "You have a visitor. Do you want to come out here to meet with him?"

"Him?" Katy and Angie exchanged a hopeful glance.

Had Derek reconsidered? But when Katy glanced over Naomi's shoulder, it wasn't Derek . . . it was Ron.

"Hey, Katherine. How are you doing?" He stepped inside the room and walked toward her.

"I told you to wait out there, sir," Naomi said, and she didn't look like she was about to back down either.

"You can go now," Ron said. "I want a word with my wife."

"I'll thank you to abide by my wishes in my home, sir." She looked at Katy, and Katy could feel the one hundred questions coursing through Naomi's mind, but the old gal held her cool. "Katy. It's your call."

"Katy?" Ron laughed.

Katy felt the hair on her arms prickle at his snarky laugh. "It's fine, Naomi. I'll get rid of him."

Naomi took off down the hall, but Angie held her ground.

Ron looked at Angie and waved his arm toward the door, like she'd take his signal and move on.

"No! You do not have to leave, Angie," Katy said, then jumped up from the bed. "I do not want you here, Ron."

Ron glared at Katy. "I'm sure your friends have things they need to do."

"I said I don't want you here, Ron," she repeated. "I don't even know how you found out where I was. You have no right to be here."

He blinked, the fast blink he did when he was mad. "You're my wife. I'm taking you home."

"No, you're not, and I am not your wife. We have signed separation papers. I have a copy of those papers right over there."

"I don't want a divorce," he said. "Not doing it."

"It really doesn't matter what you want now. You blew your chance when you took on that girlfriend. Please leave."

"I'm not going anywhere."

"How did you even find me?"

"Peggy told me you were here."

Oh great. Peggy gives in to her cheater husband, and then suddenly she's on Ron's side? How could she have broken that trust?

"Leave! Or I'm calling the police." Katy felt the room shift a little. Please don't hyperventilate here and now.

———

Naomi came back in the room with Derek right behind her. Angie looked at Katy with a smile.

Derek nodded to Katy, then leveled a gaze at Ron. "You heard the lady. Probably time for you to go." His voice was quiet, but stern.

"I don't need you to tell me how to handle my wife."

Katy stepped closer to Angie, praying her strength would rub off. "Handle me?"

Ron shook his head. "Don't twist my words, Katherine."

"Please leave," she said. "I came to this town to be away from you. I don't want you here."

"You were just mad. You're not giving up everything we've built together. We built a good life together. Katherine, women don't leave this kind of life behind after one little indiscretion."

Derek stood quietly in the doorway.

Katy was embarrassed for him to see this, but also glad he'd come to her rescue. Naomi obviously had called him, worried about what might happen.

"Good life?" She blinked back tears but there was no sadness in them, just rage. "Which part was good, Ron? The part where you made me go by Katherine instead of Katy because you felt like it would be a better career move? Or when you put having children on hold when I was ready because you weren't? The part where we lived in the big fancy neighborhood instead of in a small house with a big yard and two dogs? Or was it the part where you were running around with Melissa?"

"I really don't see you having a bunch of dogs in the house," Ron said.

"Don't tell me what I want and don't want, Ron. Not only are you a liar and a cheat, but you are selfish. We didn't go on vacation or even see each other during the week because we were both working so many hours. We didn't make memories. We just made money. How was I so blind?"

"Don't exaggerate."

"I'm not. You want to know what woman gives up that kind of life? The good life, as you put it?" Katy paused, sucking in a long breath. "A smart woman. I did!"

"Katy, I can escort him out. Or I can call the police," said Derek.

"Katy?" Ron chuckled. "He calls you Katy. You can't just run away and pretend you're someone else." He turned and looked at Derek. "Her name is Katherine. Katherine Barclift."

Ron looked back at Katherine. "This whole Katy business is ridiculous. I ought to have a psych eval done on you."

"You no longer have the ability to do that. And this is not about anyone but you and me." She marched right up to him and pushed her hands against Ron's chest. "Leave. Get out of my life. I left you. Katherine left you. Katy left you. Whoever I'd become was happy enough just sailing through day to day in a life that really had nothing to do with you anyway. You were barely there. If you'd loved me, you wouldn't have cheated."

"It was hard on me too."

"Don't give me that." It was almost hard to look at the man. "You know what . . . fine, I'll give that to you. Poor Ron. So hard to be a faithful partner when the going gets rough. You're the one who needs counseling. You cheater."

"I'd be real careful where you're casting stones right now, Katherine. I have a feeling," he glanced over at Derek, "that we might just be even."

"Love isn't a game. You don't keep score. I'm gone. It's over. I'm never coming back. I will live my life on my terms. And if I choose to have someone share it, it will not be someone like you."

Ron lifted his chin.

"Leave now. Or so help me, I will have Derek call the police and I will press charges. Do you hear me?"

Ron Barclift turned and stormed out of the room.

Naomi looked like she didn't know whether to chase him down the hall or duck, but she decided which way to go pretty quickly because she was hot on his heels and slammed the door behind him as he stepped out on the porch.

———

They all walked out to the living room. Katy, Derek, Angie, and Naomi.

"You came back," Katy said to Derek.

He glanced at Naomi. "Someone called and said you needed help."

"You didn't have to come."

"Friends help friends. It's how small towns work."

She was hesitant, but she wanted to be in his arms. He stepped closer and took her hand in his. At least it was a start.

"Well, there sure is enough stuff broken right now," Naomi said. "It's like we're under a black cloud or something. People sick, marriages falling apart, cars breaking down, storms, people out of work. I think it's time for a good change around here."

Katy sat down on the couch, her hands still shaking from the whole scene. "Thank you all for being here for me. I'm not sure if he'd have left so amicably without your support."

Angie said, "I can't really imagine you married to him."

"Ten years. We were college sweethearts. People grow. Change. And then some don't." Katy wondered what made the path diverge for people who started out traveling the same one. It seemed odd, but then maybe you can't change a person's real destiny.

———

Todd came out into the living room. The hospice nurse had left earlier, and he usually stayed with Kelly Jo until hospice came back.

"She's gone," he said.

Angie was the first to fold into Todd's arms, and he clung to her like a child holding tight to a favorite stuffed animal.

Naomi ran to Kelly Jo's room as if she could bring her niece back.

Tears fell down Katy's cheeks: a combination of relief for Kelly Jo, and sorrow for the grieving Todd had just begun.

Kelly Jo and Todd had had such a beautiful and unselfish relationship. Then there were the Rons and Tuckers of the world. They had no idea what they had. Derek's story. Naomi's. Angie's. Peggy's and even Bertie's. None of it was simple.

Life is precious—every day, every step of it—and sometimes it changes.

Tomorrows were treated like a right, when really, you never knew how many you would have. She'd wasted a lot of them herself.

Derek wrapped his arms around Katy, and she buried her face into his chest. His warm embrace comforted her, but she knew he needed comforting too.

A few minutes later, the hospice team came back in. They went straight into action, taking care of things and comforting all of them.

———

Naomi sat on the couch. Katy and Angie each sat on either side. Todd and Derek walked outside. Derek stood by as Todd walked out to the creek and kicked one of the fence posts along the way. He was mad. Derek knew the feeling.

The funeral home director showed up shortly after.

Derek walked out to the dock. "Do you want to see her again before they take her away?" Derek suspected Todd would want to have the funeral back in their town.

Todd sucked in a breath noisily and waved his arm as he shook his head. "Can't."

Derek stood there for a moment. "It's okay, man. You were here with her when she needed you. You gave her everything she wanted. You did the right thing."

Todd shook his head again, but never turned around.

"I'm so sorry you're going through this." Derek turned and walked back up to the house. He let the guy from the funeral home know that he could take her away, and then he stood and watched as a few moments later she was wheeled on a small gurney out the front door.

Kelly Jo was so tiny that it looked like the gurney was empty. Todd watched them leave from the dock and then made his way back up to the house.

Derek held the door open for him. "Come on."

Angie brought him a glass of sweet tea. "Here."

He took a sip. "Thanks." With tears in his eyes, he said, "Thank you. All of you for being a part of Kelly Jo letting me come back here. For all we've been through, I wouldn't have traded one moment with her, not even knowing how short a time it would be."

Derek rubbed his hand across his cheek and chin.

"Life is fragile," Angie said.

"She had everything figured out. Everything." Todd's voice shook.

Angie wrapped her arms around him. "We're all here for you. For her. You won't go through this alone."

"I'm not ready for her to be gone, but at least we got to discuss all the plans. The way she wanted things. I still feel her here."

"We'd talked about it too, Todd," Naomi said. "She wanted to make it easy, but that was an impossible task. The mechanics are easy.

Cremation. No big event. All of that. But the emotions, our hearts, those are impossible to prepare." She swept at her tears with a handkerchief. "Grief can consume you. The best we can do is share the sorrow, not giving it the strength to swallow us whole."

"Thank you, Naomi." Todd's words were choked.

Naomi turned to Derek. "It's not so unlike what you were talking about with your retreat. For the doctors. Or what Marshall did for his friends. It's about hope. It's about finding strength with the help of those around us. There are times when we need strength. We need each other more than ever right now."

Angie wrapped her arms around Naomi's arm. "Yep. It's about being there for each other."

"Having faith that together we can get through it," Katy said, looking to Derek with hope in her heart.

Chapter Twenty-Three

Two weeks later, Katy had interviewed for the position of festival and tourism coordinator in Boot Creek and been made an offer. It was a one-year contract, and she was fine with that. It would give her a chance to try it on for size, and she wanted to be agile . . . to be able to try and do new things if she wanted to.

She was itching to get busy with her new life. Like a thirsty tree lifting its leaves to receive the first gentle raindrops of an overdue rain, she wanted to get started. Full of hope and a renewed energy to live. Unsure of how she'd fit in on a long-term basis in the small town, this seemed like a good way to not only test the waters of the job, but what it would be like being with Derek. Being near Angie and Naomi had appeal too.

Shaleigh assured her that the divorce would be behind her quickly.

Things were moving in the right direction, like the current in the creek. Never stopping, just working its way around the rocks and tree limbs, forging ahead but nourishing everything in its path.

Angie, Derek, and Katy sat at the long dining room table with Naomi poised at the head.

"I brought y'all together because I have a proposition that I think can work for everyone," Naomi said.

Katy wasn't sure what that meant, and by the looks on Derek's and Angie's faces, they were just as much in the dark.

"Lonesome Pines has been my home. I shared this place with the love of my life. We had so many wonderful years here that although it's way too big for me, I've never been able to consider selling it. Marshall loved this place and the sanctuary that it was for the people he cared about.

"Derek and Katy, you two remind me of Marshall and me when we first fell in love." Naomi raised a hand. "Don't deny it. And if you really think you aren't, well you get back to me in a couple of months, because I can see it clear as day."

Katy tried to hold back a nervous giggle. She had hopes that there was maybe something in the future for her and Derek. But the truth was, she needed to be okay by herself before she could try it with anyone else. She was fine with taking time to figure it out, and it sure was no secret that he was still working through things, too.

But Derek reached his hand under the table and put it on her leg. Maybe he was feeling the same way.

Naomi steepled her fingers. "You dig in while I talk. I nibbled the whole time I cooked anyway."

Angie picked up a spoon and held out her hand for Naomi to pass her plate. "Works for me."

"Derek, I really like what you were saying about your idea for a retreat for doctors. It's not so unlike what Marshall did. I think it could be even broader than just for doctors, though. Like Marshall, you could do good things with this place."

"What are you saying, Naomi?" Katy's wheels were turning. The project plan was already forming milestones in her mind. "That you want to repurpose Lonesome Pines Inn?"

"It would take a lot of people to make it work, but I believe we could do it. I've got the place. I've got funding. I've got all of you."

"Like a partnership?" Derek asked.

"A business. Angie has the customer-service skills to handle any situation, and the cooking chops too. Katy, you can manage the whole darned project and daily operations. Derek, you run the program. You ensure that we set the stage and environment for proper health. Both mental and physical. And I'll need all of you to help me move."

"Move?" Everyone muttered it at the same time.

"Well, I'm thinking that instead of having an old gal like me rambling around here all the time, I could offset part of the price if Derek moves me into his house. Now that he's gotten rid of those tacky pink shutters, it's quite cute. I'll be on hand for whatever you need. I'll consult. It's what I do best anyway." Naomi paused to let them soak in the details. "Derek. I want to invest in this project. Financially, physically, and with every beat of my heart. I'm not getting any younger, and other than Nell, I don't have any family. Losing Kelly Jo, well I want to be sure I put what I have left to good use."

Angie looked at Derek. "You haven't said anything. What are you thinking?"

"That I think this plan has a lot of potential. Not just for me personally, but for the town."

"So, you like the idea?" Katy held her hands together, praying for a yes.

He stood up and stretched. "I'm beyond happy. I had control over making that connection with you, Katy, at the gas station. I saw you, and I don't know why, but I had to talk to you."

She remembered that moment. She remembered trying to ignore him too.

"We were drawn together by fate. I'm thankful for that," she said.

"But everything that has happened since then has not been on purpose or in my control. It's meant to be. You've given me a new outlook on things."

Angie reached for Naomi's hand. "It's true. Derek, I haven't seen you like this in a long time."

Naomi said, "I believe this special group here can make a difference. We can. Don't you think?"

"You are such a wonderful spirit. Being here with you has truly changed my life. Another chance connection," Katy said.

Naomi pulled out a stack of papers. "I had my attorney pull together a short agreement. It's nothing fancy, but if each of you agrees, then I think we can make this work. You in, Katy?"

"I'm in. I'm so in. You know, all I ever wanted was the happy ending, and I was beginning to convince myself that there wasn't any such thing. I think I might have found it."

"No." Derek shook his head and Katy's stomach dropped. "There aren't happy endings, Katy. I know that for a fact."

The joy she'd felt just one tiny moment ago sank to the pit of her stomach. Maybe she'd been wanting it too badly. Hadn't seen the truth for what it was. Again.

"Happily ever afters don't end." He took her hand in his. "True love never ends. So, see you've been doing it all wrong." He looked into her eyes, hoping she felt the same way. Needing her to. "I know this is fast, but it feels so right."

He was right. It didn't feel new. It felt like it had always been out there waiting for them to just find it. Her lips parted into a smile, and she nodded.

"Could you be happy forever and after with me?"

She leaned forward and kissed him. "Perfectly happy. Forever and after."

Acknowledgments

As Boot Creek, North Carolina, came to be, I'd like to thank those who helped me through the journey of this story. It would never have come to be without the help of so many people—friends old and new, family, and subject matter experts—willing to answer a million what-if questions. To name them all would be impossible, but know that whether you are called out by name or not, I appreciate you and your part in this special part of my life.

Krista Stroever, your commitment to excellence and the mentorship you've given me through six books is such a gift that a thousand thank-yous are not enough. You rock and I hope we get to do many, many more together. To my amazing Montlake family—JoVon Sotak, Jessica Poore, Kelli Martin, and the whole gang—thank you for your support, agility, and innovation to help make this career the best move I've ever made. Big hugs and high fives!

Thanks to Tracy March for always bringing the "fon" and for what seemed like endless brainstorming to get to the right title for this story.

And to my new friend, Wilson. You brought balance and restored my faith in so many things, through the craziest of times, as I worked to finish this book. You were an unexpected gift. I might just be one of the luckiest girls around.

Last, but not least, heartfelt gratitude goes out to all of the readers who've followed me from one story to the next. Thank you for sharing my books with your friends; spreading the word, the tweets, and Facebook moments; the fun pictures and notes; and even handing out Read. Relax. Repeat.® swag to help spread the word in this noisy place we live. All of you have had a part in making this Writer Girl's dream come true.

I hope this story gives back some of the joy, faith, and love that y'all have shared with me. Hugs and happy reading.